SOMETHING LIKE A
DREAM

TRACY TRIPP

SOMETHING LIKE A
DREAM

TRACY TRIPP

Thank you to the universe
for whispering this story in my ear.

PROLOGUE

Brent

Jacksonville, Florida
The Beginning

IF SKYLAR KNEW how intensely I watched her, how I hung on her every word, would it have changed the outcome? If she knew why I'd altered my path to intercept hers, would she have run the other way? Her naivety made her vulnerable to all of us.

I scanned the faces of the accountants as Bruce introduced me and the other temps. The employees at McClurry & Associates were all so unaware of what lay beneath the glum surface of their debits and credits, or at least, most of them were naïve to the crimes taking place on the other side of the cubicle wall.

She'd caught my attention when she'd stared at my coffee cup so intently. The simple act had pegged her, for no other reason than that, as my first target. I'd attempted to smile her way, but it had gone unnoticed. I depended on my charm, even counted on it, when trying to get closer. The more unaware the person was, the more vulnerable they became. It made my job so much easier.

CHAPTER 1

Skylar

McClurry & Associates
The Day It All Began

ANOTHER MONDAY MORNING during tax season, and like the groundhog sticking his head out of a hole every spring, I rushed into McClurry & Associates because I needed routine, structure, and yes, money. The air outside the CPA office stung with a damp, bitter, cold, forcing me to wrap my jacket tighter around me as I raced across the parking lot. My assessment of the weather might have been an exaggeration since Jacksonville, Florida, rarely ever qualified as bitter. Still, to a native Floridian, when the temperature dropped into the forties, and the summer's humidity settled into the air like invisible snow, the natives proclaimed an understanding of winter hardships.

The beginning of our busy season settled over us accountants like a black cloud. Sure, I'd picked my profession because I enjoyed being lost in numbers, too busy to notice the coworkers and clients that drifted aimlessly through the office. Still, tax season resembled taking a chocolate cake and stuffing it down a sweet addict's throat until she suffocated.

Before heading to my desk, I stopped in the breakroom. As

I always did, I poured myself a cup of hot coffee with an insane amount of French vanilla creamer. Reminding myself that the definition of insanity is relative, I felt no need to complicate an otherwise easy morning decision. Routines became my friends, and I clung to them.

In keeping with daily customs, my coffee-colored mug greeted me as it had for the last ten years. Its job of greeter had begun after the original mug had collided with the countertop and its service ended; the replacement had happened to be the same color and relatively the same size. In truth, if not for the unexpected future events, my routines would still hold me captive, and I would still be swinging from one dependable vine to another while carefully navigating my way through this unpredictable world.

Breakroom moments with my colleagues were already becoming tenser—get coffee, prepare to personal taste, and head back to our cubicles to avoid conversation. During the months leading up to tax season, someone would mention a show or a sporting event he or she had attended, or possibly some gossip about mutual acquaintances or clients. All that trivial conversation was now considered wasted time. As with most offices, the coworkers skilled in the art of looking busy caused the others to get dumped on periodically.

What consumed their time while I scrambled to finish their work? I assumed the critical task of studying the different forms of sugar in the breakroom or reapplying additional coats of lipstick.

Point in case, Roy moseyed in as I headed back to my cubicle.

"Morning, Skylar."

Usually, I would have returned the greeting with an equally

rehearsed response. However, Roy had informed me the week before that he'd begin his tax season with a trip to Upstate New York where he would take part in a local polar bear plunge. He would remember the moment on the long drab days to follow and allow it to serve as a reminder that he was still alive.

A vision of Roy formed in my mind—his short, stocky body, wearing a Speedo, running down a snowy beach. The whiteness of his belly blinded my imagination as I envisioned it jiggling with each step. As we stood face to face, I tried to shake my feeling of amusement, shock, and embarrassment from privately imagining his half-naked body.

"So, I see you survived the polar bear plunge," I said.

"Exhilarating, Skylar. You should try it."

"I'll get right on that," I answered with obvious sarcasm. For me, knowing my heart still beat in its rhythmic fashion served as sufficient proof of life.

On my way back to my desk, I mumbled a good morning to a few faceless characters who faded into the gray walls of the office. Rambling voices sputtered on about this or that; however, I'd trained myself to ignore them. Work called to me, so I settled into the cheap office chair, molded to my form, and powered up my computer. The land of debits and credits awaited me. The black-and-white world of accounting failed to excite most people. In fact, some might even find it exhausting and intolerable, but for me, it made the world seem safe. The rules, cemented in stone, and the columns, keeping everything tidy, allowed the story of the numbers to unfold without unnecessary color.

"Good morning, Skylar." Liz strutted past me in her skimpy black dress. Yes, I did say a skimpy black dress.

"Good morning, Liz," I responded because if I didn't, I

would look rude, which I would never intend to do. I merely kept my distance because I didn't like her. Now, I don't mean that in an offensive way, believe it or not, but, seriously, what kind of accountant wears a skimpy black dress to the office? Enough said.

"Did you do anything fun this weekend?" she continued.

Her question led me to the second reason I didn't care for Liz. She was quite aware that I rarely did anything exciting on weekends. I'd supplied evidence of this fact when I declined joining them for tequila shots on Fridays or any other function to be honest. Neither did I share stories around the water cooler on Mondays. Did I wonder what would happen if I looked up from my cozy world and saw more colorful possibilities? Sure. Who didn't imagine a different version of themselves now and then?

"Adam and I did a few chores around the house. We were beat after that, so we just watched Netflix."

The one-story, suburban home Adam and I had shared for the last ten years stayed immaculate, mainly due to having no kids and no pets. We'd grown accustomed to our quiet ways. At one point, we'd talked of marriage, yet one year had followed another, and neither of us had cared to change anything. We were content. Even though we weren't actively trying for children, we would have welcomed them. Maybe that would have made marriage more appealing.

"Well, that sounds interesting."

I couldn't quite decide which tone of Liz's I despised more—the condescending one she saved mainly for me; or the high-pitched, flirtatious one she used around all men. Every time I witnessed the hair flick and sashay of her hips, I clenched my teeth. I felt as if I had been transported into some *National*

Geographic show studying the mating patterns of humans. Since getting up and running from the office was not an option, I settled for secret eye rolls.

My general feeling when Liz addressed me remained the same. Liz intended to mock me, and we both knew it, yet being aware of her mockery created a dilemma for me. One, I could call her out on it—awkward. Two, I could give it right back to her with a witty slam of my own. I generally came up empty in this department. Or three, my favorite and most commonly used reaction—pretend she dished out the insults as an attempt to be genuinely friendly.

"Yes, Netflix lends itself to some good binge-watching on these cold days."

"I'm sure," Liz said before sauntering back to her cubicle.

Screw her. Liz had to be guilty of an occasional binge-watching afternoon herself.

Just as I settled into my work, Patty, the office secretary, popped her head over my cubicle wall.

Patty was a bit older than me—early forties—and had worked at McClurry and Associates about as long as I had—around thirteen years. The years had supplied her with plenty of material to gossip about, which she did daily. I kept a safe distance, believing every conversation served as a harvest attempt for fresh content. I had nothing to offer; nonetheless, it was entertaining using secretiveness to pique her interest. I could almost hear her wheels spinning at times.

"I've got some messages for you." She handed me a stack of white paper, all with the personalized message *From the Desk of Patty* on top.

"Thank you, Patty," I said as I reached for the notes.

If I remembered correctly, she had received that notepad

as a gift at a Secret Santa office party. Last year, I drew out Roy's name. I'd made Adam select the gift—a Starbuck's gift card and a coffee cup. That very cup had led to 'the change.' Well, not the cup; as much as the man who had mistakenly borrowed it from the breakroom and had stood holding it when Bruce, our boss, had introduced him as one of the new temps.

That day, I'd scanned the first document on my list and ignored the main office door opening and closing a few times. I'd successfully tuned out the mumbled greetings corresponded amongst my coworkers until Bruce had come out of his office and called us to order for a quick meeting. Only then had I looked up at my surroundings.

No surprise, fresh employees hovered around Bruce. This occurrence happened every year during tax season. I politely listened to Bruce introduce a woman named blah blah, a man called the same, and then Brent Foster. Typically, these temporarily-needed employees drifted into the background as nothing more than moving mannequins. As soon as the tax season ended, they suddenly disappeared from our lives, making it unnecessary to acquaint ourselves to any significant degree.

However, during this introduction, I'd possibly stared a moment too long—at the cup, of course. This action had allowed Brent and me to make eye contact, which in turn had made it the moment before the moment that had changed everything. In my defense, I'd looked away, as I'd recognized a possible exchange had threatened to take place. Despite my attempt, something indescribable had started to happen to me. The spark hadn't ignited at the exact second that we'd made eye contact, but shortly after.

Brent was nothing to look at really, the type of person who slowly becomes attractive over time and exposure. Then again, he wasn't so bad to look at in comparison to the others around me. I vaguely remembered thinking, *Well, that's a nice change*, before meandering back to my cubicle and giving it little thought for the rest of the day. Honestly, that had been the extent of it. Straining my neck for a second glimpse was not something I'd made a habit of.

The following morning, Brent and I arrived at the office at the same time. A fleeting moment took place between us as we danced around, deciding who would go through the door first. I am ashamed to say, but the awkwardness caused me to emit an adolescent giggle that did not sit well with the beginnings of crow's-feet. Sure, Adam insisted they didn't exist; however, he wasn't privy to the image that stared back at me from my magnifying mirror. Thirty-five years old, crow's feet, and working as an accountant. Did this all bother me? Subconsciously— perhaps, yes. But isn't everyone bothered to some degree? I couldn't control the speeding train of life rolling over years like they were meaningless numbers and leaving them in the dust where the next generation begrudgingly picked them up and learned to cling to them as well. Future lip lines and crow's feet were its unpreventable tracks.

Life unfolded as it should—ages changed, maturity showed, work happened. If I were honest with myself, there were times my life resembled a campfire. I built the fire by laying twigs in a heap, threw on a few good-burning logs, and encircled the fire with stone. Yet when I stood back to admire it, I could not deny one fact. Somehow, I'd forgotten to light the fire. When I giggled that morning, at the door with Brent, somewhere deep inside me, a tiny spark sent hope to the old logs lying dormant.

The spark smoldered inside of me for a few days. Over

the weekend, my mind drifted to work, and somehow the temporary mannequin named Brent found his way into my thoughts as well. Just glimpses, leading nowhere, really; nothing to cause worry. However, on Monday, when Brent entered the office and headed directly to the breakroom, I rose and followed him. Entirely innocently, of course. He used a yellow pack of artificial sweetener and not real sugar, and for some reason, I found myself ripping open the yellow packet and pouring it into my cup too. I also rushed through the stirring process so I would leave the breakroom at the same time, leading to an utterly unprovoked conversation as I raced to keep up with him.

"How was your weekend, Brent? It is Brent, right?" I stammered.

He then turned and looked me right in the eye. "My weekend was awesome. How was yours?" he said with a slight pause, allowing me to remind him of my name.

"Skylar. My name's Skylar, and my weekend, well, it was pretty uneventful, actually."

"Well, Skylar," he said while never losing eye contact, "I hope next weekend is better." He turned then and headed back to his cubicle.

That night I had the dream—the one that lit the log on fire.

It was just a dream—an unquestionably bizarre and deranged dream I wanted to shake off. Yet, something told me the illusion represented more than an odd mental transformation of daily events. In my mind, the dream served as a warning, a premonition of some sort. Something powerful headed my way.

From the back seat of the car, I stared at the man driving. My heart pounded. Who was he? Friend or foe?

SOMETHING LIKE A DREAM

Snarling noises came from outside. The zombies were closing in on us. A half-dead man, slamming into the rear door near me, clawed at the car. Sweat dripped down my forehead and the distinct feeling that a premonition was demanding attention closed in on me, much like the creatures running at superhuman speeds outside my window.

Something large landed on the roof of the car and banged and scratched at it like an animal. My heart beat against my ribs until I thought it might bust out of me. And then a decaying hand ripped through the roof. I slid from one side of the car to the other, knowing that no matter what, this creature must not latch on to me with its rotten teeth.

I pressed myself against the door. The zombie's face emerged through the roof. My breath stuck, making it impossible to let out the scream building inside of me, as the creature breathed the smell of death into the air. I squeezed my eyes closed, and the zombie's teeth sank into my shoulder.

Suddenly, I appeared in the guest bathroom of my home, studying myself in the mirror. I slid the shoulder of my shirt to the side and saw only a small trace of the bite mark. Bringing my face closer to the mirror, I searched for changes and found none. However, something about me was different.

In the master bathroom, Adam innocently got ready for bed, not knowing that a new beginning for me was sprouting. A mysterious happening was taking place just a short distance away from him, and the woman he sometimes spoke of marrying would be changed forever.

The bite hadn't turned me into a zombie, but instead, had made me powerful. Confidently, I stared at myself in the mirror as something enormous started banging against the closed cabana bathroom door. I watched my image staring back at me from the framed alternate world. Soon my power would kick in, and I would puff up to my immortal self, allowing me to demolish the being that threatened from the other side of the thin door.

I waited, yet my transformation didn't happen. The banging noise got louder.

My confident, knowing smirk faded, yet I had not completely lost faith.

A clawed hand smashed through the door. I got my first glimpse of an enormous, alien-type being pushing its way into my happy home. Again, in the mirror, I stared at my unchanging appearance. I wasn't big. I wasn't powerful. I wasn't immortal.

I screamed "I'm scared!" But I didn't just yell, "I'm scared." I called out his name, and almost in the same moment I heard his name leave my lips, I jolted awake and realized I was in my bed with Adam beside me.

In the quiet darkness of my room, I experienced a faint feeling a metamorphosis of my life had begun. I would have pondered the feeling more, but suddenly I was no longer alone in my thoughts.

"What's wrong?" Adam sat straight up our bed.

His watched me in the darkness, while waiting for a response. Still wondering what I had said out loud, I struggled to get acclimated to reality.

"It was just a bad dream." I sat up, and he rested a hand on my back. My heart was still racing.

"You okay now?"

"Yes. It was a silly dream about zombies and aliens."

Satisfied I would survive, Adam curled back into his blankets.

"Sorry I woke you."

"No problem."

I curled up as well, thankful some parts of my dream remained private.

"Who's Brent?" Adam asked through his yawn.

"He's a temp in the office," I said while still trying to make sense of my speaking his name. "For some reason, he turned into an alien—or at least, I think he did. Dreams are confusing, you know?"

"Tax season makes you crazy, Skylar," Adam mumbled into his pillow.

Before I could respond, his breathing deepened. In all the world, Adam remained the one person who understood why I'd chosen to live life behind the walls of a cubicle. And because of that understanding, I clung to him, and he never pushed me to let go.

Ours was the perfect relationship; symbiosis at its best. As I drifted back to sleep, I searched my mind for the tail end of my dream so I could grab hold and write the ending I felt sure I wanted it to have. Unfortunately, the images had already slithered to the recesses of my subconscious, where I could no longer alter them.

CHAPTER 2

WHEN I NEXT entered the office, I tried to forget that Brent shared the same space. But despite my efforts, my senses were quite in tune with his presence. His voice, soft and comforting, traveled across the room like an aroma drifting from a candle, impossible to dislike.

I followed his voice to the breakroom, where he and Patty shared a laugh about something she'd discovered in the back of the fridge. She tossed it in the garbage. "I'm sure they'll never miss it."

"I'm quite sure they won't."

I didn't like the way she smiled at him, or how easily her laugh came. I felt foolish standing behind them. Nonetheless, I couldn't turn and walk away, either. I moved around them to get to the coffee machine.

"Good morning, Skylar." Brent's voice startled me.

Suddenly, I was self-conscious about a childhood flaw that, at times, haunted me. One of my legs had grown slightly longer than the other, and if I started thinking about it, as I did with Brent's focus on me, I found it impossible to ignore.

"Good morning, Brent." I concentrated on each unstable step. "Did you save any coffee for me?"

Patty strolled past him and gently placed her hand on his back. "We'll catch up in a bit."

"Sure, Patty." As he spoke, his eyes never left mine.

20

I stood beside him while I poured my coffee. Coolness trickled down my neck. Was I sweating? Brent had not followed Patty out of the breakroom despite the fact he already had a full cup of coffee in his hand. Was it possible he felt the connection as well?

"They sure do like to keep it warm in here, don't they?" I said.

"I feel fine." He eyed me with a hint of a smile playing at his lips. "Want me to see if they'll lower the heat?"

"Oh, no. Besides, it wouldn't do any good. Thanks, though." Before the rambling could commence, I made my way to the door.

"See you later, Skylar."

"See ya, Brent," I said over my shoulder.

Don't think about limping. Don't think about limping. After a few minutes, my heart rate calmed down, and I forced my mind back to where it needed to be.

About an hour later, Bruce dropped a file on my desk. "I need you to review the forms Suzanne prepared." Since no one by the name of Suzanne worked in the office regularly, I assumed her to be the female temp earlier referred to as blah blah.

Our boss always wore slacks, a dress shirt, and a tie, and yet he still appeared as if he had just rolled out of bed. He didn't qualify as officially bald; however, only a ring of hair encircled his shiny chrome top. Through the years, his stomach had formed enough of a pouch that it hung slightly over his pants. His appearance screamed that he'd given up long ago.

Bruce, being a man of few words, headed back to his cave without any further explanation. "No problem," I said to the already empty air, even though I found it infuriating to once again have other people's work dumped on me.

I picked up the folder. Nice and thick. *Great.* Focusing on it seemed impossible. Instead, my mind drifted to Brent. The thing that got me, and I suspected others as well, was the need to be near him. He could walk into the accounting office—a quiet space split apart by cubicles—and bring in from the world, mysteries that clung to him like snowflakes glistening on the trees. However, in the stagnant air, the snowflakes never melted off, and the smile never left Brent's eyes.

I needed to glisten with his energy more than I needed anything. Roy had known something when he'd chosen to plunge into those icy, unwelcoming waters. A heart that beat in unison with all the other heartbeats until its sound became canceled out was not living. I suddenly understood the universe's plan. Brent made me want to live, to hear my heartbeat. Brent had come into my life because I'd refused to seek out the ice-cold water on my own.

Above the standard office hum, his voice warmly reverberated through the air as he answered a question Patty had asked, presumably work-related; however, I couldn't be certain. Then it went silent. When I glanced up, I saw Brent approaching. Quickly, I flipped open the folder and studied the forms.

"So, this is where you call home?"

I glanced around my cubicle. A picture of Adam smiled back at me.

"This is it. I'm considering remodeling after tax season. Maybe put in some hardwoods."

The heat creeping up my neckline assured me that, despite my words, I had not played it cool.

Brent responded with an amused smile before he moved along.

I cursed the sensation of being drawn to him like a magnet

begging for a prime spot on the fridge. There was no one I could discuss my infatuation with Brent with, nor could I explain my feelings. Slowly, despite myself, the empty places inside of me felt more exposed, and I became more desperate to fill them.

The next day, I unknowingly pulled into the parking spot beside Brent. As I came to a stop, he stepped out of his black F150 truck. At first, I couldn't tell if he'd noticed me at all. I hit the lock button, and he turned at the sound of the beep.

"Good morning, Skylar."

"Good morning."

"So, I'm hearing everyone's going to happy hour this Friday. Does that include you?"

"No." I'd sounded more critical than I'd intended. "I don't generally attend the office drunk fest."

"Generally, or ever?"

"Ever. Watching Liz get drunk and hit on everyone is not entertaining to me. She's engaged, you know?"

"No, I didn't."

"That's an interesting story. A few years back, Liz got divorced from her high school sweetheart. He caught her with their mechanic, another high school companion of hers. Rumor has it that when her then-husband Seth went to the garage to check on the progress of their BMW, he found his mechanic busy checking out much more than his wife's carburetor."

"That is interesting. And where does one go to get all the dirt on his fellow coworkers?"

"I know that story because, let's face it, we're all merely human and who could pass up a chance to eavesdrop on conversations of that caliber? I try to tune out a great deal of the gossip, though."

Brent opened the office door. "And what is there to know about you?"

As if she'd been waiting for him, Liz stood inside by the entrance. "Good morning, Brent."

"You'll have to fill me in another time, Skylar."

"Yes, another time." Maybe by then, I would have something worth saying.

As I sat in my cubicle, reapplying my newly purchased lipstick, a question entered my mind. If the universe had planned for my path to intercept Brent's, why did so many other women whisper his name? What was the universe's plan when it had decided to include all these different characters? Furthermore, if the universe had created the magnetism I'd felt, why did it seem so one-sided?

There are many reasons why two paths might intercept, with romance being only one of them. Due to this fact, I pushed guilt aside. Brent had entered my life for a reason, but only time would reveal the plan behind this encounter. Whatever the reason, I would accept it. After all, who was I to question what the universe intended for us in its elaborate plans?

Liz's flirtatious tone drifted from Brent's cubicle. She explained how surprised she'd been last weekend when after drinking a few shots, she'd experienced a hangover.

"It must have been from the sun. We'd spent the day on Atlantic Beach before going out."

The sun? Really? In winter, even in northern Florida, the temperatures cooled down. Maybe Liz had just ignored the fact she was no spring chicken but had still downed tequila shots or whatever older people enjoyed on a bender. What had she expected?

I couldn't completely blame Liz for believing Brent wanted to hear all about her adventures. Brent did bring it on himself. He had the unique ability to draw people in and to quickly become familiar with everyone in the office. By the end of week one, he seldom passed someone without addressing them by name. He held eye contact with each person, perfecting the exact amount of time that said, *I see you*, and then drifted on before the moment reached, *I'm a creepy stalker*. He had a way of making each one of us feel important to him, as if he wanted to know all of us a little bit more. Which, of course, made me curse the whole universal magnetism once again.

Up to this point in my life, I'd trusted my mind. I wasn't one to be swept up in emotion, and I'd questioned why a man I'd barely known at the time could create such a troublesome dilemma. The feeling was one I likened to touching a flame. I didn't need to know a single fact about fire, but when I touched it, the heat would still burn my hand. I hadn't known Brent. Not in any way, but when I'd stood next to him, I'd still felt his warmth. Did I feel guilty that Brent gave off unexplained warmth? No. Well, not really. A person's mind can be guilty of a multitude of sins. It was my faith in my actions that kept the guilt at bay. So yes, when Brent walked by me in the office, I might enjoy the moment, but I was confident that I would not pull up my camping chair and get too comfortable.

The weekend came, and I found myself looking for ways to fill my hours with something worth mentioning. Adam and I started with a morning walk at Riverside Park Duck Pond where ducks drifted aimlessly on the frigid water. They went unnoticed by a couple on a bench who were lost in a kiss, hands caressing each other's faces softly and lovingly. Had Adam and I ever acted so passionately in public?

As with most parks, we saw many dogs. Their owners busied themselves bragging about the tricks their dogs had mastered as if they were children. Adam and I generally laughed at this behavior, not understanding the need to treat pets like offspring. At one time, we had considered a puppy, but the thought of watching it chew on my expensive rug after defecating on it ended any chance of us following through with the idea.

We walked together silently, giving me time to wonder what other people did on their weekends that made their days a little less humdrum. My mind drifted to my parents, and the wall tried to build itself up, as it often did, to protect the young girl inside of me from yearning for them. Through the years, I had trained myself to only peek over the top of that wall, allowing manageable amounts of memories to find me. My parents would forever exist, young and free, in my mind.

Adam understood me. My need to feel safe, to grip the steering wheel of life, bonded us together. There was an understanding between us, and I had faithfully abided the unwritten rules up to now. No one rocked the boat; in fact, no one even peeked over the sides of the vessel. We were on a journey—a smooth, comfortable ride through the unknown. If we kept our blinders on as we went through this life, we were safe.

Growing up with my parents should have taught me to let go of the steering wheel, put down the windows, and occasionally take my eyes off the road. They'd fueled their lives with risks and unpredictable occurrences with an assurance that tomorrow's problems would be taken care of tomorrow. The futures problems were not allowed to interfere with the present. Any slow, steady moments had always built up to sharp drops, severe twists and turns, and loopholes that had made them screech in delight. As a child, for a while, I'd learned to live this way as well. They'd almost sold me on it.

Walking beside Adam, I tried to imagine that other me. I glanced up at him. He must have sensed I was looking at him because he smiled down at me.

"Want to get margaritas tonight? Maybe do some tequila shots?" I asked.

With one eyebrow slightly lifted, Adam stared at me. "Are you okay?"

"I'm kidding." And I was. The idea of drinking something that burned going down and with my lack of party experience, would also burn coming up, disgusted me. "What about staying overnight in St. Augustine? We could eat dinner, walk around, shop."

"Why would we spend money on a hotel when we have a perfectly good bed at home? And look, we're walking here, right?"

I glanced around at the small duck pond and wondered why none of the ducks seemed to want to fly away.

"You're right."

Adam took my hand. "Is something bothering you, Skylar?"

"I guess work is getting to me."

"It always does at this time of year. It will pass, as it always does."

I reminded myself that I'd chosen Adam because of his tame and predictable nature and tried to push my nagging thoughts from my mind. Together we formed a stable, secure relationship. But I feared my contentment was leading to my life becoming seriously and sadly mundane.

Sunday morning, I woke early and did laundry. As always, I folded the clothes in my specific way and sorted them by color in their respective drawers and closets. I pulled out chicken breasts to thaw, checked our vegetable supply, and even dusted off a bottle of chardonnay. I would prepare our dinner after returning from the adventure I had planned while Adam slept.

As I settled on which marinade to use, Adam, wearing his flannel pajamas and slippers, shuffled into the kitchen.

"You're up early," he said.

"I know. I have a plan."

"Oh, good God, Skylar. It's Sunday; a day of rest, remember?" The day of rest had nothing to do with his religious beliefs and everything to do with his enjoying nothingness.

"Resting can be interpreted in many ways. We're going to rent beach bikes and ride along the shore until we find the perfect place for lunch. Then, when we are good and tired, you can come home and rest while I cook dinner."

"It's forty degrees outside, Skylar."

"That's because it's still early. The forecast says it'll get into the sixties. It's a perfect day for a bike ride on the beach."

Adam gave me a quizzical look. "How about the movies? We can go to a matinee and save some money."

I couldn't deny my disappointment, but I nodded my approval as I poured the marinade over the frozen, bland chicken.

At work on Monday, in the moments that my brain sought out a break from numbers, I was more aware of everyone around me. Who were they outside of the office? I'd never truly cared before; however, unfamiliar competitiveness undermined my otherwise tame demeanor. My duck pond adventure wasn't going to win any contests.

Brent's voice drifted throughout the office and reached my cubicle.

"Good morning, Beth." Beth was always rambling on about her daughter going to college in Gainesville as if she attended Yale. "How was your weekend visiting your daughter?"

"Wonderful. We even managed to find some time to hike down inside a giant sinkhole called Devil's Millhopper. Ever heard of it?"

"Can't say that I have. Is it worth the ride out to Gainesville?"

"Throw in a lunch, and you'll have a nice day trip."

"I might just do that sometime."

In anyone's book, a giant sinkhole trumped a duck pond.

Trish had spent her weekend researching ideas for a vacation she said would begin, "the moment I sign my last tax return of the season."

"So, what place is winning?" Brent asked her.

"The Cayman Islands. We're going to swim with the stingrays, I believe."

"Aren't you adventurous."

"I try to be, anyway," Trish said with the voice of a mother drowning in her mundane life.

Maybe she would share her research with me, but since Adam wouldn't go to St. Augustine, I highly doubted we would be running off to the Cayman Islands together. Then again, weren't stingrays dangerous?

Brent even tried to make small talk with Bruce, perhaps unaware that Bruce was the one person in the office more boring than me. Brent had yet to notice Bruce consistently refused to engage in needless conversation. At one time, he had interacted with us, but many years had passed since then. Going through what he had could change a man.

Besides our occasional dreams of the future, time in the office passed slowly and uneventfully. Each day I tried to swallow the plain oatmeal life served me. Except now, it had become so dried out I'd found myself searching for the orange juice that would help me wash it down before I choked.

It was on a Friday; I remember because even during tax season, Bruce allowed us to wear jeans on Fridays unless a client was coming into the office. That day, for the first time, my path crossed Brent's outside of the office. I'd never worn denim of any color because I had wanted to appear professionally prepared for the unexpected. Furthermore, letting people see me dressed down allowed them into my personal life a tad, but the main reason was that I didn't own any jeans.

Liz, on the other hand, always wore tight jeans that accentuated the fact her thighs didn't come close to touching, which is, in reality, a turn-off to men. Adam had even told me he much preferred women to have healthy curves rather than to strut around on toothpicks.

The conversation may have gone a bit more like me saying, "Would you want me to be as thin as Liz?"

"Huh?"

"You know, that girl in my office who is practically anorexic, or like me?"

"Like you."

Adam's opinion served as evidence enough to me. Men like girls with some meat on their bones.

That Friday, I pulled up to the stoplight, and there he was, sitting on a motorcycle, with a passenger seated behind him. Brent's frame hid the motorcycle's make and model, or for one reason or another, I failed to notice them. My gaze settled on the passenger and the familiar tight-fitting jeans "painted" on Liz's calves that were the size of my forearms. My initial reaction was to think, *That little ho!* I acknowledged I might be overreacting, and it wasn't polite to assume the cleavage-wielding, engaged woman was a ho.

My focus drifted to her arms wrapped around Brent's waist so tightly I'm sure it was irritating him. I mean, really. They sat stopped at a stoplight. Did she think she was going to fly off? With a stupid adolescent grin pasted across her face, she said something, and he tilted his head slightly to catch her words. A small smile lifted the corners of his mouth. I focused on the curve of his lips and his five o'clock shadow.

I had become lost in some thought—I can't remember now what it might have been—when the blast of a horn brought me back. My mouth dropped open in embarrassment when I realized that the horn had been directed at me. Unfortunately, my officemates had realized it, too. For a moment, with my mouth gaping open, Liz and I locked eyes; and her smirk-like grin engaged me in a face-off. I found the gas pedal and fled.

That weekend I decided to do some shopping. Many stores were running sales on jeans since we were so deep into the winter months that everyone already dreamed of the weather giving way to spring. The deals on jeans were incredible, and being a numbers person, it only made sense for me to get a couple of pairs.

Spring fever took over. Tops were way too inexpensive to pass up. The problem was the styles were changing. Every shirt I picked up seemed to be cut lower in the bosom area than on my last shopping excursion. Not to mention that during tax season, I always managed to add on a few pounds due to sitting and munching at my desk a bit more. Apparently, the weight had gone directly to "my girls" because they seemed to stick right out. Knowing I would be losing the weight soon enough, I still found it appropriate to buy the daring attire. Even if I chose not to wear the shirts to the office, I could wear them around the house for Adam's amusement.

The following Friday, after much deliberation, I wore my new jeans. It really did make sense. Why should I appear pretentious to the people I worked with by not conforming? Unfortunately, I could not find a darn thing to go with my new jeans and ended up wearing my crossover style blue shirt that dipped dangerously low for the office. If I could have only found a darn pin, I would have pinned it a bit. It was kind of fun, I must admit, seeing Adam's gaze follow me around the kitchen as I prepared my lunch. An energy bounced between us that I had forgotten had once a part of our relationship.

Strutting into the office, I felt everyone's eyes on me and heard the whispers. Holding my head high, I continued walking toward my cubicle, confident that my coworkers' whispered conversations came from envy as most secrets tend to do. Even Liz said something that must have been of a jealous nature because she and Patty, her partner in poor judgment, laughed. I'm assuming they were surprised by what I had modestly concealed all these years.

Generally, during tax season, the other staff and I arrived in the office around seven, which held true this day for everyone except Brent. I only noticed because I passed his cubicle on the way to get coffee. My concern grew because good temps were hard to find. Not to mention, my workload increased if one of them quit. I already had enough work to do.

As the minutes ticked by, my irritation grew and caused my work to suffer. Darn temps! I got up to use the bathroom for the third time. If anyone were paying attention, it could seem like I was pacing, but that wasn't the case. Only someone who had lived in the shoes of an accountant knew how stressful tax season could be.

As I meandered out of the bathroom for the third time, Brent's voice stopped me in my tracks.

"Good morning, Skylar."

"Good morning, Brent. Late start this morning, isn't it?" I inadvertently expressed a boss-like tone. To be fair, I had worked in the office for longer than most of the employees, making me a senior in some ways.

"I'm very sorry I didn't run my client's appointment by you, Ms. Skylar," Brent said. "I will remember to do so next time."

Did anyone ever get angry with him when he cast his half-smile their way; a smile that could warm a cold stone like blanketing moss?

On one of my visits to the breakroom, I found Bruce uncharacteristically sitting drinking his coffee at the table.

"Morning," I uttered.

"Morning," he uttered back.

As I poured the coffee into my cup, a sound caught my attention. Brent had dropped some papers and was scrambling to pick them up. As I tried to decide if I should help him, I misdirected my pour, and it went across the counter. I grabbed paper towels, while trying to keep my eye on Brent to make sure everything was under control. While taking a step toward the garbage with the dripping paper towels, I tripped on the chair leg.

I finished cleaning my spill at the precise time that Brent finished cleaning his mess, which was a good thing because I didn't want to waste more time straightening someone else's paperwork. As I headed out of the breakroom, Bruce studied me intently. At the time, embarrassment was my overpowering emotion; however, looking back, I should have felt something else. At that very moment, I became the target. I had exposed my jugular to the desperate lion, and the hunt had unknowingly begun.

CHAPTER 3

THE OFFICE ATMOSPHERE weighed us down, creating a direness bordering on depression. We were all feeling the long weeks of the past, combined with the countless tedious hours of the future. The long workdays created a need for more coffee than usual. Soon my eyes pulsed; my hands shook; my heart raced; and my bladder screamed. I made a mental note to shift to decaf a bit earlier in the day. As a result of my caffeine overdose, I passed Brent's cubicle several times a day on my way to the bathroom.

Sometimes he acknowledged my presence with a quick smile. Sometimes I caught only a glimpse of his broad shoulders as he typed away on his computer. My pleasant mood only suffered when he ignored me to converse with Liz. Brent appeared far too intelligent to fall victim to her ways. During one pass by his cubicle, I heard them speaking, but did not exert real effort to overhear them. Despite this, I felt frustrated when the words refused to unveil themselves, but I reminded myself I didn't care.

The surge of caffeine pumping through my veins caused me to be more jittery than a dog on the Fourth of July. I went over my work several times to check for mistakes. Many of my coworkers had already left for the weekend, leaving only a few unfortunate souls, Brent being one. It seemed like a good time to be thorough and show Bruce that, as a dedicated employee, I remained at work.

The sound of fingers on a keyboard echoed from the cubicle by the breakroom across the nearly empty office. I cursed myself for mentally willing my path to intercept with Brent's and forced myself to wrap up my work for the day. I strolled to the door, said goodbye to the few people I passed, and left the office. As soon as I had reached my car, I realized I had forgotten my purse inside. After taking a moment to enjoy the sunshine, I reentered the office. Before retrieving my purse, I checked one last item on one of the returns and headed out. By chance, Brent decided to leave at the same time, and we both walked toward the exit together.

Brent spoke little at first but held the door open for me. I suspected the day had worn him out as it had done to me. As we approached our vehicles, he asked, "So, what are your big plans for the weekend, Skylar?"

"I seldom know where a weekend is going to take me." I did usually know where the weekend would take me—home, where yard work and laundry awaited me.

"Oh, really? It's going to be that kind of weekend?"

"Maybe." I opened my car door, placed my keys back in my purse and set it on the seat. I had an impulse to learn about motorcycles, since I had so few opportunities.

I shut my vehicle's door. "How fast can you go on that thing?"

"I try to keep it under eighty," he said with a hint of playfulness.

My eyes grew wide. "Eighty! Are you serious? That seems a bit fast."

"No worries. I'm very safe."

"I hope so." Did that seem too much like I cared? I once again said goodbye and tried to open my car door. *Locked.* My over-stimulated brain tried to recall when I had hit the lock button. Despite my effort, I could not remember the moment that my shaky finger had done it.

"Is there a problem?" he asked.

I could feel his eyes on me and turned to face him. "Um, I can't believe this, but I locked my keys in the car."

"Do you have another set somewhere?"

"At home. Adam won't be home yet to bring them to me."

With his warm yet irritating smile, he tapped his hand on the seat of his motorcycle and said, "Hop on."

So, I did.

The engine roared to a start, and my heart raced. *What was I thinking?* I clung to Brent's jacket because I feared flying off the back of the motorcycle. The leather felt like flesh in my hands, which was both comforting and disturbing. The sensation of freedom pulsed through my veins. Soon, I forgot about my arms wrapped around the man who was quickly becoming more than just an office mannequin. When Brent slowed for stop signs and streetlights, the smell of his cologne wafted through the air. While the brand of his cologne was a mystery to me, I couldn't deny the fact that I enjoyed it. I imagined a piece of me would forever search for the scent, despite knowing no bottle could contain the addictive aroma.

Due to the rush of sensations, I, like Liz, forgot to loosen my grip as the motorcycle idled at stoplights. His thin jacket allowed me a hint of his body beneath the fabric. Brent's frame, although fit, did not include six-pack abs. Instead, a soft layer of flesh created a perfect mix of fitness and humanness. If I were a different person altogether, I would have enjoyed the moment of being pressed up against him a bit too much. Instead, I shifted my focus to the wind tousling my hair and the moon peeking through the trees. Somehow, I even convinced myself that discovering a new and exciting version of myself would please Adam.

When we pulled into the driveway, my house loomed before me. Adam and I had watched the construction, had witnessed our home take form. Yet today, it seemed different; unfamiliar. A piece of the motorcycle ride clung to me as I strode into my kitchen. The daring woman who had straddled the bike convinced me to pour a bit more wine than usual, knowing Adam could drive me to my car in the morning. The woman whose hair had blown behind her in the wind tugged her shirt down to reveal what she hadn't dared to expose earlier. She prepared a chicken cordon bleu with the enthusiasm of a young woman expecting a man who was courting her. When Adam entered the candlelit kitchen, he froze. His gaze lingered on my low neckline before traveling upward. Dinner would wait. And as he studied my wine-blushed face, I dared to hope that he liked this side of me.

The stress and the coffee I'd consumed at work interrupted my sleep with strange dreams. None was quite as odd as the first one, yet nonetheless, they remained unusual. Colors were more vibrant, and messages, in baffling scenarios, seemed to be screaming at me. I was itching to experience new things, yet the demands of life kept me handcuffed to reality. No doubt, this served as a good thing, since without reality's neediness, my mind would have drifted to unwelcome territories.

My last dream was more of a quick image. An enormous, thick curtain—like in an old-time theater—slid aside to reveal another dimension. As much as I struggled, I could not view what the other dimension held. Was it dangerous? Beautiful? Most likely both. Either way, the answers remained hidden in my dreams. One thing I knew was something had happened with Brent's entrance into my life.

The last place I wanted to be when a curtain to an unknown universe flirted with revealing secrets was trapped in a cubicle. Never had numbers bored me the way they did now. I'd nod off, my head bouncing as though it was at the end of a bungee cord. I reached into my desk drawer to pull out my mini carrots. That's when I discovered a note tucked beside them.

Quite a healthy snack for a motorcycle chick. I expected fireball shots and beef jerky. If you are ever up for another ride, let me know.

Luckily, I had not placed the vegetable in my mouth yet, since I am quite sure I would have choked. I folded the paper the way his fingers once had and peered over the cubicle like a prairie dog checking for predators. Nothing was visible except the tops of heads. I sat back down and tried to calm my pounding heart.

A piece of me knew responding was wrong; despite this, wrong was a line I could control. Control would come in careful consideration of my words—nothing could be misconstrued as flirtatious. After all, I was an accountant. All things in life were black and white; they fit in boxes of debits and credits. Nothing floated around that did not fit in a box. Credits were therapeutic to my soul; debits were damaging to my soul. Motorcycle rides after staring at a computer all day were good for my soul. Straddling Brent in his chair while running my hands through his hair would prove harmful. When it came to my soul, I was strictly a credit kind of person. Since only one motorcycle ride fit comfortably in that category, I replied with my strictly platonic note.

I keep the jerky and shots locked in my other drawer. I'm afraid that being Adam's soon-to-be fiancé prevents me from accepting multiple motorcycle rides with other men. Thank you for the invite, though.

I cursed the fact that I had to refer to Adam as my soon-to-be fiancé, especially since there was no evidence to prove he planned on marrying me. Yet, the alternative—long-term boyfriend—sounded frustratingly high-schoolish.

Brent headed for the restroom, so I made a beeline for his desk. It was so darn tidy, I couldn't find a spot to place my note where he'd see it, yet it wouldn't be obvious to others. I scanned the desk, hoping the perfect spot would magically appear. The bathroom door started to open, so I settled with throwing the paper on his keyboard and scrambling back to my desk.

A giggle stuck in my throat.

"Hey, Brent," Liz said, interrupting my moment.

"Hey, Liz. What's up?"

"You know, same old thing. We missed you at the pub Friday. I thought for sure you would show up."

"I thought so, too. Maybe next weekend?"

"I hope so. Hey, you dropped something."

There was a pause; he must have been reaching for whatever fell.

"Oh, my." Liz snickered. "It looks like a love note."

Seriously, Liz? A love note? How old are you? I held my breath and silently begged that he wouldn't unfold the paper in front of her.

"No such luck. It's only my scrap paper I use to write notes to myself. I better get back to work, Liz. Nice chatting with you."

"Always nice chatting with you, Brent."

Brent had shooed Liz away so he could read my note. Of course, I would later reevaluate the situation and realize he might have thought it was his scrap paper. How, after all,

40

would he have known it was a note from me? All those second thoughts coated my happiness with doubt. Pushing the negative thoughts away, I focused instead on my original conclusion. It was, without question, more pleasing.

That night, I had another strange dream. When I woke, I remembered a journal, a gift someone had given me years before that had gone untouched. The best way to solve the mystery of my vivid dreams, I decided, was to start documenting them. After glancing at Adam to make sure he was deep in sleep, I tiptoed into the office and began writing out the zombie-alien vision and added this one to the list.

The waves softly lashed against the beach, as if tired from a day of hard play. I could see him waiting for me amongst the crowd, and I drifted toward him. An ocean breeze floated through the crowd, before gliding gently across my skin. The faces of the people around me lacked detail and had no real meaning in my life, except the one face that I focused on. He was painfully familiar, as if he was a lost friend. As I approached him, I'd felt the pain soften. Feelings of peace and happiness soon danced in the currents of the air that encircled me.

The sand beneath my feet grounded me, yet my senses were numb to its warmth and softness. My focus rested on my contented feeling, the contours of the man's face, and one other detail—the color of our clothes. The man wore a black, button-up shirt, and I wore a black dress. Both articles of clothing were beachy, despite the color. I smiled up at the man who returned my gesture with a warm smile of his own. The indistinct people on the beach surrounded us, making us the center of attention. It was our wedding, and nothing I'd ever experienced felt so right.

I purposely left names out of my dream. In the rare chance

Adam ever found the journal, I didn't want to hurt him. I would eventually work my way through my unwanted thoughts and confusion.

Next, I Googled what the color black represented in dreams. When someone dreams about the color black, it represents the unknown or danger. It can also, among a handful of other things, mean potential or possibilities.

I spent the next several minutes pondering the dream. What had come first—the feelings I'd experienced, or the dreams that were whispering messages involving Brent? Was the dream a premonition or nothing more than the result of my brain trying to figure out the mystical draw? And even if dreams could be either one, what was the basis of this one? I Googled again.

Some things even Google couldn't answer, and it infuriated me. People could create a 3D copy of a crescent wrench with a printer, yet Google couldn't tell me if my dream was sending me a secret message about the temp in my office. Baffling!

After writing everything I considered necessary, I closed the journal, tiptoed back into the bedroom, and hid it in the corner of my closet. Adam would never find it; I felt confident. I assumed that Adam wouldn't consider the mysteries of my brain amusing. My dreams were taking me somewhere; that much I could be certain of, and the journal would serve as the universe's treasure map.

When I dressed for work the next morning, I wore black, tempting Fate to make Brent also wear black. He wore blue. I cursed Google again simply because I didn't know who or what else to curse for my distracting thoughts.

The day following the coffee spill, Bruce gave me a new account. Nothing about it piqued any excitement or concern except for the fact it was more work on my plate. The account belonged to a cheesy local hotel. I stayed extra late working on it, a habit Adam accepted, and I completed it in record time. Early the next morning, I handed it back over to Bruce. He looked up momentarily and then went back to his work. Mumbling under my breath so no one could hear, I strolled back to my desk and prepared for the hours to tick by.

An hour later, Bruce called me into his office and asked me to shut the door. My heart pounded like a child sent to the principal. Nervously wringing my hands, I sat across from Bruce. Had he noticed my late nights and wanted to give me much-deserved recognition?

"So, Skylar, you've been with this office a long time now, haven't you?"

A raise? Was I getting an unexpected increase in pay?

"Yes, I started the year before Patty, so that would make it…."

"I noticed you have been staying later than a lot of the other ones as well."

Okay, so he didn't care how many years and "the other ones?" Really? It was a bit of a sub-human way of categorizing us, but back to the possible raise.

"I like to make sure I'm taking good care of my clients in a timely manner," I said. Sometimes when listening to myself, the evidence of my awkwardness even shocked me. Bruce examined me for a moment. I couldn't tell if he was judging my geekiness or reevaluating his desire to increase my pay.

"I have a special client; one who needs a bit of…well, let's say it's a unique case. He has some offshore accounts that recently came to my attention. As you are probably aware, ever since The Panama Papers, people are panicking about accounts they may have, shall we say, overlooked when we initially filed for them.

"Now that other countries are handing over their names, clients may ask us to file FBARs for them. My client needs you to go back six years and file the appropriate amendments. I have several accounts needing attention right now." Bruce shuffled some papers on his desk, as if it would prove his point. "Since you're more experienced with these types of accounts than your coworkers, I want you to handle this one."

He stared at my unflinching face. I would say that I excelled at giving poker faces, not letting on excitement or concern, except that I was truly blank. Did he really believe I was more experienced with FBARs than he was? The acronym stood for Foreign Bank Account Report and had stuck even though the legal name had changed to Foreign Bank and Financial Accounts. Beyond that, I had zero experience with FBARs.

Bruce must have decided my blank stare conveyed a lack of concern. "Would you be willing to work with my client? It may involve more out of office meetings."

I laughed louder than I intended. "Who doesn't want to get out of the office during tax season?" Heat rose up my chest. I couldn't admit to my boss I was ignorant in any area having to do with taxes, but I feared the truth would be revealed shortly.

Bruce studied me after my outburst, which created a slightly uncomfortable silence.

"I'm having a late lunch with him this afternoon. I would like you to join me."

"Definitely, yes. I would love to join you."

"We'll leave here at 1:45. Don't plan on coming back to the office today. If you have anything pressing, give it to that temp. What's his name? Brad?"

"Brent. His name's Brent." Pride that I was privy to such information hinted in my voice.

"Sure. Give it to Brent. And close the door behind you."

I took that as a clear sign to leave Bruce's office immediately. Exiting his lair, I had a purpose. I needed to find an important piece of work that needed immediate attention.

One of my clients, Mr. Stein, owned a small appliance store in the area. He thought both he and his name were pretty big deals. To keep him happy, I always tried to make him feel as though I believed it as well. In truth, I had recently bought new appliances from a completely different store because his selection had left something to be desired. When I had attempted to use his store, his young employee hadn't even been able to explain the benefits of an induction stovetop.

Adam and I had politely thanked him for his useless information and headed down the street, where we'd proceeded to spend far more money than we had planned. Thanks to Mr. Stein's competitor, I now completely understood the benefits of induction stovetops.

Mr. Stein had emailed me a list of items he wanted to know if he could write off. Yes, I could have dealt with his questions in fifteen minutes or less, but I had no intention of opening the email until I was about ready to leave. Because of this detail, I would not be able to adequately explain the reasons why or why not each item was a write-off. Due to this fact, it became necessary to ask Brent to devise an email on my behalf. At precisely 1:35, leaving only enough time to explain the situation to Brent, I forwarded the necessary information and headed to his cubicle to explain what needed to be done.

As I approached, Brent shut his laptop. Was he one of those sneaky people who searched Facebook on office time?

Very disappointing. And that kind of work ethic was why Bruce had chosen me over my colleagues to meet the unique client.

"Excuse me, Brent."

He swiveled in his chair to face me. "Well, hello, Skylar. What a pleasant surprise."

A nervous laugh escaped me. "I have to bother you with something."

"I can't imagine you bothering anyone." Again, a stupid nervous laugh escaped as I tucked my loose strands of hair behind my ear.

"I have to meet a client with Bruce." Brent's expression changed. Still interested; however, the amusement vanished. "He told me to hand over anything that needed to be dealt with today since I may not come back today." Had I said today too many times?

"Sounds dangerous. Who's the client?"

"No clue yet. Bruce said it was a unique case, is all." I even made the quotation marks with my fingers. Again, Brent's expression seemed more intense.

"Interesting. You'll have to fill me in on our next ride."

"Will do. I mean, I will, except not on a ride," I said. "Would you mind responding to this email for me? Mr. Stein is the type of client who expects an answer the day his question's asked, and I try to oblige."

Bruce's door opened, and he scanned the office. He had to be looking for me.

"Looks like it's time. Do you mind?" I asked.

"Anything for you, Skylar."

"Thanks, Brent. Oh, and he likes good detail as to why or why not."

"Sounds like someone I'm glad I don't have to deal with daily."

"They save the best ones for me." With a small smile and wave, I turned away.

I loved my unique client without even having met him. More importantly, I loved the fact that by walking out that door, side by side with Bruce, I became the interesting one.

CHAPTER 4

BRUCE STRUTTED IN front of me until we reached a black Tesla. Expert knowledge of the makes and models of cars eluded me, yet several aspects of Teslas were well-known even to me—the most significant being that I could never afford one. The fact that the key had a button on it that could make the car back up by itself was moot due to the first fact.

I tried to place my hand on the door handle and found only a flat surface. Not knowing how to get into Bruce's car was an undeniably lousy way to start our outing. When I looked up, Bruce studied me as if I were a puppy barking at its image in the mirror. The look said 'what the heck' but lacked the loving adoration.

"You're following me. Remember, I told you that you might not come back to the office."

"Oh." I looked back at the door for some answer it didn't hold and then faced him again.

"I'm actually parked out back."

He rolled his eyes. His low opinion of me was undeniable, and I flushed with embarrassment.

"Stand back." He must have hit a button on that mysterious key thing because both doors began to swing upward. How had I not noticed this car parked in front of our office before?

"Get in."

I slid into the sleek black vehicle that transported me to another dimension. Only a few lucky souls had inhabited this parallel world that would speed by the minivans smelling of yesterday's french fries. A full computer screen took up the dashboard. I wasn't worthy of such luxuries, and my boss's lack of eye contact made it apparent he agreed.

Without a word, he swung his vehicle around back to the parking lot.

"Which one?"

I pointed to my red Camry, viewing it with humbled eyes. He stopped in front of it and allowed me time to get in and start my engine. If I dreamed of Bruce that night, he would most certainly be wearing black, except in an ominous way.

Bruce kept to a slow speed at first, maybe testing my abilities to follow. As we approached the Buckman Bridge, he took off, exceeding the speed limit by twenty-one miles per hour. Why did I care? First, I had avoided ever receiving a speeding ticket. Second, I was well aware that anything over twenty miles per hour above the speed limit was considered reckless driving. I had never been an irresponsible person and had no desire to begin being one at that moment. Despite my apprehension, I had to keep pace with Bruce. What choice did I have?

I pushed my foot down on the accelerator, and several cars disappeared from my view. Many also kept up with me. There were a great many more reckless people in the world than I'd imagined. Bruce slowed down as we approached the first exit, and I followed him as he turned left onto US 17. It felt like forever before he turned into the parking lot of a small yet appealing Italian restaurant. I stepped out of my car and saw him approaching me.

"The client we're meeting, he's, how should I put it, a

private man. He'll want to know information about you before he lets you handle his account."

"Not much to know. I...."

"Be truthful and professional. Let him know you understand the ins and outs and that you are all about taking care of your clients. And for God's sake, don't ramble on. Understand?"

Did I detect fear in Bruce's voice? Sweat formed on the back of my neck.

"I understand."

We stepped into the restaurant. Only a few tables were occupied. In the back corner sat a solitary man hidden in the shadows. He stood as we approached, and the ceiling seemed to shrink to meet him as he blocked the light behind him. My eyes adjusted, and a face took form in the shadows.

"Henry, this is Skylar. Skylar, Henry Davis."

"Nice to meet you, Mr. Davis."

We shook hands, both of us eyeing each other up. Henry's tailor-made suit hugged his six-foot-tall, broad physique, and he towered over my five-foot-three frame. One could find him attractive if he didn't also seem so intimidating.

I got the impression he was a man who liked extravagant things, and I wasn't sure he saw me as fitting in that category. He gestured for us to have a seat. Both men ordered a bourbon, and in a fashion quite unlike myself during work hours, I ordered a cabernet. I glanced at Bruce for approval, and he ever so slightly showed me one finger, signaling to me that one was my limit.

"So, Skylar, how long have you worked with Bruce?" Henry asked.

Bruce shifted in his seat and searched the restaurant, as though looking for the waitress. He obviously needed his drink.

Bruce's actions were making me uncomfortable, so I redirected my attention to Henry.

"I've worked with Mr. McClurry for about thirteen years."

"He must think highly of you to let you work on such an important account."

I glanced at Bruce, and he again searched, in a panic, for the waitress. I almost felt bad for him. He had reached a point in his life where he must have realized not one person in the office would consider him to be a friend. When I had first started working with him, he'd been a different person. Every morning, he would walk in the office and greet us as, at the very least, colleagues. Slowly, many of the original people moved on to other jobs, other towns, other lives. Bruce had drifted into his office, becoming a hermit in his private world. Most of the employees had never known the old Bruce. It had been a long time since I had thought about the man he once was. Yet, after all the years of tolerating his distant personality, an image emerged from the recesses of my mind. I still remembered the Bruce that had once existed. Suddenly, a small amount of pity crept in for the squirming, middle-aged man who sat next to me.

"Well, I would like to think I have earned Mr. McClurry's respect through the years."

"What do you think it is about you that earned his respect more than the other employees? What made him choose you for this account?"

Why was I being interviewed? A nervous flush ran from my face, down my neck, and onward to my chest.

"I'm loyal and dependable. There are only a few of us originals left in the office. Well, I guess I'm not an actual original since Mr. McClurry began his business several years before I started working there, but close enough." I was rambling. "I stay until I complete my work. I'm accurate. I've never had complaints. I know the tax business as well or better than anyone in the office. Except for Bruce, of course." I gave a weak smile to my boss, and he returned it awkwardly.

The waitress approached with our drinks and took our food order. I ordered lasagna because I had never mastered the spaghetti twirl to perfection. Biting the pasta off the fork and allowing the other half to drop into my bowl seemed inappropriate in this situation. I took a large swig of my wine. The warmth traveled to my stomach. I prayed the alcohol would do its job—enter my bloodstream and numb the awkwardness of the situation.

Henry had his elbows on the table, hands folded to hold his chin up so that his eyes could study me. Something was off. This conversation felt far from my black and white world of credits and debits. Part of me screamed "Run." At the same time, another part was too scared and in a weird way, concerned for Bruce if I did.

"What I need is an accountant who knows the rules and can find every possible way for us to hold onto our money that the government has, let's say, overlooked."

He threw the statement out there as if it were that menacingly violent dodgeball from elementary school. Then he watched to see if I was a ducker, a victim, or one of the few who threw themselves in front of it, attempting to catch it before it bounced off their foreheads. How many times had I proven to myself that I was a ducker and proud of it? I could easily avoid hazards. Nevertheless, my moment of being one of the last girls standing, confidence high, generally ended with me taking a ball to the back. I would turn to see some evil boy laughing at me while I contemplated how many years it would be before he would be serving jail time.

"Understandable. That's what we all want." That was my duck. I allowed myself to stay alive, knowing I would never actually jump for the ball.

"Yes, Ms. Skylar. It is what we all want, isn't it?" Henry studied me while I tried not to squirm in my seat. "It appears I have neglected to include a few accounts. What I need is for you to file the appropriate forms to put me in good standing before a possible audit." He adjusted his napkin on his lap before looking at me again. "Your work on my hotel account appeared efficient."

So, he was the wealthy owner of the fleabag hotel Bruce had had me work on out of the blue. I had thought nothing much of it at the time.

"I wanted to see your work before taking what Bruce said about you as truth. You seem competent enough."

"Well, I've been doing this for many years. I can handle large accounts."

Henry took a small sip of his drink before leaning back in his seat. "Some people are better at finding legal ways to save the taxpayer money than others. Almost loopholes, wouldn't you say?"

"Agreed." Agreed? The word had floated from my mouth, even though I had no clue where it had come from. Did I agree to loopholes? A loophole didn't quite fit into a black and white world. It was undeniably a gray word, yet I'd said it.

I took a deep breath, knowing that forms controlled my world—forms that asked questions, to which I gave answers— correct answers. There was no loophole section, so I needn't worry. I'd merely be filling out multiple FBARs.

As for the experience with them that Bruce had alluded to, I was unaware of any—unless he considered the fact I had sat in meetings with my coworkers, the very coworkers that I'd thought ignorant of the topic as well. Listening to the recent current events about FBARs did not qualify as experience. One thing I did recall was if the IRS had not contacted Henry yet, all he had to do was file the FBARs, pay his fees, and he would remain in good standing. Possibly, he was merely paranoid. Or perhaps, he had watched one too many movies about offshore accounts.

I became brave enough to clarify. "So, I'm assuming several offshore accounts will need filing?"

Bruce's foot pressed down on mine.

Henry smirked. "You assume correctly."

"There has been a bit of an IRS crackdown on accounts that, how did you put it, people somehow 'neglected to include in their tax returns.' I also believe we can avoid penalties if you deal with everything before they force you to take action." Again, Bruce applied pressure on my foot. So much for sounding professional and knowledgeable. I took a sip of wine and decided listening would be the best approach from then on.

The waitress delivered our meals, and I politely picked at mine. Henry took a rather large bite of his chicken parmesan. He seemed to savor each mouthful as though he had hunted it down and prepared it himself; he chewed each morsel slowly and deliberately.

Several uncomfortable moments of silence passed before Henry finished swallowing and washing down his food. "Do you think our friend here chose you because you're the best at finding the loopholes?" he asked while swiveling his bourbon around the oversized ice cube.

"I suppose that must be why." I glanced at Bruce again and found him staring into his glass.

"Can I could count on you to protect my money?" Henry asked.

"Of course," I stammered. The forms would save me. I chanted this phrase in my head instead of letting him know there was a difference between loopholes and breaking the law.

"I'm trusting Bruce when I say I will allow you to work on my account. I know Bruce wants to make his clients happy. After lunch, I'll take you to my home office, where you can get started."

"Thank you for your confidence." Again, I tried to make eye contact with Bruce, but he held his glass with both hands, staying focused on only it. Even though I had very little respect for my boss, I'd never thought he would endanger me. Was I wrong?

Bruce took care of the bill.

"Thank you, Skylar," he said while walking to the cars. Then he slid into his Tesla, a vehicle that should have been unaffordable on his accountant budget.

I followed Henry's Mercedes until we reached the homes—the ones I had often dreamed of touring—along the marshy banks of the Intracoastal Waterway. What was that saying about being careful of what you wished for? We pulled up to a massive two-story home, and one of the four garage doors opened. Henry's car drifted into the dark cave. I parked to the side, got out, and waited. Should I have texted Adam and told him my whereabouts in case I went missing? Maybe, but I had made home visits before. Adam would most likely roll his eyes at my overactive imagination.

Henry's house was incredible. The expansive rooms, towering columns, and the two-storied windows overlooking the water took my breath away. I saw a boathouse with an upstairs deck. If he didn't plan to kill me and throw my body into the waterway, was it possible we could be friends?

"This way, Skylar."

I followed, taking in the artwork and the decorations, none of which looked like they would belong in my house. The paintings were so large, they wouldn't fit on my walls. He led me to his office, which had large windows overlooking the water. There was a prestigious-looking desk in the center of the room and a smaller one to the side. He headed toward it. Many files were stacked in perfect piles on it, along with a small lamp and an assortment of office supplies.

"I have an appointment in a couple of hours. Why don't you take this time to get acclimated? Oh, and I apologize. You'll need to leave your cell phone with me. I don't like cameras around personal documents. I'm sure you understand."

"Of course." I scrambled to find my phone in a purse that somehow hid everything. Again, I wondered if I should call Adam before handing it over, but I continued to trust the stranger and his peculiar demands. After all, why would Bruce send me off to get killed? That scenario just didn't make any sense.

"I'll leave you to get started. Let me know if you have any questions."

"Thank you. I will."

Soon after opening the folders, it became evident I would be in the middle of an accountant's nightmare. Who needed so many offshore accounts? Even though the number of files Henry had put in front of me seemed overwhelming, I'd sensed there were more to come.

Henry and Bruce were allowing me to dip my toes into

their frigid water to see if I was brave enough to dive in. The problem with finding myself in an intimidating situation was that I became immediately intimidated. My judgment, already clouded, could not be trusted. Sure, I could walk out of the room and say, "Excuse me, Henry, but I have a feeling that you are a criminal. Due to this fact, I have decided not to work for you. Have a great day, and, by the way, I love your home."

Another more subtle route would be better for my survival and my job security. I chose that route, and spent the next hour engrossed with numbers that would likely bore the average person. Despite my naïve hope that something would wake me from the stupor the countless hours of studying tax forms had caused, I found nothing outwardly wrong with what Henry had me working on. One glass of wine at lunch had affected me as though someone had slipped me a roofie, or at least it's how I imagined I would feel had someone done such a thing. My sleepy head bobbed dramatically, so I poured myself a glass of ice water from the pitcher provided and carried it over to the window.

Henry's presence, when I noticed him, startled me; he'd entered the room without a sound.

"So, Skylar, does it look like an account you can handle?" Henry stood with his hands in his pants pockets, which somehow made him appear less frightening.

"Oh, yes. No problem." I hoped he did not perceive my break as poor work ethic. "I've worked with offshore accounts in the past, although you have a few more than my other clients."

He walked toward me, taking only a few steps, but his less intimidating persona faded with each one. "You sound like a woman who doesn't have an offshore account herself."

"Oh, no. I have no need, really. Not that I don't have a

savings account, it's simply not so large that I need to consider spreading it to foreign countries." I ambled over to the pitcher, refilled my glass, and watched as a cucumber slice slid in with the ice cubes. I couldn't help but mentally compliment him for the nice touch.

"Now that is where you and so many others see offshore accounts incorrectly. It's not the amount of money you have; it's investing the amount of money you have wisely." Henry poured himself a glass as well and, with his cucumber water in hand, stood towering over me.

"Is that so? Am I to assume that Wells Fargo doesn't cut it for you then?" I let out a small laugh in case he didn't give my joke its due, which he did not.

"I'm a firm believer in supporting our country; however, what happens if our dollar crashes? All your money is invested in the U.S. market, which means the little bit of money you have worked so hard to save suddenly becomes a whole lot smaller."

"Well, I didn't say it was a little bit." I set my glass down and took a step away.

"We have an election coming up which could shake our economy. Are you doing your country a service if you crash and burn with it and have nothing left to help build it back up when it's down?"

"I didn't think of it like that."

"Most people don't, Skylar. They're scared of offshore banking. They don't realize that our government promotes offshore investments when our country is on the receiving end of them. Did you know that when we're paying capital gains taxes, foreigners aren't paying a dime? That's because the government wants the foreigners' money the same as other countries do, so they give incentives to invest in their own markets. Of course, countries such as ours are making it harder and harder to invest offshore by supporting the OECD and WTO."

I took a drink and tried to bury my 'what the heck is he talking about' expression behind the glass.

"The Organization for Economic Cooperation and Development is the OECD and the World Trade Organization is WTO. They're the organizations that try to prevent the unfair advantages that even our country offers." He paused, I assumed, to compose himself even though he had been speaking with an eerie calmness. "I'm sorry, Skylar. I didn't mean to go on about this topic. To put it in layman's terms, picture yourself playing an innocent game of blackjack at a casino where you can't seem to do anything except win. Then, out of nowhere, men in black suits swarm you like vultures. Do you know why, Skylar? They're afraid of your success." Henry studied my face. "When we get through this situation, I could help you find some promising places to invest your money where the vultures aren't circling."

"Tempting," I said, knowing full well it was not, "but for now, I'll focus on what's in front of me."

"It's been nice meeting you, Skylar. I'll touch base with Bruce to let you know when I can get you back out here."

"Thank you."

"Would you mind showing yourself to the door? I have a few things to take care of before my next meeting. Oh, and here's your phone. Thanks for accommodating me."

"No problem. Thank you again for trusting me with your account."

"I have a good feeling you won't let me down. Till next time."

As I strode through his palace, I tried to take in everything before me. When I was almost to the door, I noticed a tiny camera following my every move.

Henry had never actually left me alone in his office.

CHAPTER 5

THE NEXT DAY, Bruce summoned me to his office again. I expected I'd soon be packing my things, and he would send me off to the sinister mansion along the Intracoastal. Except, it was worse—much worse.

"I have another account I need you to cover for me this week," Bruce said. "It's like the other hotel account. I would take care of it on my own, except it's out of town, and I can't make the trip."

My heart sank. While my evenings with Adam were monotonous and predictable, I loved them. Not to mention, going out of town always put me out of my comfort zone. I imagined needing to travel with a partner, making small talk for endless hours, and pretending my office hellos weren't forced.

"Okay. Where is the account?" I asked.

"Miami." Never looking up, Bruce continued to shuffle through papers. It suited me fine since it meant he wasn't paying attention to my expression. "To allow for traveling time and for reviewing the account, you'll need to be prepared for two nights."

"Two nights?" My heart fell another notch. "Are you serious?

He looked at me over his readers. His parental stare dared me to continue.

"All right. Is someone joining me?" I asked.

"Yes, and I've already cleared it with him. You'll be going with Brent. After you meet here, the two of you can work out who should drive."

My heart hit the floor. Brent was much like a friend I wanted to get to know better. A tiny bit of me—a minute bit—worried my feelings were not purely friendship. Everyone understood how an easygoing guy-girl connection could become confused, even for those with solid morals.

"Br-Brent?" My mouth was most likely hanging open.

"Is there a problem?"

"Well, actually, yes. You always send women with women and men with men. Why would you send a man with me?"

"As you will learn, Skylar, when you get to the Miami hotel that you will audit, it is not in one of the nicest areas. I would feel negligent sending you there without a male partner."

"Pardon me, Mr. McClurry, but why wouldn't you send two men, then? Roy could cover it."

"The account involves more of Henry's hotels, and you have already agreed to work with him. As for Brent, he came with excellent recommendations, and I trust you will find him an asset. I would not feel comfortable sending you to this account without him."

"I'll respect your decision then, Mr. McClurry." *Since I don't have a choice*, I mumbled in my mind.

"Thank you. You'll head home Saturday, and I'll see you back in the office on Monday. I'll let you know what Henry expects from you at that time."

He opened his laptop as I stared with my mouth still agape.

"Shut the door behind you."

Silent and defeated, I left. I didn't even care that as I exited Bruce's office, Brent watched me.

That night, trying to ignore the nervous feeling inside of me, I made dinner. I needed to tell Adam I'd be going out of town with a man for a few nights. The truth was, Adam wouldn't care; he trusted me with his whole heart. My anxiety stemmed from the contortions my face would make while uttering the words; words that would not feel one hundred percent innocent.

As I stirred the sausage into the pasta sauce, I pictured what would go into my suitcase. The first items were my "there's not a chance we're getting busy" underwear. Adam cringed when he saw me wearing them. I loved my comfy undies because they spoke for me. I never had to tell Adam I wasn't in the mood. The second item would be my bulky sweatpants worn to cover my large cotton underwear.

Adam walked in the front door and immediately came to kiss me hello. I turned to him and wrapped my arms around his neck while burying my face in his chest.

"Long day?" he asked.

"Yes, and I found out I have to go out of town for the next couple of nights." I pressed my contorted face into his shirt.

"That stinks. We can plan a date night Saturday to make up for it." He kissed my forehead before turning out of my embrace. "I'm going to change, and I'll be back out to set the table."

"Thanks." I watched him head down the hallway; a warm feeling washed away part of my anxiety.

Within minutes, Adam was in the kitchen setting the plates and utensils on the dinette table. I poured the pasta into the serving bowl and placed it on the trivet in the center of the table.

"Would you like wine?" I asked.

"Wine on a Wednesday?" He paused. "Sounds good to me."

I poured two glasses, set them down, and sat across from him.

"There's more to it," I said.

"More to what?"

"Me going out of town." I begged my expression to appear annoyed.

"What's that? Are they sending you with Liz?" He chuckled. I had shared many stories that had entertained us over numerous dinners.

"Worse." I gulped a swig of wine. "A man."

"Seriously? Bruce never does that. So, you and Roy are heading off on a retreat."

Adam had met Roy several times, and Adam clearly found it amusing rather than intimidating to envision me spending a couple of nights with my coworker.

"Maybe you should get a book on tape for the car ride, so you don't fall asleep." Adam smirked.

"It's not Roy. It's a new guy that I'm assuming will leave after tax season."

"Oh, really." Adam took a bite. "What's he like?"

"Typical accountant, I guess. I'm too old to notice anything otherwise."

"Wait, is he the one who turned into the alien?"

"Yes, Brent. That's the one." I tried to cover my nervousness with a small laugh and then decided that drowning it with a drink would work better.

"Well, if you need backup, let me know. I'll be there."

"I'm sure I'll be fine."

Adam looked at me as he swallowed his first swig of wine. "You sure you're okay?"

"Yes. It's…" I stammered. "Well, you know I hate going away and for multiple nights. I dread it."

Adam raised his glass. "Well, here's to having you home Saturday, when I can show you what a good time is."

I raised my glass. "To Saturday."

That night I added another dream to my journal.

The office was quiet, or at least I was unaware of the rhythmic normal sounds: fingers on keyboards, pages rolling off the printer, and chairs wheeling around in my coworkers' cubicles. My eyes were focused on the documents before me. I stared intently at Henry's name as I tried to make sense of the numbers that didn't add up.

Something caught my eye, and I leaned in closer to better see it. At first, it looked like a smudge, and then it moved. I jolted upright as the blemish increased in size and headed toward me. From the blurry image, a spider took form and then another and another. They scrambled toward me at lightning speed. Before I'd released the scream that formed in my throat, my subconscious mind unclenched its fists on my thoughts and allowed me to resurface.

The universe was talking, and it told me to fear something or someone. I ran to my computer to verify my obvious interpretation. Bugs represented anxieties. Was that the best someone could come up with? What else would some fast-moving hairy thing represent? Then I read further. Dreams of this nature could express sexual thoughts. Now who'd had a spider dream one day and thought, "Oh, my, I must be having sexual thoughts?" Crazy, but on the off chance, I went back to bed and woke up Adam.

The next morning, I pulled into the parking lot and saw Brent standing next to a black F150 pickup truck. His taste in vehicles screamed testosterone. I had no right to be angry with him for the situation Bruce had placed us in, but then again, I didn't feel the need to ask permission for my emotions. As I stepped out of the car, he continued to lean against his oversized hunk of metal and watch me.

"So, your car or mine?" he asked with a smile in his voice.

"Have you ever heard of a company sending a man and a woman on an overnight trip?" I grumbled. "Bruce has done a lot of dumb things, but this is ridiculous."

"First, I'm sure it happens in other companies as well; and second, do you feel nervous about running off with me?"

"I am neither running off with you, nor am I nervous. I am annoyed."

"Well, then, I guess I'm a bit insulted. Give me a chance. I could surprise you, and you could find my companionship isn't as bad as you think."

That's what I'm worried about. "I'm sorry," I said. "Bruce is a bit out to get me lately. I don't mean to take it out on you."

Brent appeared to think for a moment. "I promise I'll act like a perfect gentleman. I respect you as a professional, Skylar. I wouldn't think of you as anything else."

Screw you, bastard, screamed the part of my mind I found hard to tame. I revised my wording before speaking. "Thank you, Brent. You choose the vehicle."

"I always feel better on the highways in my big truck, so if you don't mind, I'll drive."

"Perfect."

I struggled to get my suitcase out of the back of my car until Brent moved in beside me. He lifted the case with ease and placed it in the bed of the truck.

"Do you need anything from inside?"

"No, I'm all set."

I went to the passenger side and hauled myself up into the seat. Since Adam wasn't the enormous truck kind of guy, the experience of sitting so high up in the sea of vehicles was a pleasant surprise. Brent also proved to be a natural conversationalist. He listened, shared, allowed for a couple of naps, and for me to take control of the radio.

Brent's knowledge of the world shone in his stories. As we approached Opa-locka, he shared the history of the city and the famous triangle of crime.

"In the '80s and '90s, the crime in the area became so bad the city built a metal barricade around its perimeter. They hoped it would keep traffic out." We both studied our surroundings. "It's the very area that later became known as 21 Jump Street." Entranced by the tale, I hung on his every word. "Now do you think Bruce's decision to send me along seems justified?"

"I guess, but you haven't worked at McClurry & Associates as long as I have. I'm telling you; something seems weird about this whole trip."

Brent didn't respond.

We passed Opa-locka's City Hall, a Moorish-style building that stood out against everything else.

"At one point, there were hopes of revitalizing the area and making it an artsy section renamed Magnolia North."

Despite the bars on the store windows, graffiti, and some less-than-savory characters loitering about, there were hints of promise.

As we rolled into the parking lot of the hotel we would be auditing, I must admit I was happy to have a man with me. The building was in shambles in comparison to any hotel I would have stayed in. Paint peeled off the store front, the sign was faded, and the door handle was sticky to the touch. When we entered the building, the ding of the doorbell alerted the worn, elderly man of our presence. He was the manager of many of the hotels owned by Henry in the area. The man sat at the counter; a thick glass separated us. After we'd introduced ourselves, he shuffled out from behind the counter. He glanced out the window before he locked the door and directed us to a cluttered back office.

"Sam Murphy." He offered a frail hand and then waved apologetically over the pile of disorganized papers. "It's all here. Let me know if you have any questions." He retreated to go back behind the counter.

As soon as the door swung shut, Brent and I could not help but laugh at the pathetic creature. After fighting the urge to run out to buy sanitizing wipes, I began organizing the disaster.

"I can see why Bruce didn't want to take care of this account." Attempting to wipe the disgust off his skin, Brent rubbed his hands on his slacks. "Why does Bruce even keep this account anyway? He mentioned it was one of his wealthy client's hotels. Still, it makes no sense to me."

"I can't explain it myself." I thought it best to stay quiet about Henry for the time being.

We found nothing troublesome about the account once we got through the clutter, yet I agreed it was more than a one-day venture. Around five o'clock, we decided to head back to the hotel the office had booked for us. We had not had the pleasure of seeing it up to that point. The oceanfront building was incredible, and, for a moment, I forgave Bruce for sending me on another questionable outing.

Once Bruce and I had finished checking in, the view in the back drew us to it. An infinity pool, given that name for good reason, stretched out to reach the water beyond. Cozy chairs lined the pool. Some sat nestled in tents or between flower beds that created private romantic getaways. My mind drifted to Adam and how much I wished I could share the view with him. On one side, there was an outside sitting area for the hotel restaurant. Small fire pits, catching our attention as their flickering flames began to show in the setting sun, added charm and warmth to the chilly evening.

"Well, I don't see any reason to eat anywhere but here. Do you?" Brent asked.

"I don't see the reason to leave here and go back to that other hotel in the morning either, except we probably wouldn't get away with staying here all day."

Brent smiled at me. "We'd better make the most of tonight then. Meet you back here in one hour?"

"Perfect."

"I'll try to reserve us a table."

Brent walked toward the hostess while I headed to the elevator, my last words repeating in my mind. Had I said I wanted to stay at the hotel with him all day? I hoped it was not what he'd heard. My room was on the third floor, and Brent's was on the fifth. In my opinion, the farther away from mine, the better.

Upon opening the door to my room, a white down comforter welcomed me to relax and look out over the view of the ocean. Everything in the room and the entirety of the hotel was pristine with a modern flare. It was way above any accommodation Bruce had ever put us up in before. Thankfulness and cautiousness fought for control in my brain. A weird energy filled my world, and I couldn't decide whether to embrace it or run from it.

After my shower, I sat in my big white fluffy robe and gazed at the moon trail on the ocean. I tried calling Adam.

No answer. I was happy I wasn't a Liz who gave off vibes of availability even though she wasn't available. As I sat, looking out at the backdrop of stars peeking through, one thing became clear. I had nothing to fear, whatever the universe threw at me. Sure, it could toss me into a candlelit dinner with my chemically compatible counterpart. Regardless, it couldn't change me. Well, it could, but only if I allowed it to. Despite that, the idea that the universe was trying to destroy me didn't settle with me. The universe had something it needed me to see.

With a renewed belief in myself and the universe's purpose, I dressed in my attractive, yet professional, dinner attire. I gave myself one more look-over and headed down to the restaurant. Brent was already sitting at our table. He had decided to keep his five o'clock shadow covering his strong jawline. Is that what the universe wanted me to see? I doubted it. He stood when I approached.

"Well, don't you look nice, Ms. Skylar."

"And you as well."

He pushed in my chair for me and took his seat across from me.

"You're not going to believe this. When I went to get our reservation, the hostess said we already had one. Somehow, they forgot to give us the heads-up."

"That would be typical of Audrey. She's been Patti's assistant for about six months. We keep waiting for her to work out the little kinks," I said with an eye roll. "So far, well, you can tell she has not."

"Think it was her idea to put us up in this hotel? I'd like to see Bruce's face when he gets this bill."

"Oh, my Lord, I wonder if it was. Well, this may be the last overnight trip she plans." We both laughed despite it being out of character for me to laugh at someone possibly getting the boot.

The waiter approached with a bottle of wine in hand I intended to refuse. I needed to keep my wits about me. The man lifted the bottle the way waiters do to show the name. I saw Mount Veeder and 2012, yet the quality was lost on me. I bought anything under ten dollars at my local Publix, and I'm referring to the big bottle. Despite my lack of knowledge, I got the sense this bottle exceeded my general selection choice.

"A gift from Mr. McClurry." Both of our jaws dropped. "It comes with a note." The waiter handed the note to Brent, who proceeded to read it.

"Thanks for going above and beyond this week. Bruce"

"Well, I guess the hotel selection won't surprise him," I uttered, still in shock.

The waiter poured a taste into Brent's glass and allowed him time to approve it.

Brent took his small sip. "Perfect."

I felt relief that Brent had dealt with the wine taster job. The process always made me feel a bit like an imposter. Unless they'd poured me straight vinegar, I considered the wine worthy of my appreciation. Although, when I tasted this selection, I was pleasantly surprised. Even a person with no expertise like myself could tell this was high quality.

"We've been instructed to keep your glasses full to your liking." The waiter poured wine in both our glasses and turned to leave.

"Have we entered the Twilight Zone? Bruce hasn't said more than two unnecessary words to me since I've worked for him. He must hate this account, even more than we thought," Brent said, amazed.

"I'm baffled. That's all I can say." A hint of giddiness welled up inside me. The magical ocean air mixed with the adrenaline rush I experienced whenever Brent came within fifty feet of me. The night screamed trouble.

"So, do you consider yourself a favorite in the office or someone Bruce is trying to push out?" Brent asked.

"Funny you ask because I have been wondering that myself lately. Crappy accounts, amazing hotel; I'm getting mixed messages."

Brent studied me a minute. "You know, I've always considered myself a pretty observant person. But to be honest, I am stumped on this one as well. He has been trying to get you out of the office a bit lately."

"Yes."

"And this account is on the verge of being dangerous," Brent said.

"I didn't say dangerous, did I?"

"You don't think the neighborhood is safe, do you?" Brent asked, surprised.

"Oh, that hotel. I…never mind." I envisioned Henry's tall frame hovering over me and tried to force myself to stop talking, at least, for the time being. "I'll take this location over the other one. Let's keep it there."

"You've got to be kidding. The other one is in a worse place than this one?"

"No. Kind of the opposite actually. It's in an amazing place. It overlooks the Intracoastal Waterway, and I hang out in a home I could only dream of owning."

"So, what's the problem?"

"Just a lot of FBARs I'm supposed to know how to deal with and, I don't know, a feeling, I guess." His gaze searched mine. I pushed the steak around on my plate and contemplated what amount of food I should leave untouched to appear appropriate.

"Go on," Brent urged.

"Something tells me I should keep my mouth shut and see where the numbers lead me before I end up rambling on about crazy girl intuition."

Brent refilled my wine glass. "Promise me you'll talk to me if that girl intuition turns out to be something."

"Promise." I couldn't quite make eye contact when I agreed.

The conversation drifted to less tricky waters until we'd both had our fill.

"What do you say we pay the bill and get a second bottle of wine to take outside?"

After repeating a few affirmations and restoring my confidence in myself, I said, "Sounds great." It would have been ridiculous not to check out the pool area.

We found a circular couch by a fire pit that others had graciously left empty for us. I shivered due to the chill in the air. Brent grabbed a blanket that the hotel had laying out as they did with pool towels in the daytime. He set down his wine, and in a slow and comforting way, wrapped the blanket around my shoulders. When the gesture seemed to take too long, my gaze drifted to his. For a moment in time, we appeared like two lovers lost in their world.

"Are you warm enough?"

"Yes, thank you." I took a seat on the farther side of the couch so it would have been awkward for him to sit close. With my powerful, faithful mind, I conjured up an image of Adam's sweet face. I wanted to stare at his face for the rest of my life, or so I believed. I held on to the image until my quiet talk with Brent began to turn sleepy, and we headed to our separate rooms.

The next morning, we met downstairs for a complimentary breakfast of scrambled eggs and sausage links. Then we headed off for a quiet ride back to Opa-locka. Besides small talk, we busied ourselves with finishing the audit so we could get back to Jacksonville. The uninvited closeness of the night before seemed almost forgotten as we worked until sunset.

After freshening up, we met at the restaurant and found yet another complimentary bottle of wine awaiting us. I recalled the many business trips Adam had taken, the nights in hotels with younger women who had yet to see their first hint of a wrinkle. Once home, Adam shared stories about coworkers that made me cringe; stories sprung forth from indulging in a bit too much alcohol. Of course, Adam had remained an observer, yet still present, amid the temptations. I'd trusted him to come home to me the same Adam who had left me, even if he'd stood at the window of inappropriateness. So, I allowed myself a glance through the window. I allowed myself the extra glass of wine, because not only did I have faith in myself, I knew Adam had faith in me, as well.

The night air brought magic from countries far away, of adventures untold from the vast ocean. As we had the evening before, Brent and I headed down toward the fire pits. This time, the ocean, wanting to share its stories, seemed to call to us from beyond the hotel barrier. Again, with full faith in myself, I walked side by side with Brent who carried the wine bottle in one hand while I held our glasses. Attempting to block out the chilly air that sought an opening in the blanket wrapped around us, both of us held onto a corner. Also, we were not quite sure if we were breaking the rules by taking the wine we kept covered down to the beach. Like a couple of teenagers, we laughed as we tried to conceal our loot. The wind, working as the enemy, tried to give us away, which left us laughing even more as Brent rewrapped us several times.

The full moon peeked out from behind the clouds, and we settled into the sand to give it the admiration it deserved. Unfortunately, the brisk night air stung more than we'd expected. We remained huddled together as we sat on the beach. I felt I had no choice because keeping the blanket to myself would have been extremely rude. Brent's ability to create a comfortable conversation eased my tension. Even the silences passed without notice. Only a small amount of wine remained in the bottom of the bottle, which was, I reminded myself, the second bottle. I promised myself that as soon as the wine came to an end, my time with Brent would end too.

We watched the crabs scurry to their holes in the moonlight and took time to point out one after another. As Brent pointed out a large one in the distance, a crab ran over my foot, making me scream and throw wine on my face and chest. Disregarding the hotel property, I tried to clean myself up using their blanket. Brent watched, laughing.

"Well, did I get it all?"

"Not a chance." He picked up a corner of the blanket, wiped my neck, and let his hand drift downward. "I think you're good now."

Suddenly, we were both silent, staring into the dark. Did we both know we were approaching dangerous waters? Part of me wanted to run back to my room, but that voice was a whisper amongst the other voices in my mind. After a moment of listening to the waves, Brent asked, "So how long have you been with Adam, Skylar?"

"Fourteen years."

"That's a good amount of time." He sipped his wine. "Why have you never tied the knot?"

"I guess because our relationship works the way it is. We are considering marriage, or I think we are. Adam's fine either way." The silence demanded words. "Not to sound too girly, but I'm starting to want that experience. I mean, if I've found the right person, maybe it's a good thing to make it official." I had a sudden urge to take a sip of wine myself.

"So, is Adam the right person?"

I considered my relationship with Adam. A million quick memories flashed before my eyes.

I smiled. "He's definitely the right person."

I looked Brent in the eyes. I intended the action to show my devotion to Adam. Instead, I was surprised at how close faces become when two people are entwined in a blanket. I smelled the wine on his breath, and I'm sure he could smell it on mine. The moment felt too intimate, which I had not intended.

"He's a lucky man."

"He might not think that if he saw me now."

"I know you're sharing the blanket with me strictly for survival. I wouldn't think otherwise."

"I hope I don't appear inappropriate. I assure you; I've never been anything but good to Adam."

"I believe you, Skylar." Brent's soft smile touched his eyes.

"So why aren't you married?" I took a rather large sip and looked away while trying to distance myself from my desire to know.

"Just waiting for the right person, I guess."

"Well, Liz hasn't walked down the aisle yet. Maybe you can snag her."

Despite his pained expression, a slight laugh escaped Brent. "Liz is exactly the type of person I stay away from."

"Nice to know you have good taste. So, what are you looking for?"

"Someone who is smart, witty, adventurous, not too into herself. The kind that kicks off her stilettos to jump on the back of a motorcycle," Brent said. "Someone who is in awe of sunsets. Someone who likes a drink, but not so many she loses her memory to an alcohol fog."

"Sounds like someone I would like, minus the stilettos." I raised my foot to show my one-inch heel. When I glanced back up, Brent stared at me, before his gaze shifted to the ocean and somewhere beyond. A hint of sadness darkened his eyes, and I knew I had no business wanting to take it away. Somewhere through the silence, I heard the whispered voice again, but this time, the voice carried an urgency.

"Brent, I'm going to give you the biggest compliment I'm allowed to give you."

"What's that?"

"It's time for me to go."

His slight nod said he understood that my staying created danger for the one person we'd both chosen to forget about as we'd sat under the stars together. I left him to keep warm in the blanket that I feared would forever hold a piece of me.

The sound of the waves drifting through my hotel window, or was it the lingering memory of the night, allowed yet another dream to form in my sleeping mind.

I was in my backyard planting flowers when I noticed a small lake forming behind me. A childlike excitement intoxicated me as the cool water splashed across the manicured grass and slapped at my ankles. I playfully kicked back at the waves, as if they were friends coming to play. A smile naively spread across my face, and I ventured a step farther into the growing swells. The waves responded with increasing intensity, until my light-hearted laugh caught in my throat. I glanced back at my home; the waves were beginning to slam against the siding. A small uprooted daisy floated by me in the sea foam. Looking down, I didn't see the monstrous wave approaching. Unable to brace myself, my body hurdled toward my home until I felt the force of our collision. The sound of shattering windowpanes jolted me awake.

I guess some waters existed in which we were not intended to dabble in even for a moment, and I promised myself I never would again.

CHAPTER 6

S
O, I'D SAT under a blanket with some man despite his ability to permeate several of my conscious thoughts and creep into my dreams as well. A person could do worse things. For example, the safety inspectors had forgotten to replace a valve at the Piper Bravo Oil Rig. This slip up had led to an explosion that had killed 167 people and cost 3.4 million dollars in damage. Captain Hazelwood had allegedly gotten drunk while driving the Exxon oil tanker, which had caused him to steer it into the Prince William Sound. His alleged mess up had cost 4.4 billion dollars in damage and spilled 760,000 barrels of oil into the water. My quick snuggle time in the moonlight paled in comparison. Not to mention, I'd gotten up and left. I'd let Brent know that in my mind, no one could compare to Adam. Nothing had happened, which meant the solution to my undeserved guilty feeling was to allow it to subside into nothingness.

Back at the office in Jacksonville, I stood in the parking lot and studied the brick exterior of McClurry & Associates. I had spent a third of my life sitting behind a desk and staring at a computer. So many hours had passed in that way that my 20/20 vision had diminished to 20/30 at best. On a regular basis, sciatic nerve pain shot down my legs. It was their way of screaming, "Get your butt out of the budget-friendly chair." Bruce had insisted our chairs had years of life left in them despite the fact he'd purchased them a decade ago.

I continued to grow old in that office while I watched time tick by uneventfully. What choice did I have? The only adventure that begged me to run with it would leave my aging soul in despair. Who was I kidding anyway? Whoever Brent had perceived me to be as he sat on that beach was a myth. Staying faithful to the man I loved, the man I had groomed to tolerate my weaknesses and flaws, remained the best option. All possible futures with Brent should have died on that beach the moment I'd left him alone, staring at the moon.

I straightened my shirt and tried to smooth out the seat belt wrinkles formed during the long car ride. Then I lifted my chin, because, well, I don't know why one does that to appear unbeatable. I then headed into the building's stagnant atmosphere where one pulse of electricity waited to light my world on fire. Of course, I wouldn't let it, though. After the long and businesslike ride home from Miami, I personified faithfulness bordering on cold and unfriendly.

I had barely reached my desk when Bruce walked by. "Come to my office, please." What next? I followed close behind him and received many curious glances from the office staff. He let me enter first and then closed the door behind me.

"Have a seat."

I followed his instructions like a puppy, sitting poised for anything.

"So, Skylar, how did your trip to Miami go?"

"It was fine. You were right about the area. Opa-locka isn't the best part of Miami."

"Now you see why I sent Brent with you."

"Yes," I replied in the best unthankful tone I could muster while stopping short of being disrespectful.

"I hope you liked the accommodations."

"They were beautiful. We were quite impressed." Despite my distrust of his generosity I added, "Thank you. And the wine was a nice touch, as well."

He nodded slightly. "And as I promised, Brent acted like a professional." Was that a question or a statement?

"Oh, yes, of course, he was very professional."

As Bruce leaned back in his chair, he studied me with his hands folded in front of him. I crossed my legs, desperate to find a way to feel comfortable. After an eternity had passed, he cleared his throat and sat up, making the change in the subject official.

"Henry is ready for you to go back out to his house this afternoon to work on his accounts. Do you have any questions about what he expects?"

"I don't believe so. I'm merely filing FBARs for each of Henry's offshore accounts, correct?"

"Correct." Bruce studied me again. He began to creep me out, and even leaving the office to go to some account I had my suspicions about seemed like a retreat. "He would like you there at noon. I don't expect you back at the office today. Brent will be your official go-to person for any accounts needing attending to while you're out."

"Great. I'll make sure to be at Henry's by noon." Silence. "Is there anything else?"

"No, Skylar, you're free to go."

"Thank you." Again, I held back the tone begging me to uncage it.

I left his office and headed right for the breakroom for a coffee I didn't need. Brent followed behind me. Oh, the irony. You give someone the cold shoulder to push them away, and it only draws them closer.

"Good morning, Skylar."

"Morning, Brent." I grabbed my French vanilla creamer and didn't give the yellow packet a second glance.

"How was the rest of your weekend?"

"Wonderful. Adam took me out to dinner, and we got a Redbox for some quiet time at home. How about you?"

"I got a Redbox for a quiet evening at home as well. Did you happen to watch *Now You See Me?*"

"No, totally different route. We watched *The Boss.*"

Brent ripped open his fake sugar. From the corner of my eye, I watched his hands. For a moment, I remembered those hands wrapping the blanket around my shoulders. I pushed the thought from my mind.

"I may be sending you some work today. I'm going back to that client of Bruce's from the other day."

"No problem. I come prepared to stay late."

"Thanks."

I strutted by him and hid from all distracting thoughts in the safety of my cubicle, but a feeling followed me across the office, despite my efforts. The feeling connected me to his cubicle like an invisible rubber band. The desire to give in to the pull between us refused to diminish.

Thoughts of the two of us huddled together under the blanket haunted me. The memories replayed in my mind and the sensation of being pressed against him tormented me. Something that I lacked lingered on his skin. I cursed my need to be near him—to share the air that at one moment in time had circled inside of him. Why did some part of me feel empty now that I had met him?

Before leaving, I handed Brent the trivial amount of work that needed attention. After thanking him, I headed off to the mysterious home on the Intracoastal. A minor piece of me felt less afraid of Henry than of being near Brent.

A moment after ringing the pretentious doorbell, Henry came to greet me. I noticed the impeccably tailored fit of his gray slacks and white dress shirt. They accentuated his broad shoulders and tight backside, yet no matter how perfect he appeared, I felt zero attraction to him. I remembered riding on Brent's motorcycle and how his body felt while my arms were wrapped around him. His physique did not compare to Henry's sculpted one. Attraction was a strange and unexplainable force.

"Welcome, Skylar." His words were always right, always polite, yet his mannerisms could somehow belittle a person within moments. He seldom made eye contact with me, as if I were an object rather than a human. "Thank you for making the trip out here again."

"That's what we do as accountants."

"Well, thank you anyway. I hope you haven't eaten. I had a lunch prepared for you. It's waiting for you in the office."

"Thank you, Henry. That wasn't necessary."

"Necessary or not, it's there for you. Follow me." I followed a few steps behind while trying not to sneak peeks at the cameras I knew watched me.

"A few particular accounts need attention today."

"Okay."

He opened the door to the office and motioned for me to enter first.

"I have the documents for the offshore accounts on the desk, along with the necessary instructions. If you have any questions, there's an intercom button on the phone so that you may reach me." His slow, steady voice wore on me much like a whetstone wears on a knife blade. Was it stripping me of my edge or sharpening me? "Is there anything you need as of now?"

"No, thank you. I'm good to go."

"I'll need your phone again if you don't mind."

Yes, I mind, but here it is anyway. I handed it over.

"Very well. I'll leave you to your work, Skylar."

He shut the door behind him, and I shuffled over to the window to steal a glimpse at the waterway flowing by outside. I took a breath, allowing its peace to become a part of me for a moment. It would fade soon enough. A silver platter—yes, an actual silver platter—displayed my lunch of chicken salad on a croissant with a side of fruit salad. My stomach rolled at the thought of eating the food even while my fingers grabbed a plump grape off the top. I remembered the camera and decided I should get busy.

On the top of the pile sat a list of account numbers. With them were instructions explaining what I should claim— nothing major for a man worth so much—fifty thousand here, a hundred thousand there. I began to comb through the material. That's when the problem that had been pecking at my door, waiting to show itself, materialized. The actual accounts were worth double what he wanted me to claim for him. Still, in comparison to what I had expected, the accounts were not that substantial. Why not claim the correct amount? Yet the better question, the baffling one, remained. Why did he think I would jeopardize my career by signing off on inaccurate accounts? Henry had proven he did not understand the black and white rules. I stole one more grape, cleared my mouth, and hit the intercom button.

"Yes, Skylar? Is there a problem?"

"I think it is safe to say you know there is a problem. I

cannot sign inaccurate FBARs, and I am quite sure Bruce would tell you the same."

"I am quite sure you would be incorrect about that, Skylar. It appears you missed some of the instructions. Now would be a good time for you to look in the envelope on my desk."

Watching the camera the whole time, I got up and moved toward the paperwork, knowing somewhere in the house, Henry watched me just as carefully. The manila envelope, the only paperwork sitting out on his pretentious, over-the-top desk, dared me to open it. I looked between it and the camera before deciding I had no choice. The glossy finish of a photo staring back at me changed everything. In an instant, I realized that for the first time in my life, I would be doing something outside of the boxes I had learned to use for survival.

I froze when I saw the images—the romantic fire pits, the wine, the beach. A photographer didn't need much talent to make the situations look bad. All the same, this photographer's skills—the angles, the lighting— excelled beyond brilliant. I could say, "Adam, Brent and I never kissed." He might believe me, except the damn talented photographer made me question if I'd even forgotten a moment when my lips and Brent's had brushed. No, I would remember.

In one picture, Brent's hand appeared settled at the top of my breast. I could have ripped up the photos except I knew that the one copy glaring at me symbolized the countless copies Henry could produce at his leisure. I wanted to take back many moments, especially the one where I stood dumbfounded, staring at that camera. A path of wires carried my broken image through space to Henry, where I'm sure he sat, watching with amusement, in some big leather chair.

Bruce had to have been in on the plan, I thought, almost

immediately. I should have suspected something with the expensive bottles of wine, the hotel on the ocean. Like clay in their hands, I'd molded into someone I'd thought I could never be. Then my thoughts drifted to Brent. I remembered the way he'd wrapped himself up next to me in the moonlight. Had he been posing for a photographer he knew lingered in the background?

I could trust no one. I didn't even know if I trusted myself. My signature, for the first time in the history of my history, existed on a false FBAR. I signed it and sent it, making it impossible to turn back. The next day I did something else that I'd never considered doing in the past. I called in sick during tax season. On a typical day, I would fear the repercussions. Today, I didn't care. Bruce had nothing to say anyway, besides, "I'll plan on seeing you tomorrow." I hung up without offering a response.

Adam wouldn't be suspicious because I got ready for work and backed down our driveway at the same time I did every morning. Houses, trees, and schools blurred past me. The blurred effect was not due to erratic driving. Instead, it was due to me not paying the slightest bit of attention to anything. At thirty miles per hour, I tried to outrun the menacing evils I had somehow managed to make my own. As suspected, my speed was less than sufficient.

I found a park with the Savannah moss overtaking the monstrous trees. The moss created a beauty that bordered somewhere between mystical and creepy. For a while, I sat in my car and looked out the window at a world I viewed differently now. Bad people existed in it. Bad people who were so successful at being evil that they could make me bad, too.

Needing air, I started down the path that headed out to a pier. The only signs of fishermen were a few lures tossed to the side for reasons unknown. I liked the solitude. For an hour or more, I sat at the end of that pier, looking at Jacksonville in the distance, and contemplated telling Adam. Could he forgive me? To begin with, would he forgive me for the pictures? I wasn't sure we could even get over the first hurdle.

I spent a great deal of time putting myself in his place, and I couldn't imagine myself being very forgiving. Scenes played out in my mind—plates flying, tears streaming, words thrown like knives. After that, I would figure out how to trust him again. Wouldn't I? Amid the screaming, plate throwing, crying fits, I would need to admit to my indiscretions. I'd start with something simple. By the way, besides pictures, I might have lost my job, and possible charges are pending against me. That part might be an exaggeration; regardless, my world crumbled, and panic blinded my ability to make accurate decisions.

Inside my purse, my phone made the familiar texting beep. Damn, I had forgotten to shut off Find My iPhone. Adam would want an explanation as to why I'd skipped work in the middle of tax season to sit on a pier. It wasn't even lunchtime yet. As if my phone could explode in my hand, I slowly lifted it out of the side pocket of my purse. A text from Brent, Henry's possible sidekick, lit up my screen.

I heard you're out sick. I hope it's nothing serious.

After a moment of consideration, I texted back, *I'll be back tomorrow, back-stabbing bastard.* I deleted the back-stabbing bastard part before hitting send. It remained possible that Brent was a victim in these circumstances as well. For the next fifteen minutes, I thought of ways I could find out the truth about the new mysterious employee. I considered blurting out, "Hey, your photographer did an awesome job with his beach shots." I would then study Brent's face so intently that he couldn't hide his guilt. The scene turned into a *Saturday Night Live* skit in my head. Realizing I would never prove anything that way, I pushed the image of Kristen Wiig out of my mind.

The familiar beep of the text sounded off again. *Looking forward to seeing you tomorrow then.*

I envisioned myself tossing my phone far into the river, like they did in the movies, except let's face it, smartphones were insanely expensive. I tucked it back in the pocket of my purse, stared out at the water, and imagined the ripple that never came to be. The St. Johns River drifted by, carrying with it the secrets the universe continued to conceal.

CHAPTER 7

WHEN I WALKED into work the next day, I went in as someone between the me that had once existed and a person with more strength and determination than ever before. I'd never thought of myself as an assertive person. The feelings were immature buds, not knowing how to take form. Instead of wanting to live my mundane life as a fly on the wall, taking in life as a spectator, I had a strange desire to dive-bomb into someone's potato salad. My sole purpose would be to make them as annoyed with life as I was before disappearing back to my perch. In reality, what would I do about my pent-up frustrations? Well, nothing yet.

Avoiding eye contact with everyone, I proceeded to my desk and turned on my computer. My screensaver—a little hut built on a pier on some magical island far, far away—greeted me. I loved the image, yet the ocean water reminded me of the angry waves that tormented me the night before as I'd lain next to Adam, so close yet nowhere near him. I'd remained too lost in the shadowy world between consciousness and haunting dreams to pay attention to the man who lay next to me.

I ran to my vehicle through an empty parking garage. Over the concrete walls, I could see a tsunami closing in on me. My car would serve as little refuse from a wave of that magnitude, but it was my only chance. The sound of trees cracking and structures crumbling to the ground drew closer.

My heart raced as my fingers searched through my purse for the keys. After precious moments, I found them and frantically hit the unlock button. The wave was on top of the garage as I climbed inside the car, started the ignition, and headed toward the exit.

The crashing sounds became louder as the wave appeared in my rearview mirror. Within seconds, my vehicle lifted and swayed in the water. The next thing I knew, a surge of rushing water pummeled into the rear of my vehicle. With violent force, the car was pushed down the declining paths of the parking garage. The walls loomed in front of me as I barreled toward them on what felt like a waterslide. I tried to steer around the corners, yet I had no control over the car's direction. Each time, the vehicle somehow turned at the last second until the final wall loomed ahead, leaving me no time to react. That's when my brain knew to jump ship and woke me with a start.

Without the help of Google, I'd translated my dream to mean I was overwhelmed and unhappy.

The tsunami represented a tidal wave of fear and emotions I had no clue how to deal with. Not to mention, life was pushing me along my path, and no matter how hard I tried to steer myself in the right direction, I lacked the control to do so.

As I stared at my screen saver one last time before opening my emails, I heard Brent's voice behind me. Man, he was becoming impossible. Making sure I had my 'I'm not impressed look' pasted on my face, I turned toward him.

He responded with his charming smile. "I said, good morning."

"Good morning." Was he wearing a new cologne? Who cared?

"Should I grab you a cup of coffee? Something tells me you need it."

I took a deep breath. "You know, coffee would be great. French…"

"French vanilla. I know how you take it." He headed to the breakroom. My eyes remained focused on him, while I tried to decide what fueled him—guilt or lust. I laughed, only in my mind, at the thought of him being passionate about my middle-aged, slack-wearing self. On second thought, who knew what worked for him? By the time he returned, I was skimming my emails.

"Here you go, Madame. Just the way you like it."

"Thanks, Brent."

"Are you feeling better?"

"Not really. I have a feeling my ailment's going to stick around for a while."

"Just so you know, I have an amazing immune system and never catch anything from people."

"Good to know. Nevertheless, it's usually pretty hard to catch things from each other if we stay in our cubicles."

"Wow. Pretty cold for the Skylar I thought I knew."

"Yeah, I guess it is." An overwhelming sadness suddenly overwhelmed me. I had morphed into someone else, and I kind of liked the nice Skylar from before. "Sorry, Brent. I guess I'm not quite myself yet."

"No problem. If you need to throw extra work my way, feel free. I'm here for you."

"Thanks."

At that moment, I would have loved even a minute with a magical crystal ball that could assure me Brent wasn't part of Henry's scheme. Hating Brent didn't seem right.

He waited there with a soft smile on his face as if he wanted me to say more, so I did.

"So how did you get this job, Brent?"

His sweet smile faded, and my heart fell. He was guilty. His immediate reaction proved it. All this time, I'd been played by everyone, even when Brent handed over my French vanilla-flavored creamer like a Trojan horse.

"Same way everyone else got their jobs, I suppose. How did you get your job here?"

"I applied and interviewed."

"Well, there you have it." We studied each other for a moment.

"You know where I am if you need me," he said before he turned and walked away.

How could I focus on anything? A list of unanswered emails demanded my attention, but tears that threatened to fall blurred my vision. A list of my true confidants appeared before me, and I realized what a humbling, short, almost nonexistent list it was. I thought about a card I'd once seen while rifling through my options at a local drug store. The exact phrase eluded me, but it involved having a friend who would bail you out after a drunken night of committing crimes. The fact no one in my life would celebrate some amazing night of rule-breaking depressed me. My one true confidant remained Adam, my partner, and he would only criticize people's misadventures. Typically, I would be right there criticizing along with him.

"Skylar, can I see you in my office?" Bruce had crept up behind me like a panther—silent and deadly. Defeat came over me as I lifted my body to follow him. I envisioned this was how an animal would feel right before a predator devoured it. Again, I sat across from him, waiting for my next assignment, and knowing I would complete it because I had no choice.

"I have another assignment for you that will take you out of town for a night. Henry will fill you in on the specifics this afternoon."

"How many nights and where?"

"As I said, Henry will fill you in on the specifics. I suspect it will only be one night."

I could only stare at Bruce with complete disbelief.

"Is there a problem?"

"Why are you doing this to me? What have I done to make you dislike me so much that you would destroy me?"

Bruce shuffled papers on his desk and did not look up.

"Whether or not you are destroyed is up to you, Skylar."

"Is it? Because that's not how it feels."

"Play your cards right, and at this time next year, you could be thanking me for your prosperity."

"My prosperity? Really? I'm not seeing one way that I come out ahead by ruining myself."

"Maybe you need to come off your high horse a bit to see the possibilities. Henry is expecting you at noon." The silence settled between us. "You may go now."

I pulled in front of Henry's house, rang the bell, followed him to my torture chamber. There, like a puppet on a string, I awaited the next form of destruction he would throw my way.

"We'll be flying to the Bahamas this afternoon."

"Who's we?" I asked, terrified of the answer.

"You and I are going together."

"Hell, no." I surprised myself a bit.

"Excuse me?" Henry said, much like a father hearing the same words.

"I don't know what's going on here. I can't up and run off to Miami or the Bahamas whenever you and Bruce want me to and do whatever it is that you're doing with whomever." I had to stop my hands from flailing frantically in the air. If I'd had more time to edit my wording, I might have said something like, "Take care of your own illegal shit. I'm out."

"Skylar, maybe the trip is not what you think. It's your time to find out what I've been trying to show you."

"And what's that?"

"To know more, you have to trust me and come with me." For the first time, I sensed vulnerability in his voice.

We stared at each other intently until the weaker one of us had to speak or look away.

"I need to go pack," I said.

"The trip is all-expenses-paid, including clothes and toothbrush." Was that a friendly smile?

"I have expensive taste."

Henry looked me up and down. "I can tell." I tried to straighten myself into my 'you can't insult me' pose. "I've estimated you to be a size 6. A suitcase will be waiting for you at the airport. All you need is your passport."

"How do I explain a suitcase of new clothes to Adam?" I may have yelled.

"I'm assuming Adam is your husband?"

"Well, not yet."

Henry's expression wobbled between amusement and pity, and, if possible, I despised him even more for it.

"Your lover then."

"He's not my lover."

Henry raised his hand to let me know he had grown bored with the conversation.

"The suitcase will come back with me. That way, you'll be ready if there's a next time."

"Well, then, I guess you solved all the problems," I said with as much sarcasm as possible.

When we boarded the plane and settled into our first-class seats, I imagined a life where money was no object. The flight attendant handed me my cocktail, I think vodka and cranberry. She then brought me a blanket and eye mask. Leaning back in my seat, I became lost in Henry's world of luxury.

For a moment, I questioned myself and many of the situations in my life. What if Henry wasn't evil? What if I truly stood on the brink of an opportunity? What if Henry was a patriot for our country and not some criminal with millions of illegally earned dollars? What if my phone wasn't lighting up with texts from Brent begging me to contact him if I needed anything done? What if I wasn't searching my mind for some complex task only so I could communicate with him?

During the flight and the drive to the harbor, there was no conversation, no eye contact, nothing. Henry led me onto the most incredible-looking yacht I had ever been on, and even though I fought hard against being impressed, I was. Music came from within the cabin, and when we entered, a dozen people greeted me, smiling at me as they would react to the guest of honor. Could these people be my future business partners for a legit company that only by chance needed falsified FBARs and multiple offshore accounts?

"Can I get you a drink?"

Henry's arm grazed across my back, and even though I entertained the idea of trusting him, his touch still felt like a snake sliding past my bare skin. I'm sure he sensed me recoil a bit. Since the couple of drinks from the plane had worn off, leaving me groggy yet still mentally aware, I figured I could have one more. Plus, I felt entirely out of my element. A drink would help.

Henry disappeared behind the bar and then reappeared. His back faced me as he mixed my drink. A well-built man, maybe mid-thirties, whispered in his ear. Henry nodded in my direction, and the stranger looked right at me. If they'd tried to be inconspicuous, they'd failed.

Henry introduced me to the cheery shipmates, and despite myself, they grew on me. One woman in her mid-thirties, blond and fake everything down to the eyelashes, offered to help me prepare for the evening. Before I knew it, she'd whisked me away and dressed me in a beautiful yet casual black evening dress. Along with that, she applied my makeup perfectly, and I smelled so good. In fact, I had never looked better or felt better or smelled better. I learned the other women's names—Cynthia, Charmaine, and Kate—and I loved them. I really loved them. Somewhere in the back of my mind, I thought, this is strange. I don't love people that much, and especially not women like these women. Regardless, I loved them.

We walked out into the main room of the yacht. Maybe someone had changed the music. Perhaps the blame fell on the breeze coming off the ocean, or the stars shining down on us, but somehow, instead of strangers, these people were family. Every one of them, even the weird-looking guy in the corner who didn't quite fit in, was family. Maybe he had felt like an outsider his whole life and merely needed someone to love him. While studying him from across the yacht, I decided he would be the first person I pulled to the dance floor.

I can't remember loving dancing, yet nothing felt better. After what seemed like hours, still not enough time, Henry took my arm and eased me away from the crowd. We were connected, Henry and I. We were in the middle of something big, making us some sort of soulmates.

"Do you trust me now? Do you see how good it can be?" Henry asked.

"This is the best night I've ever had. Thank you."

"Good. I want to get you back to the dance floor. The night is far from over, so I need you to do something for me."

My initial dance partner, holding a pen and some paper, appeared in the doorway. I only needed to sign a few things and get back to my friends. Pretty easy. I remember writing my name over and over, and for a long time after there was something else on the edge of my memory. It toyed with the idea of coming into focus like a picture on a staticky television. My instincts told me to remember the numbers, yet the task proved impossible. It happened so quickly; like a blink of a star's light, one second when the universe lost power. I may have even hugged Henry before skipping back to my friends.

I awoke to the sun glaring in my eyes. My head throbbed, and I felt unbelievably thirsty. I was still on the yacht, but the room was empty. I lay sprawled out in my underclothes; underclothes that reminded me of how Cinderella felt after the magic moment had passed when she looked down at her ragged dress. Searching under the bed and dresser, I scrambled to find my phone. It was nowhere. Behind the fear, an incredible urge to cry, or rather sob uncontrollably, emerged. Everything appeared dismal; my job, my life, my relationship with Adam. Why hadn't he ever wanted to marry me? And I would have let myself curl up into a pathetic ball right then, except the sliding door of the bedroom opened, and there was Henry, holding my phone.

"Looking for this?" He tossed the phone on the bed and turned to leave.

"Thanks," I mumbled.

"Breakfast is ready on the deck when you're dressed."

Shit, he had just seen me scrambling on the floor in my grandma panties. I pulled on a fluffy white robe; the only item of clothing left in the room. The suitcase containing the all-expenses-paid clothes had magically disappeared along with my dress from the night before. After brushing my teeth with the toothbrush that he'd so graciously left behind, I went upstairs. Even the clear blue water and the cloudless sky couldn't lift my despair. I was empty, and at that moment, I thought I would always be empty.

Henry sat at a small table, covered with a white tablecloth. A yellow flower stood at attention between the two plates. His eggs benedict was half-eaten, but he pushed the plate aside, as if he'd lost his appetite when I approached.

"I don't know what happened last night," I said. "I'm not used to drinking that much, I guess."

"No harm done. The plane leaves in a few hours if you want to shower first."

I was having one of those coyote ugly moments without having had the sex.

"What about making me understand that things aren't what they seem, that they're actually good?"

"Did you have a good time?" Henry asked with a businesslike tone.

"I thought I did, but I'm regretting it now." Regret was an understatement. I'd had hangovers before from one too many glasses of wine. Very seldomly, but still, I'd had experienced a hangover. I had never endured anything like the misery I felt at that moment. Maybe I could blame the mixed drinks, or perhaps the number of them, but something told me there was more to my situation. I tried to recall how many glasses I had downed. It was impossible, and the effort nauseated me.

"Well, for now, why don't you focus on how you felt last night?" Henry paused while I took a bite. Something about the way he watched me made me very aware of the disgust he felt for me. "Your clothes have been cleaned, and someone will bring them to the bedroom momentarily. I will also give you one outfit to fly home in; a token of my appreciation. Everything else you'll need you'll find in the bathroom. I'll meet you up here in an hour."

The warm water ran down my body, while I tried without success to wash away the pieces of me that weren't really me. Dancing under the stars with strangers? What the heck? Who were those people I loved so dearly last night? They were like ghosts that had disappeared with the sunrise. How many times had Adam and I had a couple of drinks over dinner while sitting across from each other, people watching? We'd both admired each other's ability to find fault with people's parenting, hairstyles, shoe choice. We'd sat in our glass bubble, judging the people we had no desire to get to know. No amount of hot water could stop my head from throbbing or my world from spinning or make it possible for me to hide the truth. No amount of alcohol in the world could make me love those people.

Images of myself dancing, hugging, and laughing raced through my mind that scrambled to uncover something. Other memories, the truth, and then a vision came to me. I'd held a pen. Yes, I remembered. I signed papers, and what had seemed like many papers. As more images surfaced, bile rose in my throat. Failing to stop the progression, I vomited violently until nothing more would come up, leaving me feeling more desolate than I'd ever felt before.

By the time I was ready to meet Henry on the deck of the yacht, my jaw had clenched with rage. I wanted to go to battle, yet I was as prepared as a soldier with bullet wounds and no weapon. When I found him, he was looking out over the ocean, unaware, or so I thought, of me approaching.

"What did you put in my drink?"

He turned with the cocky smile of a demon.

"What makes you think I would put something in your drink, Skylar?"

"I don't like people. I don't do fancy. I don't get drunk. And I don't sign papers when I have no idea what they are."

"The very reasons I don't care for you. Despite that, you were the perfect choice."

"Perfect choice for what?"

"As an accountant, of course."

"How's that?"

"You have time to travel and do the extra duties that this account demands since your social calendar remains pretty empty."

A wave of anger swelled inside of me that I rarely had, if ever, felt before.

"I enjoy my life exactly as it is, thank you."

"To each his own."

When Henry chose to make eye contact, it was always after he believed he'd won a battle, and he was drilling home the victory flag in the middle of my chest. I envisioned myself pushing him overboard, his head hitting an anchor hanging from the side, blood spilling into the water, and finally, sharks circling to finish the job. Instead, I stood, dumbfounded, my head swirling. Where the hell were the awesome one-liners? Where was the hidden pistol in the back of my slacks—pants he'd bought a bit too small to add to my humiliation?

"The car is waiting for us."

I followed Henry, still his marionette, but one thing was for sure, the strings were beginning to fray.

CHAPTER 8

AFTER THE BAHAMAS trip, Adam began acting strange. What was I supposed to do? Distract him from the fact that I was distracted? Yes! So, I bought a negligee, wine, and take-out Thai food from our favorite restaurant. I even lit a candle, and waiting in my overpriced nightgown, stood by the table. I heard Adam's car pull in and adjusted my pose, trying to find the sensual side of me that only made rare appearances.

That's when the door opened, revealing not only Adam but his coworker, Scott. Shocked, I knocked over the candle and spilled wax into the Thai food. While trying to prevent a house fire, I flashed our guest and then, mumbling apologies, ran out of the room. The last vision they had was of me and my jiggling backside scrambling down the hallway.

Once in the bedroom, I paced until Adam joined me about ten minutes later. His face was solemn, which stung more than had he laughed.

In one hand, he held the bottle of wine, and in the other, he held the two glasses.

"I hope both of those glasses are for me," I said with a pathetic half-smile.

"I'm afraid I may be needing one as well," he said with a grin.

"I'm so embarrassed. Why did you bring someone back to

the house tonight of all nights? You never bring anyone back," I pleaded, not so much to him but to the little cosmic nymph that was having a heyday in the clouds somewhere.

"It was just one of those days at work, and I thought a cold beer would be nice. Next time, we'll go to a bar."

"Please do. So, did Scott say anything, or did he turn and run?" Too upset about the whole fiasco, I didn't question Adam's rare desire to drink with his coworkers.

"He bolted out the door right after he asked if he could share the story at the water cooler tomorrow."

Since Adam had not yet poured the wine, I smacked him in the arm once before grabbing the bottle myself.

"I would never speak to you again if you allowed Scott to repeat a word about this night."

Adam held out his glass so I would fill it. "Being the new world traveler, you may never even hear about it. Then again, it is a good story. It may travel." Adam smiled and took a drink before wiping his lips with the back of his hand.

"I'm sorry. I don't want to be traveling so much. Trust me."

"You haven't worn a negligee since, well, ever."

"I'm more of a cotton person. Seriously, I might be getting a rash." I searched my chest for redness but found nothing.

"I've heard that when your partner starts dressing in sexy clothes, is running away on trips, and is losing weight," Adam said solemnly, "a guy should start worrying."

"Do you think I'm losing weight?" I intended my question to be comical, except it fell short. "Adam, I don't have much choice."

"Have you ever tried telling your boss no?"

"I can't. I would lose my job."

Adam got quiet for a moment. "Well, I guess I will have to

trust that you won't forget me when you're gallivanting around the world. Just promise me, Skylar, you will never make me that guy who didn't see it coming. Promise me that you won't make a fool out of me for trusting you, for believing in us."

"You know I could never do that to you."

I wanted to shout from the rooftops that I would never fail him. As if screaming the words would make the alternative impossible. It's one thing to feel tempted. It's another thing to act on the temptation. Adam served as my island, and it was from that island, I would stand firm, watching the temptations drift by. Some things might catch my attention, they might even call to me as they passed, but I wouldn't let that change me. From my island, these distractions were small clips from someone else's movie. I'd bought my ticket to this one, and I would see it to the end.

Overpowered by my renewed devotion, I shimmied my lace-covered body a bit closer, intending a passionate kiss. The moment felt forced. Our bodies remained stiff, and our gazes refused to connect. I let the moment die.

"Do you want to tell me what's going on with work, why you needed to bring a coworker to dinner?"

Adam remained silent as he eyed the bed. Him avoiding the question served as enough incentive to reignite the flame.

"I have a better idea," I said. "Let's forget about both of our jobs and enjoy a little dessert before the Thai food."

We became two people going through the motions if only to avoid speaking.

When I next walked into the office, I felt like a ghost, watching rather than living, drifting between the cubicles. I straddled two realms. When Brent had entered my life, I'd been sure he'd brought with him a mysterious presence. I remembered wanting it. Had my secrets formed into mystical snowflakes that had covered my body the way I'd felt they'd covered Brent's. No one had looked up at me or noticed me in any way. My snowflakes had not glistened to them.

The sound of Liz giggling in Brent's cubicle brought me back from the other realm. Seriously, did the woman ever work? A sliver of the old me that used to care, tried to rear its ugly head. That little sliver tempted me to peek over the cubicle and interrupt their conversation. *Did I hear you say you were at the local pub doing shots again? You're amazing! And to think all I did was run off to a million-dollar yacht and possibly drop acid, but I'm not sure what it was. Whatever it was, it made me dance throughout the night under the stars and awake in someone else's bed. But, you know, the bar thing sounds good, too.*

A petrified feeling clenched my heart when I thought of what had happened during those hours on the yacht. The tale morphed back into something too sickening to brag about to anyone.

I worked nonstop until around four o'clock when Bruce came by my cubicle to tell me to wrap up what I was doing and swing by Henry's. Bruce promised it would be quick. Did he realize that the drive to Henry's on its own couldn't qualify as fast? After about half an hour, I went to the breakroom to wash my mug before heading out. Brent came in behind me. An unwanted relief washed over me as if I had been holding my breath until that moment.

"So, mystery woman, are you heading off into the unknown again?"

"I have to make a quick stop by my client's house. That's what Bruce tells me anyway." For some unfair reason, the caffeine must have hit me because my heart raced, and my hands became unsure of their grip on my mug.

"Did your recent trip have anything to do with the men in suits who came into Bruce's office while you were away?"

"I don't know anything about that, so I guess not."

We stared at each other in expectation until Brent broke.

"When are you going to give up being a mystery lady?"

"Why should I? Don't men find mysterious women intriguing?" Yikes, I'd edged too close to a line. Why had I blown on dying embers?

"Not always. Sometimes we just find them annoying." He turned and walked out of the office. Dammit, how could he flatten me so effortlessly?

For some reason, Brent's words took their time sinking in. After about ten minutes of driving to Henry's, sheer panic emerged from the growing pit inside of me. Who were the men in suits at McClurry & Associates, and why were they there? Blindly, I drove the rest of the way while wrestling with possibilities my simple mind could not quite process. When I pulled up to Henry's house, I saw another car parked in the driveway. I rang the bell, and one of Henry's staff members I had not met on previous visits answered the door. For the most part, the help was only noticeable in the completed tasks and perfection throughout the home.

"I'll bring you to Henry. Please follow me." I followed the lanky man down a hallway. In case his identity would be valuable in the future, I studied him. He wore dark slacks and a white button-up Oxford, and I guessed him to be in his mid-fifties. I began to question everything, even my perception of his age since I often thought of any mature-looking adult as older than me. I'm often surprised to realize that we are the same age, or worse yet, they are younger. I mentally filed my observations and attempted to dig for other details.

"So, are you the one responsible for my wonderful lunches?"

"Henry is right in here." The staff member opened a door I had not even noticed before, and Henry stood inside the room with another man I had not met. Then the man who had greeted me at the door disappeared down the hallway. So much personality in this house, it became hard to handle.

The room appeared to be either a formal sitting area or a library. Seeing how both did not exist in my own home, I couldn't be sure. It had a mini wet bar in the corner and shelves lined with books. In the opposite corner, the spectacle-wearing bald man that Henry had yet to introduce fidgeted with a camera. The camera faced a screen much like the one I had stood in front of each year for my school mugshot. The man finished his task and turned toward me as Henry spoke.

"Skylar, this is my business photographer. He'll be getting your photo for your personnel file."

"My what?"

"Your personnel photo," he said, not wavering.

"Why? I'm not part of your personnel."

"Skylar, wasting minutes arguing a point you won't win isn't in any of our interests."

I looked at the nameless photographer to sense if he, by any chance, could be on my side. His cold, dismissive eyes stared back at me. No help there. Of the many actions I had taken up to that point, was it worth worrying about a stupid picture? Taking my place in front of the blue drop-down screen, I smiled like an adolescent forced to look happy on a family vacation and then stepped away.

"Would you mind showing yourself out? We have no further need of you today." Without a word, I grabbed my purse and headed for the door while mumbling profanities that would shame a trucker. In my car, I tightly gripped the steering wheel. A desire to go in and take back something he'd stolen from me overwhelmed me. I remembered a time an aggressive salesperson, promising their product from deep in the sea would make me youthful again, had accosted me at our local mall. I'm a Dove soap and occasional Noxzema kind of girl, so when I'd gotten back to the car that day, and stared at the receipt for five hundred dollars' worth of nonrefundable anti-aging products that remained hidden in my closet, I could only wonder how I'd become snared in the salesman's trap. This time, there wasn't a receipt to give my loss a value, even though I feared it was great.

CHAPTER 9

I FELL ASLEEP TO the ceiling fan clicking as it did every night. Neither Adam nor I, being about as mechanically inclined as sloths trying to pick a lock, had been able to find the source of the mysterious sound. I must admit that besides mumbling obscenities and promising to look at the fan in the morning, we hadn't attempted any repair. So, as usual, I decided to force myself to fall asleep by making the noise a part of a calming dream. The strategy worked almost without fail. Letting go of all the day's events, I envisioned, until the image gained its own life, an unenthusiastic teacher tapping his finger on the desk.

The room was hot and stale. Light filtered through the window and glistened off dust specks that floated in the air. Around me, my classmates' sleepy faces stared forward at the teacher who sat at his desk. He wore a white button-up shirt. The sleeves were rolled up, most likely due to the uncomfortable temperature.

We sat in silence except for the teacher's thick finger, tapping out a hypnotic rhythm. A pendulum on his desk demanded my attention. The sound that lulled me now emanated from the colliding silver balls. I remained entranced until the tick-tock became so loud and fast that I awoke in a sweat. In the darkness of my bedroom, the ceiling fan clicked rhythmically, bringing the strange teacher and his pendulum into reality.

Later that day, as I sat at my desk, I took a break from the credits and debits and consulted Google. My search revealed my dream might serve as a warning that lies and rumors surrounded me. Really?

As if on cue, some strange-looking people came in, and Patty directed them to Bruce's office. Moments later, the visitors reemerged. The three of them stood in front of Bruce's door, and he announced he needed our attention. It was time; we would all get some answers.

"Due to some things brought to my attention, I am requiring that all employees submit to a random drug test. Everyone will need to meet with these healthcare professionals privately and give both blood and urine samples."

"Are you kidding me?" Liz exclaimed.

If guilty sweat hadn't formed on the underarm areas of my blouse, I would have raised my arms and shouted, "Hallelujah! Liz is going down." Instead, I stole a look at Brent and caught him studying me again. He always watched me like a guardian or a vulture; I'm not sure which one.

"Before everyone freaks out, I will discuss the results in private with each of you. We will deal with the outcomes on a one-to-one basis. It does not necessarily mean termination. The healthcare professionals will take over from here."

He motioned to the men and then slid back into his office. They began calling our names. Suddenly, all my coworkers needed coffee, and the complaints were running rampant. Some of the staff sat Googling their civil rights even though I highly doubted most of them had ever touched anything stronger than a glass of wine. *Calm down, everyone.* I wanted to shout. *Bruce couldn't care less if you are shooting up heroin in the bathrooms. The drug test is about one person and one person only, and that person just got another noose around her neck.*

After my humiliating moment of handing my urine over to a stranger, Bruce sent me off to Henry's again. Once there, Henry walked me to my usual spot in his home office and gave me some files from McClurry & Associates; my regular, everyday drab accounts instead of his personal accounts.

"Why do you have these?"

"I got them from Bruce. You can work on these today."

"Can't I work on them from the office?"

"I think it's best if you work here this week. Some things need to settle down right now at McClurry & Associates."

"Are you referring to the men in suits or the random drug test? Nice touch, by the way."

I noticed a slight lift of his lip that may have been the admission of guilt, except no comment followed.

"Is someone going to tell me what's going on?" I asked. "The men that talked to Bruce are going to talk to me eventually. If they want to, they can find me at my house."

"We're aware of that. It's about time you knew a few more details."

I sat up, ready, ears perked, but then he simply turned and, without a word, walked away. The walls surrounded me like a prison cell, and I feared I might need to get used to the feeling of captivity.

Around lunchtime, Henry entered with a Panera lunch. The kitchen help must have had other things to do. Henry handed me a folder and sat, dangerously close to me, with half of his backside on the desk.

"We have a new client you will deal with from time to time. Her name is Brenda Carter."

Some memory in the back of my mind opened one eye at

the sound of that name, but then quickly closed it again. "Okay. So, when do I meet her?"

"You won't be meeting with her. Your interactions will consist strictly of emails. It's best that way."

"Fine. Whatever." I looked back at the new forms in front of me, hoping he would go away.

"She owns a business—construction—that I use for repairs on my hotels."

"Anything I should know about this construction business?" I refrained from making quotation marks in the air.

"It doesn't really matter what you want to know. Does it?"

"Of course not."

He smirked down at me.

"Well, I should get back to what I'm doing."

His smirk remained until I turned away, and, I'm guessing, long after he'd slithered down the hallway, leaving a trail of poison behind.

The first communication from Brenda Carter came in the form of an email. Soon after I had downed my Panera sandwich—Asiago roast beef, usually my favorite—I followed the directions given and transferred money from a bank in the U.S. to an offshore account in the Bahamas. I noted the fact that the account was in a Wyoming bank. Accountants knew Wyoming had once been referred to as the "Cayman Islands of the American Prairie." I guessed that having an "offshore" account in the U.S. was beginning to get too close for someone's comfort.

As Brenda's accountant, I was able to complete deposits and withdrawals from her accounts. Henry assured me that Brenda had granted me permission and both banks had cleared me. Even though I had doubts about how clean the money was,

I couldn't quite see how my part would be illegal, so I would do what they asked of me. Sure, some form needed filing if I suspected money laundering. Except, this was nothing more than a company spreading its wealth, or so I told myself. Even so, Brenda Carter was now up there on my list of people I despised.

It disgusted me how easy it was to click some buttons and take what I assumed was illegal money and deposit it in, I was sure, an illicit offshore account. After that, all I needed to do was send Brenda the confirmation number. With a big chug of sweet tea, I swallowed the acid rising in my throat.

Before long, I got back to my legit computer and my legit accounts. I logged on to Steve Stark's account. He owned a seafood store in the Jacksonville area. Whenever I entered the premises; Steve greeted me with a smile that appeared friendlier than I deserved. They always carried an assortment of once-living creatures that entertained me and sickened me at the same time. Frog legs for instance. Who really ate those things? Sometimes his adolescent son worked behind the counter with him. He had such excellent manners, and he always answered my questions. As people went, they were some good ones. They didn't make much, but they served their customers as if they loved what they were doing. Steve, once nothing more than a client, became a spark of much-needed goodness in my otherwise bleak reality.

CHAPTER 10

THE RESULTS SHOULDN'T have surprised me. I'd failed my drug test. Bruce came to Henry's the next day to share the news. Staring out at the Intracoastal, I slathered a bagel with strawberry cream cheese and poured some orange juice. Feeling bold, I plopped down in Henry's chair, hoping to leave breadcrumbs all over it. I took a large bite, making sure that I faced away from the camera so I could enjoy the thick, chewy bread without his judgmental scowl. That's when the door opened and in came Bruce and Henry. The two of them stood over me like disappointed parents.

"Well, Skylar, I guess you are not as clean-cut as you like to pretend," Henry said.

"Excuse me?" Darn the thick, chewy bread. I reached for my orange juice but didn't have enough room in my mouth for it.

"You failed the drug test," he continued, hands in his pockets like he was deciding what weapon to pull out next.

"Are you kidding me?" That's what I said, except what they heard through the bread likely sounded different.

"Bruce tells me it's grounds for dismissal."

Finally, I swallowed. "You know why I failed that test."

"I have no clue what you are trying to insinuate, but I assure you, your accusations will not stick."

"That's fine with me because I will get another job, which

will make me much happier, I'm sure." Why was my voice cracking? Why did I want to cry every time someone made me this mad?

"Skylar," Bruce chimed in, "where would you go for a reference? I would have to tell any potential employer why I let you go, wouldn't I?"

"You're both bastards." I stood and grabbed my things.

"Hold up, Skylar," Henry said. "No one wants to wreck your career because you tested positive for the drug Ecstasy. Correct, Bruce? Since you have been so helpful on my account, Bruce has decided to let you stay as long as you continue to be a good sport."

Henry smirked, and Bruce squirmed. I hated them both almost equally.

"I suppose something big is coming my way?"

"Nothing you can't handle, Skylar. We have faith in you." They turned almost in unison toward the door. "For your efforts, why don't you take an early day? You can leave by four," Henry added as if he were my boss.

"Thanks," I said right before I took the rest of my bagel slathered in strawberry cream cheese and threw it at the door as it closed. The bagel slid down the paneling until it hit the doorknob and plopped onto the hardwood. The realization that my only weapon was a bagel sickened me. Somewhere inside of me had to be someone who wasn't so weak and pathetic.

I was almost home when Brent's text lit up my phone. *Any chance you would want to meet for a drink?*

Definitely. My response created zero guilt, because I felt too defeated to have an inappropriate thought. I needed a friend. I needed Brent. An hour later, we met at an out-of-the-way bar, which only the locals would enter; far enough away that we wouldn't know anyone. The choice of bar had everything to do with keeping my social life private from Bruce and Henry. Brent was already there when I arrived, and he rose to pull out my barstool for me.

"What'll you have?" Brent asked.

"I'd like bourbon on the rocks, but that may not go well for my drive home."

"No kidding? I didn't take you for a bourbon girl."

"I've never actually touched the stuff," I said with obvious disappointment in myself.

"That's a good thing, Skylar. I like that about you." He got the bartender's attention with a simple raise of his hand. "How about a chardonnay?"

"Perfect."

We sat in comfortable silence until the bartender set the drinks in front of us.

"What's making you want to cross the line to the hard stuff today?" Brent asked.

"Nothing. Everything." I rested my face in my hands.

"I'm a good listener," he prompted. I stayed silent, hiding in the darkness of my palms. "Why don't you start by telling me about this client? What do you know about him?"

After a deep breath and a sip of wine, I sat up. "Well, I know he owns hotels, a few big ones. And a chain of run-down ones reaching down to Opa-locka. Starting to ring a bell?"

"What's his full name again?"

"Henry Davis."

"So, he's the one that's making you drink tonight?"

I nodded.

"The accounts looked pretty clear cut from what I saw."

I was sharing too much. "Oh, yes, they are. It's just, well… he's not a very nice person to work with, that's all."

"I know a bit about him. His father was quite wealthy. He owned several hotels at one point, but he died some time ago. Henry must have made out well with the inheritance."

"Apparently. Henry's house is on the Intracoastal and quite nice. Yacht parked by the shore. I would say he does all right."

"In other words, he's a rich, cocky bastard?"

"Pretty much. Very particular and demanding. And very used to getting his way."

"What does he want from you? You're only an accountant. What can he be demanding of you that's legal?"

There was so much I wanted to say as we sat staring into each other's eyes in that dark bar room. Some of it might have come out if my phone hadn't started ringing. Bruce's name stared back at me from the lit-up screen.

"I need to take this. Sorry, Brent."

"No problem. I'm going to run to the bathroom." Brent walked away, leaving his wallet on the bar. As I answered the phone, I couldn't help but run my hand over the wallet while wondering about its contents and why he would trust me with it. I guess he knew he was buying my drinks anyway.

"Hello?" I said, knowing the voice on the other end was one I didn't want to hear.

"Skylar, I'm going to need you to go on another trip for us."

The rage that Henry and Bruce so easily created within me scratched its way to the surface. There were a million responses I wanted to give, but I answered the only way I could. "Where? When?"

"The flights are booked for tomorrow afternoon. You'll be

working on Henry's hotel accounts again. Sam Murphy manages these hotels as well."

"Sam Murphy. Oh, yeah, the man who manages Henry's run-down crappy motels in Miami."

"Yes, but these hotels are in the Bahamas. Brent will join you again."

Again, if I chose to argue, Bruce would win. Telling Bruce that spending nights away with Brent was like an alcoholic being expected to drink club soda at a bar would not help the situation either. In fact, Bruce would probably enjoy the fact he'd put me in an uncomfortable situation.

"I can go to the Bahamas on my own."

"No, we need Brent to go along with you. Get used to it, Skylar."

"Why? I need to know. Is Brent in on this with you? Why does he have to follow me everywhere?"

"You'll know what you need to know when you need to know it."

"I'll ask him then."

"That would be a horrible mistake, Skylar. Sometimes strange things happen when you travel out of the country. Sometimes people don't make it back."

"Are you threatening me? Did you just threaten to have me killed if I talk to Brent?" My hands shook with both fear and anger as I clung to the phone.

"Skylar, I want you safe. For that to happen, you have to listen to me, please. Go to Henry's in the morning, and he will give you your tickets and instructions."

"I'm going to work on hotel accounts, I thought."

"Go to Henry's in the morning." Bruce hung up.

With perfect timing, Brent came back.

"Well, we're going to the Bahamas tomorrow," I said.

"More of Henry's hotels?"

"How'd you guess?" Even though he could have guessed, I couldn't ignore the momentary flinch—an awkward shift in eye contact—as if he'd said too much. I hoped I was only paranoid.

"Well, it's what we did in Miami. I assumed it would be the same." He tipped his glass back and finished it. Was he nervous? I hoped not. I couldn't trust my instincts. A wave of nausea came over me. Brent motioned to the bartender for another beer, a visible sign of nervousness. Brent was hiding something.

CHAPTER 11

WHAT DO YOU want me to do, Adam? It's my job." I'm not sure who was more surprised by my harsh tone, Adam or me. I heard it yet couldn't stop it. "I don't question every overnight trip you need to go on, do I?"

"When does Bruce ever send you to the Bahamas?"

"Every year is different, Adam," I said, exasperated. "He's always trying to get new accounts, and this one's big with hotels in many places. It is conceivable he has confidence in me, and that's why he chose me." I left out the part that I'd failed my drug test and my job was on the line.

Inside, I screamed, *Stop! For God's sake, stop the lying.* Except I couldn't, and I proved to be an angry liar. Psychologists would have a grand time explaining my puffing up like a rabid badger to protect myself, but Adam was not a psychologist. He didn't know that what I desired most was to run to him and cry for endless hours on his shoulder. Instead, he became somber, ate, and offered to clean up while I packed. I sat on the edge of my bed, trying to predict how my spiraling fall would end and what shape I would be in when Henry and Bruce decided to release me from their hold.

That night Adam held me close as we slept, and the next morning we shared tender kisses before heading out the door. I hated everyone at that moment, except him. What had I gotten myself into? What had I gotten Adam into? Were we both in danger?

I met Brent at the airport. He stood there in his jeans and fitted T-shirt, looking like a kid about to go off to camp. If he knew my real mission, he might lose that confident grin on his cocky face. If I told him, could he help me figure out a way to save myself? The problem remained, I had not decided whose team he was on, let alone pegged him as my savior.

"Well, good morning, traveling partner."

"Good morning," I replied, not offering more.

"That didn't sound like much of a greeting. Hell, we have an all-expenses-paid trip to the Bahamas. What could you be in a bad mood about?"

"I never asked to go to the Bahamas."

"Okay, so where would you prefer to go?"

"You know that's not the point." I finished checking in at the kiosk and, dragging my carry-on luggage, wheeled past him. He followed like a far too eager puppy. It was strange and empowering being the one not trailing him or caring to, either. "Brent, this is going to be much more professional this time." I faced him. "I allowed myself to get too close to a line by going to the beach with you. It's a line I never intended to cross. I assure you, it won't happen again."

"I respect that."

"Do you?"

"More than you know."

"Fine. At least we're in agreement."

I was sweating everywhere. Brent had to have noticed that my hands were shaking. I had orders to find a tall man with light brown hair and blue eyes located in the TSA line I had to go through to have my luggage scanned. He would be the one watching while we took off our shoes and jackets. Next to him would be the second friend of Henry's, bought and paid for, who would watch as my carry-on slid through the scanner. What if Henry's helpers aborted the plan? What if they called me out on the stacks of money well beyond the ten thousand dollars I should have claimed?

I easily picked out the tall man amongst the women and shorter pudgy men. He made subtle eye contact, and I headed in that direction.

"Skylar, this line is much shorter. Come over here."

Brent looked at me with a quizzical expression. He had to wonder why I would avoid the shorter line. He must have assumed I attempted to keep distance between us.

I scrambled to throw my shoes in a bin. "I'm already unloading. This is fine."

After an eye roll, he left me to continue as I saw fit. It seemed to take forever for my bag to pass through the scanner. The man, conceivably to appear engrossed in his work, stayed hidden on the other side. A more likely reason was to remain unseen by other people, meaning me, wrapped up in Henry's web. Finally, my suitcase made its appearance, and I breathed a bit easier. Grabbing my things, I scrambled to get away from security.

I walked toward our gate at a fast enough pace to make it awkward for Brent to catch up. As soon as I was able to sit, I tried to lose myself in my book but found that I kept reading the same paragraph over and over. My stolen glances often met with Brent's as he sat across from me reading a paper. He would grin, I would ignore it, and then he would catch me again.

It infuriated me that in a world of attraction, where the

continuation of our species depended on magnetism, we had no control over it. Adam and I, well, we were like the earth and the moon, circling the universe together, never leaving each other's side because we had no choice or desire to change. Without each other, one of us would go spiraling until we slipped into someone else's gravitational pull. Up to this point, nothing had come close to bumping us off our path. After all, what were the chances one would pass another object at the exact moment that its speed matched with the pull of that unknown object creating a new orbit altogether? And if that did happen, whose fault was it?

For years I'd spiraled around the universe as happy as could be. And then, I'd become aware of the sun. Due to the sun's enormous size, the moon's gravitational pull to the earth paled in comparison. Now that the sun had revealed itself behind the eclipse of the moon, it was impossible to ignore.

If only I could decide if the sun was there to blister my skin or give me life. One minute I swore to myself that Brent was out to destroy me; the next, he made adrenaline rush to every part of my body. How could I explain my feelings even to myself? These were feelings I'd never asked to have or wanted to have, yet I couldn't, no matter how much I tried, deny them.

As we caught each other in mid-peek again, his smile, warm and inviting, like a crackling fire, lingered in the air. Suddenly, I knew exactly how he made me feel when around him—like I was home, in a place where I could curl up with a cozy blanket and chat about anything. I wanted to hear about all the parts of him. Who were his parents? Did he have siblings? What would be his perfect weekend?

Being around him reminded me of one of the adventures I'd most enjoyed with my family, the winter before everything had come to an end. We were in the Adirondack mountains. My parents, determined to teach me to ski, had spent hours picking me out of snowbanks. Despite their efforts, my favorite memory hadn't been on the slopes. My favorite memory had formed as we'd watched the crackling fire, laughed about my lack of skills and sipped hot chocolate. Outside, snow had blanketed the trees and created a wonderland. The warmth from the fire had seeped into the memory, and for the longest time, had kept me warm when the memories had become too painful. Except this wasn't the cabin I'd once shared with my parents. It was some stranger's cabin I wasn't invited to visit. Brent felt right, and yet he was so wrong.

"We are now boarding flight 4590 to Nassau," a woman's voice spoke over the intercom. Brent stood, walked toward me and reached for my bag that I had kept tight to my leg so I could detect any movement.

"Could I help you with that?"

"Oh, please. Like I can't handle a little piece of luggage," I said in my best attempt at a joke. If Brent were to lift my bag, he would find the weight of it suspicious. Who knew money weighed so much?

"Suit yourself," he replied.

We scanned our tickets from our phone and walked down the jetway and into the plane. The hairs on my neck stood alert as if an attack from behind was imminent. Nothing happened.

"Did you bring your suit?" Brent asked from behind me.

I glanced over my shoulder, looking disgusted even though the image of us swimming together was not unpleasant. "No, I did not bring my suit. Didn't I already tell you this would be a much more professional trip?"

"Yes, Ms. Skylar. My apologies, but it seems you are making

my question a bit more risqué than I'd intended. I'm not sure you're acting very professional, insinuating I was coming onto you in some way."

I rolled my eyes, which I'm sure he couldn't see and hoped the redness in my face would disappear before we reached our seats. With a glance, he asked if I wanted help lifting my luggage into the overhead bin, and with another look, I told him no. Without words, we settled into our seats. I sensed a change in Brent's attitude. He was getting sick of me, and a part of me wanted to say anything to fix it. I didn't.

I watched out the window as the luggage handlers loaded the suitcases and thought about Adam, which then made me think about Brent. I became aware of the feelings that were somehow missing in my otherwise perfect relationship. This unsettling awareness crept into the forefront of my mind. I likened it to the ache one felt for his or her ordinary life after traveling for a long time.

Adam had been a fourteen-year vacation from another life, and I'd begun to feel homesick. I'd spent years running, trying to avoid taking my hands off the wheel the way my parents had encouraged me to do. They'd always adventured together—hiking, kayaking, taking trips. *Life was meant to have some zest*, my mom had always said. And, maybe had I not lost my parents, I would have believed her more. Adam had been my steering wheel that I'd clung to for safety, and the idea of ever letting go petrified me.

The plane took off and reached cruising altitude. I sensed Brent looking at me. I remained in my thoughts, allowing in momentary memories of a time when adventures had been part of my life too. Was Brent's purpose in my life to bring me back "home?"

"Skylar." Brent's voice broke into my thoughts. A flight attendant stood beside us. "Do you want anything to drink?" Brent asked with slight agitation.

"Oh, no, thanks." I peered out the window and wondered what lay ahead at Customs. My blouse had not even completely dried from the sweat created from going through security at the airport.

I could almost feel my mother sitting next to me, smiling that smile she always had when setting out into the unknown—although I was quite sure she would not have approved of criminal activity. Sitting there petrified of the hours to come, I also missed my parents, their bravery, their excitement. I had let a piece of me die with them. Brent created a feeling essential to humanity, my humanity, a need for completion, that almost felt negligent not to fill. Something about him reminded me we weren't supposed to grip the wheel with white knuckles. He couldn't sense what was on my mind as I glared at him, a person I didn't even know well, with such distaste. Yet some part of me felt I had known him forever. He couldn't know that my feelings of distaste and angry glare, sprouted up from feelings that were so opposite.

Brent cleared his throat. "I'm guessing you know that Bruce told me I'd be auditing one hotel, and you will be auditing another."

"He did tell me that."

"Do I sense bitterness?"

I closed my book that had sat open on my lap.

"Let's just say, Bruce and I would not be great friends outside of work. Same for Henry." And then I had a thought. I would try to trip Brent up, make him admit that he knew him. I was desperate to know where Brent fell in all of this. "What is your impression of Henry?"

"Well, if you feel such adversity toward him, then I expect I would feel the same."

So much for that.

"Can you tell me what exactly makes you feel so uncomfortable about him? He's never been inappropriate, has he?"

Concern swept over Brent's face.

"No, he's never been inappropriate." I looked out the window for guidance but found none. "You know, Brent, I should get some sleep, so I'm prepared for when we get to the Bahamas."

"Okay, Skylar."

I closed my eyes, somehow knowing he was watching me.

"I'm here if you need me."

I swallowed, trying to erase the burning cry forming in my throat and turned away from the warmth of Brent, the sun in my solar system.

After a quick and uneventful layover in Miami, the plane landed with a startling thud at the Nassau airport. I associated the thud, at least in my mind, with the talents of a novice pilot. Always good to know I was hurtling through the clouds in a missile driven by an amateur. The young pilot had probably been wiping the sweat off his upper lip the whole time. I released my grip on the armrest. Right when I was about to feel safe, Brent tapped my hand, like a parent not wanting to overstep his bounds with a testy teenager. I yanked my hand from the sting of his touch and placed it on my lap.

"Seriously, you'd think they would cover landing a bit better in pilot school before they let them off into the world."

"Skylar?"

Skylar what? He left the question hanging with a million

possibilities. *Skylar, why are you so on edge? Skylar, why are you acting like you don't want me to hold your hand and make you feel safe through this nightmare? Skylar, why are you flying to the Bahamas to become a criminal?* Instead, though, he stared at me with genuine concern in his eyes. An image of myself regurgitating the details of the wretched events, forced upon me by a corrupt man, filled my mind. What if I did allow myself to recall everything like the fast-talking child retelling events of a horrific scene on the playground? The image became more humorous than impossible. It amused me enough I was able to take a deep breath and reevaluate the situation.

I hadn't completed Henry's next task yet. A million events could intervene. I might suddenly become a braver version of myself. On second thought, a hurricane from nowhere would be more realistic. Outside, thinking of me as nothing more than another tourist escaping reality, the palm trees waved hello. Brent stood to get our bags from above. I heard him behind me as I focused on the waving branches. I didn't fight him.

"I thought you feared planes. Shouldn't you be pushing people over to get off first?"

I stared right at him, digging deep with my gaze, begging him to stop me from following through with the plan. Instead, he did a 'wow; this chick is weird' chuckle and a headshake before handing me my bag.

"Did you pack a few bricks in this thing?"

I didn't answer.

I didn't want to add any other crazy descriptive words floating around in his mind about me. Standing, I took my bag and followed single-file down the aisle that led to the mature-looking pilot. Where else had my perceptions been off target?

"Should we share a cab, or would you be too offended to sit near me?" Brent asked.

"You can sit in the front." A half-smile, tired of hiding for so long, tugged at the corners of my mouth.

"Great idea. Probably better company up there."

"Unfortunately, you may be right, even if the driver can't speak English." I wanted Brent to know I understood his frustration. I wouldn't want to sit by me, either. He glanced at me from the corner of his eye. He might have thought he had an opening, but I refused to look his way.

And then he walked ahead of me, leaving me to stare at his back. I could have run up to him to apologize, but instead, I kept an even pace three strides back. The pull was strong, though, much like the pull a mosquito feels to the bug zapper. Yes, I reminded myself, it was possible to be drawn to the very thing that could destroy you.

Outside Brent waved down a cab and jumped in the front as the taxi driver came around the side to put our luggage in the trunk. I watched my bag until he'd slammed the trunk shut. My door remained closed. Deep inside of me, alarms sounded, "Someone is mad at you, someone is mad at you." For a person who had few close friends and wondered if I liked people much at all, this new concern was unsettling. I enjoyed disliking people from afar and wanted them to have enough mutual respect to do the same. Brent wasn't hiding his distaste for me at all. I couldn't take it on top of the other stresses encircling my mind. I opened my door and slid in the back.

"So, I would have dinner with you if you're interested," I offered.

"Let's see. I could have room service with the remote all to myself or sit across the table from a woman who hates me for no apparent reason. Room service is sounding great."

"You don't understand. There's a lot..."

"There's a lot on your mind," Brent said with annoyance. The cab driver settled into his seat and buckled his seat belt. He was a hefty man with a strong scent of cigarette smoke emanating from his sweat-stained t-shirt, which added to my building nausea. "How about me?" Brent continued. "I'm being shipped all over the world with you. One minute I was enjoying conversation and wine, and yes, I wondered what you were thinking. The next minute you acted like I'd thrown you down in the sand and had my way with you. I have been nothing but good to you, Skylar."

A flush rushed across my face "Brent, not in front of the driver!"

"We already decided he couldn't speak English."

"I speak English." The taxi driver probably wondered how he'd become a part of our argument.

"I am aware of the fact you didn't throw me in the sand." The heat in my face deepened. "I'm not upset about that."

"What are you upset about then? Are you mad I didn't throw you in the sand, or are you mad that you wished I had?"

"This is the last time we'll be going away together. I guarantee you that."

"Oh, really? That's disappointing."

I started to cry—and not a few tears trickling down my cheek. I'm talking about hiding my head in my hands; an I-could-use-a-tissue, kind of cry. I heard movement and mumbled complaints from the cab driver. When I looked up, Brent was coming over the seat to comfort me. The next thing I knew, I was sobbing on his shoulder. Everything I couldn't say poured out in my tears—how much I hated myself, how I hated Bruce and Henry, and how I wished I could trust Brent and needed to trust him.

"Can you just believe me that there is more than I can share going on right now?"

"Yes." His capable hand rubbed my back. Despite the danger, I wanted Brent in my life, because, at that moment, he was the second-best friend I had.

I called Adam after getting settled in my room, a room that was nice, yet not as impressive as the one in the Miami hotel. Evidently, Bruce had decided the seducing part of our relationship had come to an end. He had already trapped me.

How could I make Adam trust my loyalty? I couldn't let him down. Although I knew if he could see into my heart, I already had. In some strange way, I would have appreciated, even enjoyed, hearing him say: *Skylar, there's a woman at work I can't seem to keep a clear head about. Let's run off to a romantic island together and rekindle our relationship.* And then I would say: *That's so weird. I'm going through the same thing.* We would have a good laugh at the irony of the situation, him hiding his feelings, me hiding mine. All we actually needed to do was tell each other, and the unwanted feelings would fade away. Everything would turn out to be another bonding experience—not the likely outcome in reality. The conversation instead followed an almost scripted narrative starting with: "How was your day?"

After freshening up, Brent left to handle an account at one hotel while I pretended to head out to another hotel nearby. Instead, I took a cab to a much different place. I stepped onto the sidewalk in front of a massive, ornate building; a building responsible for legitimate transactions. Yet, someone who worked in that bank knew criminals like me wandered amid the other patrons. In my bag, I carried a suspicious amount of money. Where had the money come from? My guess was from a deal that would only sicken me. I was, whether I wanted to admit it or not, part of the dealings that I was of aware of and the dealings that lurked under the surface.

Craning my neck, I looked up to the peak of the four-story building. My life was spiraling. The sun, soft like a smile from above, beamed down on me. As if it was encouraging me, I said what may have been a prayer. *Give me an answer, universe. Give me a way out.*

A passerby jarred me out of my conversation with the unknown. Unaware of our encounter, he continued to walk down the street. Was he my out? Was the stranger strolling through the crowd the one with the solution? Most likely not. He passed a park bench placed there for people awaiting a bus or other public transportation.

Holding tight to the bag of cash, I strode toward the bench, ready to push away anyone who entertained the idea of taking it from me, and plopped myself uninvitingly in the center. No one expected me inside the bank for several minutes. I could sit and wait for an answer.

It was as if I were watching myself from above; a girl in a dilemma. Doesn't that stink to be her? What will she do? Minutes ticked away, and I continued to watch in anticipation. An inexperienced criminal, alone in a foreign country, trapped by her actions. More minutes ticked by without event. I descended back to reality, unable to stay at a distance.

A yellow cab appeared, and in a thick Bahamian accent, the universe spoke.

"Do you need a ride, lady?"

"Yes. Yes, I do."

The driver pulled back into traffic. "You must tell me where to take you."

"Oh, yes. Umm, I would like coffee." I thought for a moment. "And a muffin."

"I know just where you need to go."

He drove only two blocks and stopped in front of a small shop. I ignored the obvious truth that I could have walked, handed him the payment for the ride, and stepped out. Who cared? It was a whole new world for me.

I drifted, giddy, into the cafe as if I had chewed through the rope used to handcuff me. Freedom—all I had to do was not do anything. What could happen, really? I was ready to find out. Maybe I would tell Brent. Perhaps I would scream the truth behind my behavior from the rooftops. Wouldn't that throw a wrench in Bruce's Tesla motor? Henry's plan would be destroyed. They would be scrambling to figure out their next move while I buried them deeper in their paperwork of lies.

The cab driver was correct about the shop having coffee and muffins. It also had the local paper. I grabbed *The Nassau Guardian* and paid for my items. Spotting a quiet corner, I picked up my steaming mug and muffin and headed to my hideout. After an hour or so, I could check in with Brent while pretending I needed to handle the account in the comfort of my hotel room. We would be heading home the next afternoon.

I planned to read the paper and drift away into some other country's mundane troubles, so I could forget about my own. Except, as I opened the newspaper a headline stating, "Files Leaked from the Bahamas" greeted me. While I scanned the article, the crease between my eyebrows folded into a future wrinkle. Over a million files containing information from the corporate registry were being investigated.

I'd half-studied this subject, never thinking I would need to know it to save my life, just like FBARs. Yes, I had heard of the Organization of Economic Cooperation, easier said as OECD, and Automatic Exchange of Information referred to as AEOI. I'd listened during that part the same way I listened to a waiter reeling off the specials when I already knew I was ordering Bang Bang Shrimp. Unless some culinary masterpiece jumped out and grabbed me, I settled on my shrimp. I had chosen the type of accounting I'd do, and international was not it.

The leaked documents included the names of corporate intermediaries in recent history. I recognized one name the article referred to—Mossack Fonseca & Co, the law firm whose leaked files had begun the Panama Papers investigation. It had started the intense scrutiny of offshore accounts. Henry had tried to educate me on why offshore accounts were beneficial for everyone. He'd tried to hold back his frustration with the new confining restrictions and transparency countries were forced to have. Working for Henry had marked the beginning of why I cared about the Panama Papers and OECD and why any of that had made me view the new agreements through the eyes of a criminal. I'd read enough. After folding the paper back to its original neat form, I placed it on the table behind me. To take my mind off the subject, I people-watched for an inordinate amount of time until my cell phone rang.

"Hey, I'm about ready to head out," Brent said. "I can take some of this back to the hotel. How are you doing?"

"I was able to finish my business early today as well." I squeezed together the remaining crumbs of the second muffin I had purchased to form the last bite. "I was about to grab a cab. I'll have the driver swing by and get you."

"Perfect."

At dinner, Brent noticed my cheerful mood. I'm sure the ease with which I drained my glass of wine caught his attention as well. I rambled on about things that meant nothing, which felt amazing. For the moment, the suitcase full of money hid in some closet in my mind. Unfortunately, my lighthearted conversation clashed with his much more business-like one.

"Seriously, Brent, we're done for the day. Let it go."

"What's the issue with talking about our accounts? I know you're dying to hear about mine."

"No, in all seriousness, I'm not. I want to drink wine and walk on the beach and not think about anything."

"Why the one eighty in your attitude? What happened to being professional?"

"I didn't say I was going to act unprofessionally with you. I'm just going to enjoy some down time."

Brent was quiet; eerily so. He watched my every move, studying me. Lately, he had become more and more curious about my accounts yet had never asked me direct questions; the ones I feared he would ask soon enough. Still, what hid behind his intense stare? I recalled from a world of long ago, a similar glare my father had given me as I sat across our kitchen table from him. He would interrogate me about my weekend plans, but I'd had no adventurous plans, no joint hidden up my sleeve, no vodka bottle lying under my mattress. I'd never been sure if this had disappointed my father. Now I sat across from Brent with the equivalent of a vial of crack cocaine in my possession, or whatever this generation called it, wondering what feeling was worse.

"Well, if you must know. I went into the hotel office and found the paperwork laid out in neat piles. I plugged in some numbers, and that was about it. Hardly worth the plane trip, if you ask me," I replied, hoping to end the conversation.

Again, Brent studied me as he took a rather large swig of his wine.

"Same here. Almost mysteriously easy. I'm not quite sure why Bruce is sending us way out here when we could deal with the accounts through snail mail and email. Makes me wonder."

Did I gulp? I believe so. "What does it make you wonder?"

"It makes me wonder if there is more to Bruce than it appears. Maybe not everything he does is on the up and up."

I took a large swig. "You've watched too many movies."

"Or maybe you haven't watched enough."

"So, what are you thinking?" I asked. "What menacing tasks could he have in mind for us down here?"

"I'm not sure yet, but I'm crossing every T and making sure I do things by the book. I definitely wouldn't trust that Bruce has my—or your—best interests in mind."

My heart raced. This would be the time to blurt out the truth. Except, how could I tell Brent, the noble one, how I had failed? He hadn't done one thing to give Henry and Bruce leverage over him, and I was already defeated. My shame and fear that I could have endangered not only myself, but Adam as well, silenced me.

"I guess I'd better watch my back as well then."

"Look at me, Skylar." His voice was calm and demanding.

"You're wrecking my good mood, Brent."

"I'm worried about you."

"Seriously, I'm not in a good mood that often. Why are you wrecking the moment?"

"Will you please talk to me?"

With my favorable mood officially gone, I said as much as I could. "Have you ever felt that somehow in life you got in way over your head?"

"Well, I've always been a pretty good swimmer, so I would have to say it doesn't matter if you're in over your head. You just need to know when to grab on to the life preserver when you need one. Don't let yourself sink."

I had to laugh. Brent made it seem so easy, simple and matter of fact. *I'm fine if I don't sink.* Some of the weight lifted from my shoulders until I remembered the cement block tied to my ankle. I didn't read many crime novels, but it never ended well for the folks attached to the blocks. Brent must have seen the darkness encompass me again.

"So, are you a good swimmer?"

"Normally, I can hold my own, but as we know, even the best-built ships can sink."

"As long as we know to grab the life preservers, we can survive any catastrophe." He lifted the wine bottle and, with a slight look, asked if I wanted more. I did. "We always have more control than we think we do."

I felt warm tears, the ache in my throat. "You're very wise for an accountant, Brent."

"To being wise." We clinked glasses, and I was pretty sure I heard only goodness in his warm voice.

CHAPTER 12

I LAY IN THE hotel bed that night, and I needed to grab on to something that could save me. With the help of the wine, I was ready to depart from the disastrous journey Bruce and Henry were taking me on and arrive, scars and all, on safer ground. So, I would have to explain some pictures. I would have to beg for forgiveness. Perhaps couples counseling was in my and Adam's future. I would pay some fines or penalties for signing false FBARs. Maybe it wasn't too late to report my suspicions without incriminating myself. And Adam would believe me, without question, that I hadn't taken drugs, or at least had not meant to take them.

The next step was too big, though. It would be too obvious an act for an accountant to do willingly. The numbers said it all. Avoidance. Deception. I couldn't proclaim my innocence if I went through with the next task, which, for the moment, made my decision easy. I would tell Adam and Brent the truth instead of wading deeper into Henry's dark waters. My wine-foggy brain drifted to sleep, happy to know that the next day would be the beginning of my walk back to my normal life. But instead of a night of peaceful sleep, another dream took form in my mind.

My cell phone rang with a faraway sound, as if muffled by a pillow. Frantically, I yanked back the covers and tossed the bedding to the side. The demanding device was nowhere to be found. I jumped from the bed and searched the room, including my suitcase and under the bed. Pausing and giving one final listen, I heard a faint ring coming from the closet. Digging through my shoes, I saw the lit-up screen, and answered the call before the ringing stopped.

"Hello. Hello," I yelled.

Through the static, I heard the familiar voice of a man, but I couldn't decipher a word he said. As if my life depended on the conversation, I pressed the phone as tightly to my ear as possible.

"You have to listen to me," he said.

"I'm trying."

Before I could comprehend his words—and trust me, I wanted to understand him more than anything—the hotel phone woke me. On the other end of the line, Adam's voice reminded me that my reality was anything but blissful.

"They fired me."

"What?" I bolted upright, rubbing my forehead as if it would bring clarity.

"Work called to say don't bother coming in because they are looking into some issues."

"I don't understand, Adam. What could they be talking about?"

"Skylar, I promise you, the whole thing is crazy. It makes no sense."

My stomach clenched. Something was wrong; something more than Adam losing his job. I saw a folder by the door that someone had slid under it while I slept.

"It's okay, Adam. We'll get through this."

"There are accusations and possible lawsuits. We need my income, Skylar. We need my job. At least we have benefits through yours."

Adam worked in HR for a large company that shall remain nameless. I knew Adam. I knew his beliefs and his morals. He hired people who were the best people for the job; flat out they were the most qualified. I also knew, even then, that those people willing to lie were somehow connected to Henry. The scariest fact was that I was me, and Henry was Henry, and no matter what I knew, if Henry wanted to win, he would win.

"Yes, at least we have my job." My head spun from wine and morning fog. I headed toward the door and bent to pick up the folder. Inside were names, pictures, and accusations from beautiful women. Some names I had heard of, women I knew Adam had hired. Everything became clear. I must let the life preserver drift by on the rocky waves.

Soon a video recording would exist of me, Skylar Shaw, walking into the bank with a suspicious amount of cash. The authorities would have evidence I deposited it into Brenda Carter's accounts; accounts that Henry and Brenda had never intended to claim. What accountant travels to the Bahamas to do such a thing for a client she has never met? Only a guilty one. Only an accountant who did more than balance debits and credits. Only an accountant who'd received something on the side. And that's where the money order would come into play. The one made out to Skylar Shaw herself; the one that would open the first offshore account in my name, making my future official. I needed to avoid that future, yet when I looked backward, each misstep already taken sat like a boulder blocking me from escape.

Later that night, I would tell Brent about my dream—the one where he tried to tell me something, except I couldn't hear him. That's when he assured me that it symbolized my yearning for a stronger connection with him. Next time, I would remember to ask my friend Google before discussing my nightly visions.

When I returned home from the Bahamas, I would like to say I was the same Skylar Adam knew so well. I wasn't. By Thursday, Adam realized it wasn't merely a passing mood. I feared he would perceive my moodiness as disappointment in him or that I questioned his innocence. As much as I tried, I couldn't fake being happy. I walked in the door and smelled the aromas of garlic and oregano filling our kitchen. Adam had eased his boredom by busying himself with the list of household chores and cooking our meals. It worked well for me.

"Welcome home, baby." Adam came to kiss me. He wore my apron and held a wooden spoon. Usually, this would have amused me, except that would take energy, and I had none.

"Dinner smells good."

"It's my specialty. Homemade meatballs and sauce. I could get used to this domestic thing."

"Really?"

"Not a chance." His smile faded, and stress momentarily clouded his face. He tried to be strong for me, the person who had caused it all.

"I didn't think so," I said.

Adam placed a glass of wine in my hand. Again, the mere idea of a sip began to ease the fear that now lived deep inside of me. For someone who hadn't used to care about alcohol, it was finding a solid place in my life.

"I need to change first." Showing I had complete control, I set the glass on the counter before I could take that medicinal sip and walked to our bedroom. Instead of changing, I rested on the bed and stared at the ceiling for what I thought was only a moment.

The door creaked open.

"Aren't you eating dinner?"

Startled, I jolted up. "Oh, I'm sorry. You know how tax season drags me down. I'll be right out." Without a word, Adam walked away, and I scrambled to put on leggings and a sweatshirt. *Find your energy*, I told myself, *Adam needs you.* Nothing would come.

We ate in silence.

"So did your travels to the Bahamas wear you out that much? You've been home for a week, and yet you don't seem like you're mentally here."

"I'm tired, that's all, Adam. And, yes, sometimes traveling when you never get a break to recoup can wear you out for a week." Was there an edge to my voice?

"Is Brent still tired?"

Angrier than I had a right to be, I gave Adam a stern look. After all, I would have said something similar, except I would have said such things days earlier. I took a deep breath and tried to remember that he had the entire day to sit around, wondering what had happened in the Bahamas.

"Adam, you have too much time to worry about stupid stuff. Me being tired doesn't mean there is something to be concerned about."

I'd used an unnecessarily harsh tone. Adam calmly got up from the table, set his napkin down, and without a word, walked toward our bedroom. So much for taking a deep breath so I could choose my words wisely. As I sat, eating the delicious homemade meatballs and washing them down with my wine, only one thought crossed my mind—it was nice being alone and not fearing what the conversation might bring. I only wished I hadn't hurt Adam.

The next day, before getting home to Adam, I tried to lift my spirits. I listened to upbeat, energetic music in the car. I even tried singing. My vehicle was the only one with the windows down, forcing in the fresh, uplifting air. When that didn't quite do it, I practiced smiling in the visor mirror. In three hours, and I would be in bed. For only three hours, I needed to be the kind of happy partner he'd always had. I could do it.

I opened the door, and the smells of garlic and butter hit me, and another scent as well. I couldn't quite place the aroma. The plates and glasses sat on the table waiting for some meal, and in the background, soft classical music vibrated through the air. After plopping my purse on the counter, I crept into the living room, and that's when I saw Adam. He cradled a ball of fur in his arms. Yellow legs kicked the air, and Adam's whispers quieted a soft, whiny cry. With an enormous smile, Adam brought the furry stranger toward me, presenting him like a proud father.

"Adam, what did you do?"

"We needed something, Skylar. And I'll do anything."

In an instant, I was madly in love with both of them.

We named him Ted. He was a rescue puppy, likely guilty of chewing one too many household items. This unfortunate habit had begun his demise and had led to days of watching the world through cage bars. How many people had strutted by, stopping for the occasional peek before moving on? And then Adam had strolled by while heading into a department store to purchase an underpriced, name-brand T-shirt. Adam never gave a second look at the animals, begging with their sad eyes for another chance, another couch to chew. On that day, for whatever reason, he'd paused long enough, and Ted had become our baby.

Saturday morning, we found ourselves at the park, right in there with everyone. "What type of dog is he?" "We got ours as a rescue." "He chews everything." "What vet do you use?" Sometimes, Adam and I could hardly contain the desire to laugh at ourselves and Ted's silly antics. We left the park knowing one thing—we would be good parents, and the bond of knowing that meant something to both of us. We even set strict rules such as Ted was not allowed on the furniture. It meant we sat on the floor leaning up against the couch so he could rest his head in our laps. We quickly learned that remotes, shoes, sunglasses, pillows—everything was considered a chew toy. Instead of talking about the Bahamas, we tallied the daily losses over dinner. We had a new source of joy and a way to distract ourselves from our frustrations. Ted was a good thing.

CHAPTER 13

MONDAY MORNING, MY alarm clock proved unnecessary due to the vivid dream that awakened me. The pleasant nature of the subconscious vision allowed me to fall victim to its message.

I sat at my kitchen table eating bacon, one of my all-time favorite foods. Ted, whimpering for a taste, sat next to me. I wouldn't share, though. Instead, I looked into his sweet, desperate eyes and continued to shovel the calorie-free dream bacon into my mouth. As dreams go, I couldn't complain. Until I took another bite, and the bacon tasted of death. The putrid taste jolted me from my sleep.

In my opinion, the vivid dreams were the universe's way of helping my simple mind understand my desperate situation. Despite this, I still needed expert advice to help me clarify Her attempts. Grabbing my phone, I Googled once again. That's when I noticed Adam was already up and somewhere else in the house. Keeping an eye on the door, I typed in dreams about bacon.

So, dreaming about bacon had to do with having the staples in life. The analogy made sense, seeing how I had gone to bed concerned about Adam's lack of employment. Still, what was the reason for my mind's cruel twist, giving my much-loved snack a putrid aftertaste? According to my research, I was in some sort of forbidden situation.

145

I slid the covers off me and strolled down the hallway to find Adam. He sat at the kitchen table, newspaper open to the classified ads, coffee set out for the two of us, and eggs ready to fry. I didn't see or smell any bacon, so that hadn't caused my dream. Just as well, since my desire for my favorite breakfast treat was now nonexistent.

"Isn't that a little old school going through the classified ads looking for a job?"

A small smile struggled to appear on Adam's lips. "Last time I had to do this, it worked."

Sliding into my spot across from him, I picked up my oversized mug and studied Adam's expression. He looked so defenseless in his flannel pajamas and matching T-shirt. If only I could tell him none of his situation was his fault. Guilt weighed on me, and I craved crawling back into bed with Adam and forgetting the world.

"I could be a bus driver or a maintenance worker. Actually, there's a good chance I couldn't be either." He chuckled. "Do you know what's sad? Despite my degree and experience, I'm starting to realize I wouldn't even qualify for most of those jobs. Well, I guess they would consider me overqualified. Regardless, I wouldn't get the job. Crazy, isn't it?"

"We'll figure it out."

"Thank you, Skylar."

"Of course. I'm always going to be your cheerleader."

"No, not for that. Thank you for not questioning whether I did those things. Thank you for having faith in the fact that I'm not that kind of person."

"You would do the same for me." As the words left my mouth, I realized how true they were. I could hear the allegations against me and see Adam's amused face. "Yeah, right?" He would go to bat for me, and I would make a fool of him.

Could I have misjudged Adam? Could he be guilty?

All of the accusations came back to me. The woman who'd said Adam had stared at everything except her face and then asked personal questions about relationships. She'd said he'd later come around the desk and sat next to her, close enough so that their knees could touch. When she'd pushed away, the interview had ended, and the company had never called her back.

Another woman had accused Adam of implying that the company liked their personnel to be appealing to the eyes. According to her, Adam had said her attire should attract their customers' attention. The company didn't want their customers' minds to wander to their competitors. Honestly? First, I believed one-hundred percent that Adam would never say such things. The idea of it almost made me laugh out loud. Second, I'd been in Adam's office many times, and there were people whose appearances demanded a second glance, and there were people more like me that only turned a head if their skirt was tucked in their underwear. The hiring process seemed to create a miniature, representative human population.

"Do you think the investigation will go beyond the company?" I asked.

"Right now, the women are only dealing with us. I assume they are hoping to get money without going to trial. It depends on what my company will do to quiet the situation."

"How far back are these cases?"

"So far, they're all recent—which is weird and reassuring, too. I'm hoping my boss will consider my many years without any complaints when they're trying to decide whom to believe."

"Are you saying all the accusations happened since tax season started?"

"Yeah. Why?"

"No reason. Just trying to get a timeline in my head."

"The other thing going for me is these women, in all honesty, weren't the strongest candidates. I didn't even bother to call references for either one of them. From the start of the interview, I knew they weren't right for the position."

"I'm surprised Bill fired you without questioning everything more." Bill had been Adam's boss for most of the time Adam had worked for the company, and I would, to some extent, consider them friends.

"It's all about the bad publicity. The women were willing to stay away from the news if I got terminated immediately. That gives the company time to investigate things without being under the microscope. I talked to Bill yesterday. He's on my side, but he has to do what he has to do."

We both sat in silence for a while, taking a few deep breaths and the last sips of our cooling coffees.

"Are you ready for your eggs?"

"Let me jump into the shower first." I stood and kissed Adam, letting the stubble of his beard pierce my lips. When was the last time he'd shaved?

I drifted down the hallway so my tears would fall in the privacy of my shower. At the same moment I shut the water off, I heard my phone ding. Reaching for it with a dripping hand, I saw Brent's name on the screen. A warm familiarity rushed over me, and then I read his text. *It's going to be an interesting day.*

Scrambling, I responded, *Why? What's happening?*

The annoying dots hung on the screen. The pace at which

Brent typed infuriated me as I again clung to the possibilities his words could bring.

I'll let you find that out when you get here.

From the kitchen, I heard Adam telling me the eggs, that now sounded unappetizing, were cooked. I dressed and got ready in under ten minutes, forced down my cold eggs, and hurried out the door.

My heart raced as I sped down the road. I envisioned the scene awaiting me—swarms of police, flashing lights, and guns drawn. Megaphones blared out the words, "Skylar Shaw, exit the building, and no one gets hurt." The eggs churned in my stomach, and the nasty taste of my dream bacon wreaked havoc on me as well.

Approaching the drab, quiet building calmed my nerves until visions of what awaited me inside ignited them again. Yet the office was quiet inside. Only then did I admit to myself that my imagination had been on overdrive.

I walked straight to Brent's cubicle for clarification. "Were you trying to give me a heart attack? Why the text?"

A curious smile on his lips, Brent swiveled around in his chair. "Why would you have a heart attack over my text? Did you think one of us finally flipped?"

"Anything's possible during tax season. So?"

"So?" he repeated with a smirk.

"I don't have time for this. What happened?"

"Okay, already. It's obvious someone is not in the mood for a mystery."

"I have enough on my plate with Adam losing his job. I have no desire for more mystery, thank you."

At the exact moment Brent was about to spit out his news, Bruce came out of his office, his expression determined, his jaw tight. He headed for the breakroom. Without concern for the fragility of the coffee cups or pot, he poured a cup and jammed the pot back on the burner. Since I was unable to turn from the train wreck in time, he caught me staring.

"Don't you have enough work to do Skylar, or should I find more?" Leaving his threat hanging in the air, he continued back to his office.

"Well, that explains part of it," Brent said before turning back toward the computer.

"I guess we can catch up later."

"Good idea," Brent agreed.

Coworkers filled the office, yet the only sound to be heard was them typing on keyboards. Like scolded children, we worked in silence. At first, I didn't even dare to pick up my phone, but as my curiosity grew, my resistance dwindled.

So? I texted.

After you left last night, some blond chick in a rage stormed into the office. She went right to Bruce's office and slammed the door. She was holding what looked like a necklace box on the way in and did not have it on the way out. That's when Bruce's bad mood started.

Did she have fake boobs?

I didn't notice.

Yes, you did. Answer the question.

Strong possibility from the quick glance I took.

I hope you hurt your neck, taking your quick glance.

Luckily, it feels fine.

Whatever. If I were to guess, the woman was Bruce's ex-wife.

Bruce was married?

Many years ago. Her name's Chrissy, I believe. She left him for a rich CEO of something. Bruce has never been the same.

Kind of makes me feel bad for him.

Just a bit, I replied.

The office door opened again. Our conversation stalled as I slid my phone into my drawer.

Of all days, I ended up working late on mundane and ordinary accounts. Throughout the afternoon, I tried to avoid Bruce. Since no one dared to speak, the hours ticked away slowly. I plugged away at the necessary forms with little thought, which usually was fine. However, I created more errors than I had ever experienced before. Other accountants may have been in trouble for their negligence. My unwanted alliance with Bruce would, I hoped, be an asset for me when it came to consequences.

My life, in some ways, resembled a chess game. Many of the pieces, including me, shuffled around our office. I was a lowly pawn, restricted by small movements and only to places that remained unoccupied. This thought led me to Brent. I pegged him as a knight because it seemed fitting. Bruce served as the queen, second in rank, and I'd guess the one with more ability. We roamed the board and protected a king who only cared about what we could do for him. A little fact I recalled about the pawn was that I captured in a different way than I moved. I was not on the offensive if I kept moving in my usual method, and it was vital I stopped living on the defensive. The pieces and their roles mingled in my mind until Liz strolled past, giving me a half-hearted smile. She was the piece that abided by no rules or regulations, who would go into occupied spaces and take what she wanted. I returned her half-hearted smile and watched her drift toward the breakroom and Brent.

At seven o'clock, the office staff, one by one, headed out the door. I, on the other hand, was still busy double-checking a simple tax form for the fifth time. I returned Brent's wave as he passed by on his way out and tried not to let my eyes linger. Several of my colleagues were going straight to the bar across the street, and I assumed Brent would follow suit. Did that make my heart sink a bit? Maybe. *Focus*, I told myself. I did not want to be alone in the building with Bruce, even though he hadn't left his office in hours. I took one last look over the forms and grabbed my purse, ready to depart within minutes after the last person. Then I heard Bruce's door open. I resisted looking back, but after the creak of his door, there wasn't another sound. The silence started to feel creepy.

Bruce, looking out over the office, leaned against his doorframe. I wasn't sure if he was aware of my presence. He took a step toward the breakroom, and that's when I realized he was drunk, like fall-down-on-his-face drunk.

"Are you all right?" I asked as any responsible person would do when someone in that condition was in one's proximity.

"Skylar?"

"Yeah, it's me."

"I thought everyone was gone."

"Everyone is except me." He stumbled a few more steps. "Would you like me to bring you something?"

"Coffee."

He stumbled back to his desk. The coffee was cold. I wasn't in any mood to brew a fresh pot for him, so I added an extra creamer and microwaved it instead. Then I remembered he took it black. When I entered Bruce's office, he was resting his head on his desk.

"Here's your coffee."

He looked up, with visible effort to steady his gaze. "Have a seat, Skylar."

"I need to get going. Adam's sick of the late nights."

With glossy eyes—I could not tell whether from tears or alcohol consumption—he commanded me again. "Have a seat, Skylar."

I hated myself for following his orders, but I was also curious about what blindly-drunk Bruce would say. I shoved some papers to the side and set his coffee down in front of him before having a seat. He never looked at the coffee. Instead, Bruce opened his drawer, pulled out a bottle of whiskey, and poured some in a pathetic old glass he had stored with it. With an unsteady hand, he lifted it to me as an offering. With a shake of my head, I declined. I wondered if once the staff had left, he ever slipped into the breakroom to wash the glass. For some reason, I found it depressing, thinking of how dirty it most likely was. He replaced the bottle's cap and sat back.

"So, what do you think of our friend Henry?"

"What do I think? I think he's not my friend," I answered.

Bruce laughed. "You're a smart girl, Skylar." He took a swallow of whiskey. "Henry is no one's friend. Oh, he can make you think he is, but let me assure you, he is not."

"Then why did you get me involved with him?"

Again, Bruce laughed. "I'm sure you learned about survival in some science course along the way. Fight or flight." Drunk people should never try to sound intelligent by trying to say fight or flight. "Sometimes, people need a few more options, though."

"What papers did I sign on the yacht?"

Another long sip slowed his response as he stared at me over the rim of his glass. Man, I hoped he wouldn't start vomiting in front of me. Looking at his skin, how his body swayed in his chair, made me envision all his organs pickled, wanting to purge out the poisons.

"Are you going to tell me?" I asked again.

"Did I ever tell you that I was married before?"

"I know that. I was here before the divorce, but what does that have to do with the papers?"

"Nothing. Everything. If I had never been married, you wouldn't have had papers to sign."

"You're going to have to explain it a bit better than that."

"In the beginning, we were happy. Really happy. Chrissy was from a good family, very affluent." Again, affluent—not an easy drunk word. "I couldn't give her everything she was used to." Bruce paused; his eyes glistened. "She made me believe she was okay with that. Maybe she was, and maybe she wasn't. Her family wasn't. I was never enough."

"Am I supposed to feel sorry for you?"

"You can feel whatever you want to feel. It felt horrible for me, the day I found out she was having an affair with Jackson. Jackson was everything her parents wanted me to be, and, admittedly, he was everything I wished I could be. But I would never make that kind of money doing what I do. Chrissy is the type of woman you wanted to pamper, needed to pamper. I hid my stress when the bills—huge bills—came in from salons and stores. She was beautiful. I was so proud to have her by my side. You may not understand it. You don't seem like the type to have your nails done."

Now I wanted to vomit as well. Still, I held back my tirade of why I was a better woman, slid my neglected nails under my thighs, and let him continue his story.

"No matter how hard I worked, how honest I was, how good I was, Jackson was going to win. And then one day, a day when the world fell out from under me, I signed the papers giving up my wife. I went to Henry's on a regular visit. He could tell I was a mess. Hell, I may have even been a bit drunk that day.

He offered me something that made it all go away—Ecstasy. I was happy, beyond happy. Happiness is an addictive feeling when everything is black in your life."

"That's what Henry gave me too."

"I'm not sure what went on while you were gone, but according to your drug test, I would agree."

Bruce had apparently forgotten I wasn't looking for his confirmation.

"The next day, it was worse; it was so much worse. I thought about taking my life that day. Instead, I decided I would take back my life. Henry offered me a way to do it. He assured me we could go under the wire, and that a hard-working man shouldn't lose the love of his life because people's salaries were unfair. I signed papers, took Ecstasy, signed papers, and took more Ecstasy. But you know what? She never left Jackson for me, and Henry and I didn't stay under the wire."

"And that made you think you had the right to pull me into all the corruption? It's okay to destroy someone else because you screwed up?"

"Fight or flight, or in this case, divert." Then he laughed, a drunken, pathetic, beaten-sounding laugh.

"What, you're trying to make it look like the whole scheme stems from a corrupt accountant and not the business owner? That won't even work, you know."

Bruce let out a laugh that was more confusing than any words he could have spoken.

"Why are you bringing Adam into all of this? He's innocent."

"Innocence is a funny concept isn't it. The line is very fine at times."

"That's all you're going to tell me about the accusations?"

Bruce took another swig and swiveled the whiskey around in his mouth. His ice-cold stare answered for him.

"You're a bastard."

He swallowed and set the glass on his desk. "Maybe I am Skylar. But I didn't start out that way. Good guys never seem to win."

"And what have you won?"

He took another swig, and darkness clouded his face. "Nothing."

"Are you going to tell me what I signed?"

"I already did, Skylar. Diversion. It's all diversion."

All night, I thought about Bruce and his attempt to take back his life. Strength could be very deceiving. Take Gandhi, for instance. His strength had come from a determination to stay true to his values. His power had come from the belief that when one person was brave enough to stand up for goodness, it could empower others to do so as well. Navy SEALs, they had strength, too—strength as in, do it my way or live to regret it or maybe not live to regret it. Yet, both were so different.

Bruce had done things that took courage and determination, yet he was so misguided. Who was I? As a puppet, what courage did I exhibit? How would I break my strings and kick the bad guys in the throat? Bruce and I both had the desire but no direction. We were both the same and so different at the same time. I refused to end up the drunk, beaten victim, yet I had no idea how to change my path.

CHAPTER 14

I'D NEVER BEEN officially introduced to Chrissy, but I hated her. As I pictured her bouncing around some country club tennis court with her fake tatas, the nagging annoyance grew. The idea of Chrissy tipping back her mimosa, while some unfortunate Asian woman scrubbed the callouses off her feet, infuriated me. The image of her crew going on about some tennis scandal while my life crashed around me no longer just smoldered inside of me. It had become a full-on blazing fire.

According to Bruce, everything wrong in my life had come as a direct result of Chrissy and her snobby, selfish personality. My hate spawned a small obsession. I even opened a Facebook account with the sole purpose of spying on her on Facebook. Picture after picture showed her perfect little life.

She now had a daughter who looked about ten from what I could see on the public images. There were a surprising number of them. Then again, Chrissy apparently wanted everyone to see how glorious her life had become since she'd run off with the successful, wealthy CEO her parents had envisioned for her. Then I thought of Bruce. Had he spent hours scanning her photos while the whiskey had slowly found its way to his liver, damaging him even further? I knew the answer.

There were pictures in front of a home I thought at first was their country club. In addition, there were tons of tennis pictures, trips overseas, an African safari. Damn, I would have loved that trip. And then I saw a photo of Chrissy and her girlfriend sharing a warm beverage at a little coffee shop. The caption was very telling. "Another Monday morning meet up with my BFF. Love you, girl!" I chuckled at the thought of myself ever posting something so absurd and fake. Then again, maybe it wasn't phony to her. More importantly, I knew the establishment and knew they met there on Monday mornings. For whatever reason, I needed to meet Chrissy, the person responsible for everything wrong in my life.

Henry expected me at ten o'clock. I fudged the time a bit to Bruce and drove the twenty minutes out of my way for my overpriced cup of joe. I wondered if they served my French vanilla creamer. There was an open table for two under a small tree. The beneficial aspect of coffee shops was that if I opened my computer, I appeared cool instead of lonely. Suddenly, I was thankful Henry had told me to bring my computer with me that day because it served its purpose well. Opening Facebook, I searched for another glimpse of the BFF who should be showing up at any moment.

And then there they were. My plan came together with surprising ease. I chalked it up to the universe, patting me on the back and saying, *Great idea*. Chrissy and her BFF sat within earshot, only if I kept full concentration on my part. In the first minutes, I gathered that the BFF's name was Brittany, and that she used it interchangeably with Brit. Brit had an issue. Something about marriage. What would she do? How could he have done that? I felt no pity for her. A little piece of me may have even thought, *Serves you right*, except I couldn't quite figure out the logistics of my thinking. They began whispering, and then they glanced my way. Moments passed, and their conversation continued. Chrissy reached over, hugged Brittany, and rubbed her back. Her actions appeared genuine. I didn't realize I was staring again until a couple of ladies passed, looked at me, and followed my gaze to Chrissy's table.

Time for me to go. I closed my computer and threw my remaining coffee in the garbage. As I stepped off the curb, I heard the distinct rumbling of a motorcycle engine. Glancing in the direction of the sound, I saw a man heading to the exit on the far side of the parking lot. Daily, countless black motorcycles crossed my path. The probability was high that the driver would be wearing a dark leather jacket and black helmet. Why did I believe the motorcycle was the one I knew too well? If I could have walked faster in my one-inch pumps, I would have tried to follow the man, but there was no way. Instead, I settled for texting my curious friend.

Anything crazy going on in the office this morning?

I waited for several minutes. No answer. I stared so long at the last place I had seen the disappearing motorcycle that my eyes blurred. I was starting to realize that this often happens when you search too hard for answers that weren't ready to surface.

At the office, Bruce remained silent about our drunken stupor conversation, although his avoidance of me spoke volumes. Brent apologized for not getting back to me. "Crazy day," as he put it. Yeah, I bet. It was hard to stalk people and get all his routine work done in the same twenty-four-hour period. His unwanted interest had helped ease the confusion of the friendship versus attraction struggle. No honest, faithful partner went near the border if the safety gate wasn't secure. If Brent was going to stalk me during his private time, I needed to take ten steps back. One of us had to be strong always.

After a couple hours of staring at my computer screen, my head bobbed. I needed my coffee, no ulterior motives necessary. I walked by Brent's cubicle. Liz had pulled a chair up so close I hadn't heard her high-pitched giggle until I was on top of them. The strangest part of the situation was that Brent laughed with her as they stared at the screen. He had real problems. Their heads blocked most of the screen, but I saw they were on Facebook. At about the moment I had seen enough and was about to look away, Brent swiveled around in his chair. "That's a good one, Liz. Thanks for sharing."

Our gazes locked for a millisecond of faked indifference on my part, and I continued to my desk.

I waited, without being conscious of my desire for Brent to come to me, hoping that with or without words, he would tell me that the moment with Liz meant nothing. We could share our secret look that said, *She is so annoying.* We could go about our day with the unspoken knowledge that we were still the "friends" I was starting to take for granted. Moments passed, and my mind stayed frozen in its unproductive stance until, finally, it gave up. He wasn't coming.

The following day, Bruce stayed in his office most of the time. The day was mundane, like a gray cloud blocking fireworks, until it wasn't mundane anymore, and the fireworks burst through. Two men marched in as out of place as polar bears in the desert. We all stared as they disappeared into Bruce's lair.

The office was silent, and then I heard my coworkers' chairs sliding backward. I peeked over my cubicle and saw my colleagues peering at Bruce's door, at each other, looking like prairie dogs searching for predators. Roy threw in the last bite of a protein bar and chewed nervously. He scanned the office before disappearing into his hole again. Then I looked toward Brent. His eyes didn't wander or waver. They stayed focused on me with an urgency I couldn't quite understand and found unsettling. I slid back into my seat, as did everyone else one by one. We all stayed there for the fifteen minutes the authorities remained in Bruce's office.

The door finally opened. I didn't look toward it, yet my hairs rose, alerting me of the men's presence. As they walked down the aisle, toward the exit, I sensed them growing closer to me. I could no longer resist the force urging me to look their way. Staring at them from my cubicle, I became transfixed. Time slowed as they closed in on me, each step landing silently. They turned their attention to me knowingly, yet they continued on past my desk and left the office. Sometime, maybe minutes later, I breathed again.

Bruce let enough time pass before calling me into his office. He'd also called several other people's names at various times. I wondered if that was to throw everyone's curious minds in many directions, or if there was some legitimate business. Mostly, I questioned what kind of business it could be.

He paced frantically. "Is there anything on your computer? Anything at all?"

"No, Henry always has me use a different computer when I'm at his house. I rarely bring mine anymore."

"Good. Has anyone asked you questions?"

"No, but the men looked at me as if questioning me. Why would they look at me like that?"

"I don't know. Just play dumb if someone asks you anything. Don't bring up Henry's name."

"I am dumb about this. I don't know what's going on." Part of me even believed myself when I said those words, but in truth, I knew too much, and I couldn't avoid that fact forever.

"It's for the best for now. Stay under the radar."

Bruce was a terrible criminal. I shook my head and left.

I got to Henry's and, as usual, walked by the cameras following my every move and handed over my phone. Instead of leaving the room, Henry pulled up a chair and directed me to have a seat.

"I hear Adam lost his job. Very unfortunate."

"Are you seriously going to act surprised? You slipped papers under my door."

"I'm quite sure you have no proof to back up such an accusation; however, I have looked into Adam's case since we're business partners, so to speak."

"I'm your accountant, not your partner. There's quite a difference."

A knowing smirk crossed Henry's face. "Either way, I wanted to look into the matter for you to see if I could be of any help. My network of contacts is, how should I say it humbly, quite extensive."

I was quite sure—no, positive—that this conversation was all about giving him more power over me. Even so, I had to bite. "So, can you help Adam?" If having a soft, believing expression would have helped me earn Henry's sympathy, I would have been in trouble. My jawline had tightened as I'd forced out my plea.

"Well, I must say, it doesn't look good. Some women from as far back as a year ago may support the recent accusers' stories with their own."

"So, are you saying you can't help him?"

"I'm saying it would take a good deal of effort on my part to quiet these women and have them retract their stories. Probably my own money as well. These are things I do for friends and colleagues who have earned my respect. I don't do favors for just anybody, but, yes, we could find a way to get Adam back behind his desk."

"Thank you." Knowing he had me backed against the wall and was about to strike, I clenched my jaw again.

"What do you know about cryptocurrency, Skylar?"

"Nothing; absolutely nothing."

"No problem. You can learn on the job."

"And you can assure me Adam will have his name cleared and you will leave him out of this from now on?"

"Again, I am only here to help Adam get out of a situation that is of his own doing. I have nothing against Adam personally. Can't blame a guy for looking when a ten walks into his world where only a four exists."

"Excuse me?"

"I'm going to keep this simple. Cryptocurrency is like money, except banks or governments do not control it. It's the wave of the future. Sure, there are some kinks to the system, but before long, we'll all be buying and selling with cybermoney, and the dollar bill will disappear. I consider myself a man ahead of the times. Therefore, I keep some of my money in the cyber world."

"Sounds suspicious, if you ask me."

"I didn't."

"How does cryptocurrency involve me?"

"My colleague, Brenda Carter, is expanding her construction business, and the profits are rolling in. You'll notice that the accounts you deposited her money into are growing rapidly. I'm quite happy for her success but have suggested to her that she expand her horizons. Brenda is a very busy woman and will need you to work on buying the cryptocurrency. Some you'll purchase with the money in her account and some with money before it hits the U.S. banks. The banks in our country simply don't understand Bitcoin the way other countries do and are becoming more hesitant to work with it. I am forced to look elsewhere, and I'm choosing the Netherlands."

"The Netherlands! Are you kidding me? And why is the U.S. government not a fan of cryptocurrency?"

"Control, Skylar. They lose control if we are not using the fiat money system. Our government does not like losing control." Part of me wanted to ask what fiat money was, but I decided that looking it up later might fare better for me. "Because of this, U.S. banks are becoming more and more skeptical of the system," Henry continued.

"Why are they skeptical? Is this legal?"

Henry stared at me; his expression blank.

"You are so naive. It's quite pathetic. You live in your little accountant world unaware of the bigger picture. You may thank me someday for the education you're receiving."

"Somehow, I doubt it." Henry had a unique way of using silence to intimidate. I hated the man, yet if I took one thing away from the situation, it was how to win a fight without saying a word. "So, what do I need to do?"

"Since Brenda is busy and you can work with her accounts as her accountant, I am having you do the legwork. You are going to open a bank account in Brenda's name. The man you will work with is a rather good friend of mine and has agreed to let you do this in her place. This means that you will also sign for her. Brenda and I will oversee giving Lucas the necessary documentation." Henry's tone was that of a teacher reading the directions for a standardized test. He described each detail as if

I were a child, and I wanted to throat punch the condescending tone right out of him.

"You are going to deposit money into Brenda's account," Henry continued. "Lucas will then help you create a cyber wallet. After that's created, he will put the necessary applications on the phone that Brenda will give to you beforehand, or rather, she will give to me. Then you will bring the wallet and whatever information is needed for the account back to me. I will get it to Brenda. Clear enough?"

Even though I didn't want to have to ask, I did anyway. "A wallet?"

"Yes, a special wallet that has a key. You're going to take money, a rather large amount, to that bank. You're going to deposit the money into the bank account which will be used to fund the Coinbase account Lucas creates for Brenda. He will then transfer the money into the Coinbase account, and you will purchase as many Bitcoin as possible. You will then bring the key information back to Brenda and myself. Pretty easy."

"I'm carrying all this cash in my carry-on again. What about security?"

"I have my people set up here. As for entering the Netherlands, there is always a risk. I'm assuming Adam is worth it."

As I stared at his smirking face, a wave of nausea rushed over me.

"If I do this, then you'll make sure Adam gets his job back?"

"It won't happen overnight, but yes. We'll work together to make sure both our lives are running smoothly."

"That doesn't sound like you are asking me to do only one thing then."

"As I said, this is going to take a good deal of effort and money. One day at a time."

"I'll ask again, is this for something legal?"

"Yes, Skylar, cybermoney is very legal," Henry said with what may have been an eye-roll.

I ignored the fact that he didn't answer my actual question. "Fine. When do I leave?"

"Monday morning. Bruce will have the money for you to take with you from the office."

"And if security questions me about the money?"

"Play dumb, Skylar. I have faith you can pull that off. And it would be best if you don't mention my name."

CHAPTER 15

FULL OF ENTHUSIASM and curiosity for the sunshine and air, Ted led Adam and me around the park, and we watched him. My innocent, furry child had a zest for the pond despite the dog-eating alligators lurking beneath the surface. Oh, to be unaware. I envied him since the concerns about my next mission, along with Bruce's drunken warnings, bogged down my mind. Would people share the same disgusted pity for me that I felt for Bruce? Adam was less than pleased to hear I would be leaving again, and I hoped our walk would calm the tension.

A picture of Chrissy had hung in Bruce's office long after she had left him. Maybe it had been there as inspiration, to help him feel brave enough to do the things Henry asked him to so that he would be good enough for her. She was the type of person I hated, everyone should hate, yet life had given her everything. It wasn't fair. I was so distracted by my thoughts that I didn't hear my name at first. Then it broke through my haze straight from another world; a world so far away I didn't fully realize how separated it was until it collided with the one that I existed in with Adam.

"Skylar," Brent called.

Both Adam and I turned.

"Brent." Adam's hand tensed in mine. "What are you doing here?"

"I try to run on the weekends. You know, work off the stress."

"Brent, this is Adam. Adam, Brent."

The two of them politely shook hands. Brent was smiling; Adam wasn't.

"So, you're Brent, the man running off with Skylar all the time." Adam had chuckled when he said it, but I'm sure no one had felt the humor.

Panic filled me. I had chosen not to tell Adam where I was going on the next trip. It was a quick two nights. I would be exhausted from the ten-hour flight to the Netherlands, one day of work, and another ten-hour trip home; however, I was determined to be strong enough to hide my fatigue. The idea of explaining it without mentioning something incriminating seemed more stressful than simply saying I was going to the Bahamas again. Now, I questioned my decision.

"Not my choice," Brent said. "Not to say Skylar isn't a great colleague but traveling for work isn't my favorite thing." He bent down to greet Ted. As I watched him ruffling Ted's fur and talking to him so naturally, I realized there were many sides to Brent that I would never get to know. I felt a loss inside of me. "Maybe you can join us one of these times, Adam, when Bruce sends us off to do his dirty work."

"Dirty work?" Adam asked.

It wasn't the part of the sentence I had focused on. I was still stuck in a mythical restaurant with Brent on one side of me and Adam on the other.

"Bruce sends us to crap accounts he doesn't want to deal with himself. I'm sure the office would run fine if he weren't there for a few days. This next trip is over the top if you…" At the precise moment my neglected details would have been revealed, a squirrel crossed the path. Ted barked and tugged frantically. By the time Adam had him settled, Brent had forgotten where the conversation was going. My heart still pounded on my chest wall. "Oh, by the way, sorry again that it took so long to respond to your text the other day, Skylar. As I said, it was a crazy day. I didn't talk to you much the next day either with those men coming in and all."

"Oh, no problem. I can't even remember why I texted you, so it couldn't have been too important."

"Either way, I didn't mean to be rude." After giving Ted a last pat on the head, Brent stood. "Well, I'd better get going before my legs stiffen. Nice to meet you."

"Good to meet you, too," Adam replied.

"Bye, Brent." I resisted the desperate urge to watch him as he jogged away from us.

"What was the text about?" Adam asked as soon as Brent was out of earshot.

"As I said, I don't even remember what it was about anymore."

"If it wasn't important, then why would you have to text him?"

"I must have thought it was important at the time." I squeezed Adam's hand. "You have to trust me, Adam." I wanted to tell him I'd simply needed to know if Brent had been the man on the motorcycle stalking me, but I didn't think that would go over very well. "You know, Adam, I don't believe you did those things at your job, although I would love you anyway."

Adam squeezed my hand back and smiled. "Thanks, Skylar, but no, you wouldn't."

"Yes, I'm telling you, I would. How can you say I wouldn't?"

"Because if I had done those things, I wouldn't be me. If

I were capable of being that immoral, everything about me that makes you think you know me would be false. How could you would love someone that you don't even know?"

There was nothing else to say.

This time, telling dreams did not disturb my sleep, but rather a nagging thought.

"It's about diversion," Bruce had said.

I woke up determined to start changing my life and digging myself out of the grave Bruce and Henry had thrown me in, but first, if I was going to save myself, I had to understand my situation.

At three in the morning, when Bruce's drunken slurred voice still refused to leave my mind, I looked up Bitcoin. Bitcoin sites came up looking all professional and almost kid-friendly. The wave of the future, Henry had said. I was, in fact, naive in the world.

Upon reading, I learned many things. The success of Bitcoin was associated with a mysterious pseudonym known as Satoshi Nakamoto, the person or persons who had authored and implemented it as a currency. Nakamoto had created software where money bought codes that represented money. The codes were then used to buy products; a pizza of all things, had been the first known purchase. Satoshi Nakamoto had created this system in about 2008, right after the stock market had crashed. People had not trusted our banking system and fiat money, which I learned meant paper money.

What confused me was that anyone could install the software and begin buying and selling right off their phone, so why send me to the Netherlands? Banks were supposed to report any suspicion of money laundering; nevertheless, with the right incentive, anyone could look the other way. Perhaps

Henry had learned that even though the powers that be were starting to notice his accounts, he might still be able to buy some time by working through Brenda's accounts. Throw in some Bitcoin, and the authorities had one more layer to dig through before his scam came crashing down on him.

I also learned that a large computer system known as a block chain recorded every transaction. As I studied an internet photo of the warehouse referred to as a Bitcoin mine, I wondered how much information could be stored in the massive system. How long would it take for someone to suspect Brenda Carter, find her offshore account, connect her to Henry, trace her Bitcoin purchases, and catch her buying something illegal? Years, maybe more, or possibly the authorities would never know. When would my nightmare end?

So yes, cryptocurrency was legal, but even the kid-friendly website seemed to scream that it was not secure and not a place to invest all your savings since values dropped in a heartbeat. Then again, values also jumped in a heartbeat as well.

My research only supplied more evidence that Henry supported Bitcoin because something illegal was going on behind the scenes of his hotel business and Brenda's construction business. I'm sure they'd figured it was better to lose illegally-earned money in a fragile market than to let the government know you had it in the first place. Either way, I was not connected to the funds that would be buying the Bitcoin, and I had no actual proof that something illegal was being purchased with them, either. With these details in mind, I decided I would buy the cybermoney for them and get Adam back to the world he used to know.

Waiting for me with asparagus and cheese omelets and hot coffee, Adam sat at the table.

"I thought I would send you off on your trip with a nice breakfast."

"It's perfect." I gave him a quick kiss before sitting across from him. "What are your plans today?"

"Scanning the Internet. Trying to find purpose."

"You have a purpose, Adam. I promise you that things will work out."

"I'll pretend I believe you. Two nights this time?"

"Two nights, and I'll be home to help search the Internet for a backup plan, but remember, your company hasn't replaced you yet. Bill could call anytime saying you can come back, and this mess could all simply disappear."

"Wouldn't that be nice." Adam stood to clean his dish.

As I watched Adam's defeated frame cross the kitchen, my determination strengthened. I would do whatever it took to make his situation right, even if it meant shutting off my location on my phone and adding one more lie to the mix between us.

I met Brent at the office. He offered to drive us both to the airport, and I agreed. Before heading out, though, I needed to get the money from Bruce. Without invitation, I walked into his office and closed the door behind me.

"Do you have something for me?"

He reached under his desk and pulled out a carry-on case. "Do you have any questions?"

"A million. Do you have any answers?" I opened the case. It appeared as if nothing were there. The black lining was created entirely to make it look like an empty carry-on. I would throw in some files to give the case purpose.

"Brent has the accounts you'll be looking into. Henry owns shares of a small boating company not far from the airport. I don't know a great deal about it, except I suspect it will prove to be a simple account."

"Anything else?" I asked.

Bruce studied me for a moment. "Good luck, Skylar."

I ran to the bathroom before making one last stop at my desk for the extra files. A Post-It on my computer screen said, *Meet me at my truck.* I looked around the small office, and I could only see the tops of the heads belonging to my colleagues who were busy at work. I had a familiar feeling, without the warmth and coziness, of walking into my home after being away at college and wondering how the walls had shrunk when I'd been away.

Brent stood by my car, speaking quietly into his phone. Even though I had no right to wonder who he was talking to or any reason to think I had the right to know either, I did wonder. The feeling only grew when, before I reached him, he quietly ended the call.

"Was that a lady friend?"

"Something like that."

Why had I simply assumed he didn't go home to anyone at night? Had I ever asked?

"Something like that?" I pried with my best attempt at playfulness. "What's that supposed to mean?"

"Aren't you full of questions today?"

"I don't have a lot of questions," I retorted.

"No, my lady friend," he said, using the quotations around lady friend. "You don't ask enough."

I opened my car door to grab my suitcase, and waiting for more, I watched him. "What do you mean, I don't ask enough?"

He tossed my suitcase into his backseat and gave me a small smile. "Just what I said. We better get going."

I climbed up next to him in the front seat of his truck. "Well, you asked for it. I'm going to exhaust you with questions the whole trip."

"And, I will gladly answer."

"So how serious are you and your lady friend?"

He finished backing out and put the truck into drive. "I didn't exactly say the person on the phone was a lady friend." He got quiet for a moment, and I could tell his mind took him far away from his vehicle's cab. "There's no one in my life right now. There used to be until she went down a dangerous path. I couldn't save her, so I haven't felt like going down the relationship road again."

I sat quietly, contemplating my boundaries, and then I remembered he'd told me to ask away.

"I'm sorry, Brent. Can I ask what happened?"

"We were young, still in college. My girlfriend was the wildest, most carefree person I've ever met. Being around her lit up my world. The crazy thing was she couldn't see that in herself. When it was only us, our relationship was amazing. Everything would change when she got in a crowd; it was as if instead of being the life of the party, she would be sucked into the background. I think the idea of being boring petrified her.

"We were young, and I didn't care much about the nights she drank too much, danced on the tables, stumbled home. We would laugh about it the next day. I would bring her a burger, and when the hangover had gone away, she was back. The real her would once again say let's go, and we would, and whatever it was we ended up doing, it was great.

"I always got the feeling that she felt like she owed the people around her; she owed them her smile, her humor, her energy. Sometimes, though, she hadn't had it to give, so with a little help, she pretended. One night, I got to the party a bit later than she had, and a friend told me my girlfriend had taken LSD. Someone had been walking around with little innocent-looking pieces of paper, and she'd said, 'Sure, I'll take some.'

"I was shocked and disappointed." Brent paused as if reliving a moment in his mind. "Regardless, I took care of her through it. We talked about it, and she promised she would never do LSD again. And she didn't. Instead, she tried cocaine. And then a few weeks later, she did it again. And then she did it again. And then she did it her last time. She'd barely had time to officially become an addict. Sometimes, I wonder what would have been worse. It would have killed me to have watched her become a true druggie, to change from the person I'd known, but I would have liked more time to make her believe she was amazing without all the partying."

"I'm so sorry you went through that, and I'm sorry if I shouldn't have asked."

"I told you to ask, didn't I? It happened a long time ago. Still, it changed my life. Even though I've dated other people since then, I've never stopped looking for her in everyone. Maybe at the young age of twenty, I thought I knew what my type would be for life. It wasn't until I stopped searching for her in everyone that I realized, maybe she wasn't exactly what I needed. Maybe what I'm looking for is a mature version of her. Someone who appreciates the mundane without forgetting how to live either."

My heart sank. Besides having been forced into the life of crime, I was possibly the most unexciting person who'd ever lived. Even though I had no right to assume I'd be a good match for Brent, it hurt not to be his type.

"What was her name?"

Brent paused as if preparing himself for the pain the sound of her name might cause. "Emily. Her name was Emily."

"Well, I don't know where to go from there. How about you tell me about the job you had before this one?"

"Another reason I haven't settled down. I move from place to place, from job to job. It's a good way of life for me right now, or at least it has been. Settling down in one place gets tempting at times, if it were the right place, anyway."

"So is Jacksonville the right place?"

Brent gave me a warm smile before looking back at the road. "It's the closest to perfect I've found so far, but close to perfect isn't perfect, now, is it?"

Was he talking about me? Was he pointing out that I wasn't the perfect fit? "No, close to perfect isn't perfect." I reached for the fan button because all of a sudden, the air seemed thicker than soup, and I was suffocating in it. "Would you like music?" I hit the power button without waiting for his answer.

Brent turned down the music a touch. "Can I ask questions now?"

"Sure."

"So why no kids?"

"You met my child at the park."

"Aw, yes, Ted. I also finally got to meet Adam. He seemed nice, quiet."

"He's very nice. He's just been under a lot of stress with losing his job."

"That's a whole slew of other questions, but kids, why none?"

"They haven't happened for us naturally, so we decided it's our fate to be childless."

"How do you feel about that?"

"Almost always, I feel okay, but sometimes I wonder what kind of mom I would have been. My mother-self, well, it's like a second me that I will never get to know. I'd like to think I would have been a pretty good mom."

"You would be an awesome mom."

"Do you think that for real, or are you just being kind? What part of me makes you believe that?"

"Why would you be a good mother? Let me paint a picture. Your kids would come home to a clean house, eat a healthy snack, and everything would be completely orderly, but then one of them would accidentally drop chocolate milk all over your perfectly organized life. Somewhere in the middle of trying to scrub up the mess, you would realize how much you truly like people and the messes they bring with them."

I laughed, knowing I too often didn't like people, until the realization weighed down on me. "What if I didn't? What if I was one of those moms who never laughed or played or took my kids on adventures?"

"Skylar, you are capable of a great deal more than you give yourself credit for. You're clinging to a branch and scared to take flight is how I see it."

My throat burned with tears. Brent had described me better than I could have explained myself; better than Adam could have described me. Dreaming of another me, I found myself smiling out the window. "You might be right."

On the long plane ride, Brent and I both fell asleep several times. I tried not to watch Brent peacefully breathing next to me, yet I found myself studying each intricate detail I would never be able to stare at if he were awake. I studied everything until my eyes grew heavy, and I drifted off, feeling his warm breath encircling my face like the palm of his hand.

By the end of the flight, I knew the length of his eyelashes, the contour of his five o'clock shadow, the plumpness of his lips.

We got to the hotel and, as usual, went our separate ways. As soon as I checked in, I decided to do more research on what awaited me. I'd already learned Bitcoin was legal but also used for many illegal things. In 2015, there had been an investigation into Silk Road and the website moniker, Dread Pirate Roberts, who'd made millions from the purchase of cybermoney. Cybermoney that, as expected, was used to buy drugs, porn, and even murders. I didn't put Henry above doing any of those things; nevertheless, my bet was on drugs.

Another notable arrest for drug smuggling involving Bitcoin had taken place in the Netherlands. And several other significant arrests took place there as well. Even the U.S. government had investigated whether it should develop its own cybermoney but had not yet created a system. Speaking of systems, I found that, as Henry had said, money in the cyber world was not backed by any bank or government. On top of that, the keys used to open the wallets made it challenging to trace.

I awoke before the sun rose, ate the hotel breakfast, and got my cab, all without running into Brent. We would be going to a small motel in the afternoon, and the less Brent knew of my other planned excursion, the better.

Once at the bank, I asked to see Lucas—exactly as Henry had told me to do. Shortly afterward, a woman brought me into a private room. A tall thin man with a strong Dutch accent introduced himself as Lucas and asked what he could do for me today. I picked up the black carry-on and allowed him a small peek at what lay beneath the lining. He nodded and reached for the bag, letting me know he would take it from there. I handed over the carry-on, and he removed an envelope with the word 'services' written on the front. I suspected it was full of cash. Lucas slipped it into his drawer. Well, that explained his loyalty to Henry.

Henry had apparently discussed with Lucas before I'd arrived what he would find inside the carry-on. Lucas opened and examined another hefty stack of money in a separate envelope. The stack had to be the funds that would never see the bank.

"I need to open an account for Brenda Carter and was told you would assist me in buying $100,000 in Bitcoin."

"Ah, yes, as our friend explained." As I sat back and picked at my pathetic cuticles, Lucas busied himself on the computer. He rose. "Everything is complete. Bring this paperwork to our friend."

He had sealed the envelope to hide its contents from my prying eyes except, this time, I was sick of playing the victim. As soon as I got to the hotel, I put my iron on steam and opened the envelope. When I looked at the letter, I saw nothing but gibberish. Twelve meaningless words stared back at me as if they were all part of the joke the universe seemed to be playing on me. It was all I had, so I copied every nonsensical word down and sealed the envelope back up.

At dinner, I nervously rambled on about Ted and his silly antics, clearly not even listening to myself. My brain scrambled to figure out how the list of random words could stop my life from spiraling down further.

"Any chance you want to tell me about where you went this morning?"

I must have looked surprised.

"I saw you walk out," Brent added. "I was drinking coffee at a corner table."

"Why didn't you say hi?" I tried to act as casual as possible but knew I wasn't pulling it off.

"All day, I have waited for you to mention what you were up to earlier. If it were nothing, you would have told me about it."

"I went to check out the area. Nothing more to it."

"By yourself? That's a great idea." He eyed me without another word.

"Are you going to have this attitude the whole night?"

"I saw you leave Bruce's office with that black carry-on. What was in it?"

"How did you see me? You had gone to the truck."

"I waited to leave until after you'd come out of the office and gone to the restroom. Something told me I should see what you were up to."

My mind went back to creepy stalker for only a moment and then headed right to complete fear that Brent was on to me. I scrambled for an answer. "The bag had stuff for the account. Why?"

"Because I think there is a reason he usually sends us to different accounts, and I think what was in that carry-on might explain why."

"Oh, my." I tried to lighten the tone. "Am I being interrogated?"

He smiled at me in an, *I'm messing with you*, kind of way, yet I knew better.

"If I say yes, will you give me something interesting for my efforts?"

"I'm an open book," I replied.

Unflinching, I stared right at him. Fear could create excellent liars.

"What was in the carry-on?" Brent set his wallet on the table and settled back on his seat.

"Bad back?" I asked.

"Excuse me?"

"Adam always says his wallet bothers him in his back pocket."

"Well, there's another thing he and I have in common."

"Another thing?"

"What was in the bag?" Brent continued quickly.

"I truly have no idea, except for a sealed envelope. I was told to give it to the manager of the hotel. As for the carry-on itself, Bruce said it was a thank-you gift."

"You okay, Skylar? You seem nervous."

"No, well, yes, but I don't know why. I guess it's because I don't like being interrogated."

There was always a chance Brent's job was to see if I would crack under pressure. If I said too much, could I be endangering myself? Adam?

"I guess it doesn't matter if there's nothing to find out, right?"

"Right."

"You worry me, Skylar."

"Me, too," I mumbled so he could not decipher my words with one-hundred percent accuracy.

I finished my meal and took my last swallow of wine. "You know, I think I need to go walk by myself tonight." The idea of being questioned any further was too daunting. "I saw an interesting area this morning that I would like to see again before leaving. Would you mind paying the bill, so I can head out before it gets too late?"

"You can't head out on your own here."

"I need to. I promise I'll just go for a quick walk, and I'll check in with you, so you know I made it back to the room safe."

"I can't let you do that."

I stood. "You don't have a choice."

Our hotel overlooked Schereningen Beach, so I felt safe enough to be alone with only the sand beneath me and the moon guiding my path. My thoughts drifted to the me that had existed such a short time before. My life had been boring, albeit nice. I had never lied to Adam, ever—except for the very occasional purchase that I'd made at a 'let's tighten the belt' kind of moment, but I'd wanted it anyway. I'd bought it and hidden it in my closet until the 'let's tighten the belt' moment had passed, and then it had magically appeared. That was it.

Adam had given me no reason to lie, and I really stunk at it. One more reason why I couldn't believe I was in the position I was in and was possibly pulling it off. Only Brent had occasionally raised an eyebrow. I might have had a more sinister side tucked deep inside of me after all, a possibility that frightened me and yet also slightly impressed me. Wrong, I know.

I held my cell phone in one hand, while awaiting the perfect selfie that I wasn't quite in the mood to take; my sandals dangled in the other. I felt free and trapped and scared and alive; a lot of feelings for one small moment. The moon drifted from behind a cloud, revealing the perfect picturesque moment I sought. I punched in my password because I had never figured out how to open the camera without the password and saw a missed call from Adam. The phone had been in my hand the whole time. Honestly, couldn't I have felt the vibration? At least now, I would have a voicemail to replay every time I needed to hear his voice.

Desperately, I forced the phone close to my ear so if it were at all possible, I could feel his breath. Instead, I heard a voice very unlike Adam's, distant and agitated from the first word.

"So how are the Bahamas or wherever you are with what's his name? Brent, right? I got a funny call from your boss today asking how you're feeling. He thought it was unlike you to be taking so many sick days during tax season." Silence. When Adam spoke again, he sounded crushed. "I guess we need to talk when you get home. Bye, Skylar."

I fell to the ground, dampening my knees in the wet sand. I couldn't let Henry and Bruce destroy us; however, the problem had gotten too big for me. Alone, I couldn't stop them. I knew that now. Like a child, I ran, seeking help from the only person available, yet still not knowing if I headed into more darkness. I had to find Brent. He had to know.

For the first time since we'd traveled together, I knocked on Brent's hotel room door. I heard him shuffling across the rug inside and drawing closer. I listened to the lock being turned, and then the door swung open. Brent, shirtless, stood in front of me wearing briefs that worked as nightclothes. Seeing his bare skin threw me, and I was suddenly at a loss for words. The sight of him was so familiar, as if I had seen him a million times before, and sadness washed over me knowing that even on my best day with Adam, I would always be missing Brent. "I'm going to bed now." I turned away to hide my tears; tears for Adam and me. Tears that Brent could never know would fall.

"Goodnight, Skylar." I waved over my shoulder and didn't look back.

I tried to call Adam too many times to count. He refused to answer.

As I boarded the plane, one text came through.

I'm begging you, Skylar, come home with a reason.

I promise you I have one. Have faith in me. I love you, Adam. It's time I tell you everything.

I had kept the text message to myself and carried the weight of it throughout the day. If I'd told Brent about it, I would have had to explain everything that had been going on since I'd met Henry, and I wasn't prepared to do that just yet. I'd needed time to think, and time to speak to Adam. All day, I'd feared how the conversation would go, and that I wouldn't be able to make Adam understand. For the first time, I'd envisioned a life without him, and a sickness in my stomach began to grow.

When Brent fell asleep next to me on the plane, I studied him again. Many emotions struggled for control in my mind, and I was sure sleep would never come. Eventually, my eyes grew heavy, and within a short time, I drifted off. Despite my fear of losing Adam, I dreamed about Brent.

My only focus was on the hand I held. I knew the man, and in my waking hours I would have been aware of the fact I shouldn't be holding his hand. But I wasn't awake, and my mind allowed me a moment that reality could not. Only the image of our fingers locked together and the feeling of completeness the bond created within me stood out in the dream. I wanted to stay in the warmth of the moment forever, where everything felt good and right. The vision was the most intimate one I've experienced because the man touched places I've let very few people explore. Somewhere in my alternate world, his hand is still wrapped around mine.

This time I didn't run to Google because I didn't care what Google thought.

CHAPTER 16

PULLING INTO MY driveway, I immediately noticed Adam's car wasn't there. My heart sank. When I entered the house, everything was quiet, which was normal except it wasn't normal. I always wondered what people meant when they said things were too quiet. There is either sound or no sound. But at that moment, the meaning became crystal clear. Quiet is a person sitting next to you but not saying a thing. Too quiet is the person sitting next to you and not breathing. It's an overlooked sound because we expect it to be there until it's not. Something was wrong with the regular cadence of my house, and every inch of me knew it. So, I kept moving forward, hoping the skipped breath was nothing but a glitch in time, and the world was about to reset.

I placed the keys on the counter and listened to the clinking sound carry down the hallway. Then I heard it. A barely audible noise—as if something was being shoved across the carpet—from the back bedroom. My head pounded while I tried to hear something through the silence that followed. I forced myself to take one step in the direction of the bedroom. Only one, because I was still deciding whether to run back out the door.

Out of nowhere, a thought barreled into me. Ted had not greeted me. That was the silence. How had I missed it? He was still frightened to be home alone and would run to us, leaping and licking with excitement. He should be jumping up on me,

186

begging for attention. Nothing. And then I heard it again—the shuffle across the carpeting in the bedroom. I pleaded with my body not to breathe, but despite this, my body insisted it was necessary. With desperation, I listened for another sound while cursing my heart for beating too loudly.

Then there was a clunk of some sort—a drawer shutting.

Still, I stood and listened, a real hero in my own story. Minutes passed, and yet Ted didn't come bounding from the room to greet me. Did something slip by my window? Could someone be watching as I stood defenseless in my kitchen? I glanced around the room, realizing I didn't need to be defenseless. The knives tucked away in their drawers, called out to me.

After tiptoeing to the counter, I pulled out the knife we saved for special occasions like the Thanksgiving turkey carving. I held it and waited until it became insane to wait any longer. Baby step by baby step, I crept down the quiet hallway and peered into my bedroom. The breeze blew in from my open window, letting the night air circulate my room. I never left my window open. Other than the whisper of the breeze, I heard silence. There were endless errands Adam might be running, except Ted only went to the park with us. Since it was already dusk, this wasn't a possibility. The fact was undeniable. Ted was missing, and someone had been in my bedroom.

Yes, Ted had eaten my favorite fake Kate Spades. Despite that, I loved my silly, drooling, shedding dog. I felt what I had heard people refer to as the Mama Bear Syndrome taking over. Why would someone take my dog, of all things? Nothing made sense.

How was I to tell Adam that someone had kidnapped our pet while I was also trying to explain why my boss had said I'd called in sick? If only Adam would have taken my calls, then I would have... Then I would have what? Explained by saying: *Oh, no, honey. You have it all wrong. I'm not having an affair. I'm flying off to foreign places to create fraudulent accounts to hide illegal money. However, I wouldn't have done that if someone hadn't photographed me snuggled in a blanket with Brent. And then right after the romantic beach scene, forced me to sign false FBARs. Now, don't you feel silly?* Then we would laugh and realize Ted had only run after a rabbit because Adam had forgotten to close the window. I would probably refrain from scolding Adam.

Where was Adam? Maybe my paranoid criminal mind had overlooked the obvious. Adam had lost track of time and was still out walking Ted. He would be back at any moment. Or worse, Adam had left me, and to punish me, had taken Ted with him. Except, what were the sounds I had heard coming from the bedroom? I texted Adam and waited several minutes before giving up on a response.

The house still creeped me out, and I had no one else to call except Brent or the police. Neither seemed logical. Would it have hurt me to have made a few friends at the office? Hadn't every movie I'd watched taught me that bad people seek out lonely souls who are easy to manipulate? I located the Find My iPhone button and stalked Adam. He was offline. Was he going to start playing that game? Under Favorites, I touched the only number there—Adam's. Maybe he didn't hear the ding of my text, but it went to voicemail. A message saying the box was full sliced my hopes. The silence encompassed me like a wave again. I sent a Find My iPhone sound, three times, maybe four, but not more than five. Nothing.

I had to lock the bedroom window, at least. Grabbing my knife, I crept into the blackness. The breeze tugged at my shirt like invisible hands and caressed my bare skin like a warning of its presence. For a moment, I stared into the night before finding the courage to raise my arms to reach the pane. Scrambling, I pulled it down and locked it. Not feeling safe enough, I yanked the window treatments shut. Still, I could not shake the feeling someone was out there, watching me. Every drape called to me, and I raced from one room to the another, checking locks and sealing myself away from the outside.

With a racing heart, I leaned back against the wall, and tears began to fall. I needed Adam. As I cried into my hands, a sudden thought occurred to me. What if the quiet dragging sound across my carpet had been Adam? I was cracking under pressure.

With my phone in one hand and the knife in the other, I curled up in the corner of my living room. From there, I could see every angle, and no one could surprise me from behind. I listened so attentively that the silence became deafening. A hum in my mind took over, and I considered turning something on, anything, to get rid of the nothingness.

If I called the police, I'd be turning myself in for my crimes. I was willing to do that, except what if I endangered Adam by making the call? I could call Brent, but how would that look to Adam? Adam could, for all I knew, be at the grocery store, about to return home at any moment. The garage. I needed to check the garage for his car, yet the door seemed miles away with windows lining the path. I sat frozen in my little corner. My only option was to wait. If someone were watching the house, I was ready. All I had to do was show my turkey knife, and they would drop their weapon. Or not.

My phone beeped, alerting me to a text. *I need time to think. I'll contact you soon.*

What? How could Adam have run off when I'd told him I could explain everything?

Adam, I told you I could explain. Please come home. A cry escaped my throat. *Please.*

I will. Give me time.

What about Ted? He's not here.

I know.

Where is he?

Nothing for several minutes. *I took the things that mattered with me.*

After further investigation, the story panned out. Adam's car was not in the garage, and his suitcase was missing, along with his wallet. Adam had chosen to leave me. With each passing hour, the sound I'd heard coming from the bedroom softened in my memory. Soon, I could no longer be sure I had heard anything.

That night, I lay alone in my empty bedroom that no longer felt familiar. Had I lost Adam? As much as my feelings strayed without permission, I wasn't ready to say goodbye. The drapes, closed, let no moonlight into the room. My inability to sleep allowed my brain to wander back to my very first dream—the alien bursting through the door into my home. The bite should have empowered me; I should have defeated him. Two novel ideas that had never quite clicked the same way with me until that very moment went through my mind. The first realization was that when I'd called out, "I'm scared, Brent!" I'd somehow thought Brent had been busting into my home and messing everything up.

Perhaps that's not what had been happening in my dream, or the vision had double meanings. What if I hadn't been telling the alien that I was scared? It's possible I'd said it to someone not in my field of vision. I'd called out to Brent for help, and he hadn't been the terrifying thing at my door. The second realization was that, up to that point, I'd neglected to puff up and fight off the gigantic alien. In my dream, I'd known I had the power to do so. After all, the zombie had bitten me through the roof of my car. Yes, dreams were entirely bizarre. Still, there was something to them, and at that very moment, I was aware of two things. It was time to call out for help, and I was ready to puff up and kick some alien ass.

CHAPTER 17

WHEN I ENTERED the office, about half of the staff was already there. A palpable tension was in the air. Making a beeline to Brent's cubicle, I ran smack into Bruce.

"Skylar, follow me."

To my surprise, he didn't have me follow him into his office; instead, he headed into a supply room. Before I could ask him why he had called Adam and lied about my absences, the urgency of the current situation erased my words. I wouldn't have gotten the answers I sought anyway. Sweat dripped down his forehead, and as he closed the door, his hands shook. His fear overshadowed the awkwardness of standing in the confining room with him.

"What's going on?" I asked.

"Do you have anything of Henry's on your computer?"

"No, I only use the one at his house. I've told you that. Why?" Bruce's eyes darted as if he was on a caffeine rush. His nervousness made one thing apparent—he wasn't cut out for this.

"Act normal."

He swung open the door and was gone. All I could do was head to my desk and watch as Bruce disappeared into his office. A couple of people in suits had been waiting for him by his door. As I walked toward my cubicle, I caught a glimpse of

Brent's concerned expression. My heart raced. I knew that I was in the middle of something big, and I was on the wrong side of things.

What the heck is going on? I texted Brent.

Not sure; those people are here looking for things again. Some people better come clean because their time is about up.

Who are they? Police?

I never heard their names. They went into Bruce's office for quite some time and then stopped by some of the cubicles. They were at yours for about ten minutes.

They were at my cubicle? Why?

No idea. You okay, Skylar? You seem nervous.

No. Well, yes. I don't like strangers going through my desk, of course. Who would?

I guess it doesn't matter if there's nothing to find, right?

Right.

What did you do in the Bahamas? You know, the time I didn't go with you.

I sat silent for a moment and then said the only thing I could. *I don't know.*

What do you mean you don't know?

I don't know. That's what I mean.

You're not making much sense.

When you said you think people need to come clean, what do you think they have to come clean about?

We're an accounting firm. Some obvious issues could be going on. I hope only Bruce is involved and not half the office. The authorities will be looking at each one of us.

Who do you think is involved in whatever it is? I asked.

Could be anyone. Do you have any ideas?

I typed *yes* and let it linger, knowing Brent watched the

annoying text messaging dots on the other end. My finger hovered over the Send button, and then I decided to delete the word. Instead, I texted, *We need to talk.*

At lunch time, we rode out to a small park where the dock reached out over the Intracoastal like a finger pointing to Henry's home. It was bizarre to me that of all the places we could end up, I would be staring my dilemma in the face. Brent's warm hand curled around mine, and I looked down at it as if it would make more sense that way.

"Skylar, for a moment, let me be there for you." I couldn't answer. "It's only a hand, Skylar. You need one right now."

I nodded and laid my head on his arm as we gazed at the water together.

"You are quiet for a woman who said we needed to talk."

"I'm trying to find a way to tell you everything I need to before the sun sets. Then again, since Adam left me, I have plenty of time to talk."

I could have sworn disappointment shadowed Brent's face, which mystified me.

"Adam left you? Why?"

"That's where the whole story ends. Let me work backward. Adam left me because Bruce told him that I had called in sick and that he didn't send us off to another account."

"I'm baffled right now. Why would Bruce do that?"

"He would do that for the same reason he's done everything else, I suppose. To destroy me so he can save himself."

"What's going on, Skylar?"

"Can I trust you, Brent? Can I trust you with everything that I know and with my life?"

"Absolutely."

I studied him for a moment, even though I had already decided to believe him.

"Look at me, Skylar." He turned my shoulders toward him, and I found myself face to face with his searching eyes. "We accountants need to stick together. If you need to complain, need advice, whatever, I'm here for you." In any other situation, I would believe he was hitting on me, but right now I felt like I was being searched.

"Have you ever wondered if you were a good person or a bad person?" I asked.

"What do you mean? I can't imagine you being a bad person."

"I mean, it's usually easy to be good, but what if there was a gray area we didn't see coming? What if we couldn't choose to be good as easily as we'd thought we could?"

To my surprise, Brent took me in his arms, sort of in a big brother way. "Skylar, you're an accountant. You know black and white, right and wrong. There is always a side to choose; you just have to decide which one you're going to pick."

His words made sense. I'd needed to hear them. Yet, I feared I was already in too deep to pick the one I had selected my whole life. Maybe this time I couldn't choose right. Then again, maybe I could.

"Brent, I've done things I never thought I would do. I'm in way over my head. I'm drowning; my ship has collided with the iceberg." My voice shook. I buried my face in his protective chest to avoid looking him in the eyes. "I didn't want to. I didn't want to do any of it. I'm only an accountant for God's sake. I don't know how to deal with bad people."

Brent again took me by the shoulders and made our gazes meet. He watched me without a word and seemingly without judgment. His expression, which appeared slightly amused, didn't fit the situation.

"I've signed false FBARs. I've deposited money that I am quite sure was illegal. I've opened accounts for criminals and deposited money in offshore accounts under my name. I've bought Bitcoin for God's sake. Do you know what a Bitcoin is?" I didn't wait for his answer. "My name is on everything. Adam was fired because of me. He left me. I need help. I need your help." Then I dared to look him in the eyes again, and there was definite amusement on his face. "Are you laughing at me? Don't you believe me?"

"Yes, Skylar, I do believe you," Brent said. "What else would explain all the crazy stuff going on in the office?"

"I'm going to jail. I'm the biggest rule follower that ever lived, and I'm going to jail."

Brent pulled me close and with tenderness, stroked my hair. "I've got a better idea, Skylar. Let's get your life back."

"That's definitely a better idea." For whatever reason, I believed that together, we could do precisely that.

Side by side, we walked down the pier toward his motorcycle. Next to his bike, I also saw a dark van parked. Something about the vehicle aroused my suspicion, and I looked at Brent to see if he'd noticed the van as well. He stared at it without wavering. "I have some confessions as well."

"What's going on, Brent?"

Outside the moment I'd sat alone, knife in hand, on my floor, I'd never been as close to hyperventilating in my life. My heart raced and nausea churned inside of me. All along, I'd wondered if Brent was good or bad; all along I'd had my doubts. And now I walked at a pace fueled by the steps Brent continued to take and headed toward the van that awaited us.

"Please talk to me, Brent."

"Everything will make sense soon, Skylar."

"I trusted you."

"Did you, really? Skylar, I don't think you have truly trusted me."

"You don't understand. I couldn't trust anyone." Tears rolled down my face, and I wiped them with my sleeve. "I wanted you to be one of the good guys."

"Skylar." In an instant, I went from rolling tears to a sobbing voice. "Skylar." Brent lifted my chin. "I'm good. You can trust me. I'm just not what you thought I was. At least, not exactly."

Again, I wiped my tears with my sleeve. "What do you mean? I'm so tired, Brent. I'm just so tired. Please tell me what you mean."

"I am an accountant, but I'm not only an accountant. I'm a forensic accountant with the FBI. I've been working a case against Henry."

"What?" I sobbed.

"Inside that van, special agents are listening to our every word. They've been listening to us quite a bit, actually."

"You've been working me?" I looked him straight in the face, the face I wanted to slap, except it was probably illegal to hit an FBI agent.

"I've been working a case, and you just happened to be in the middle of it."

"You've been trying to arrest me?"

"That was never my intention. I wanted to help you. I wanted you to trust me, but I also needed you."

"Needed me?"

"Yes. You were our person on the inside. It was better

you didn't know. It may have affected how you acted and what information you were able to obtain."

"How do you know I have any information or that I would share it with you?"

"Skylar, it's your way out."

"You didn't even care if I was in danger. You didn't care that Adam left me. I thought...I...never mind. Let's go visit your friends in the van."

Anger welled inside of me, and I stormed over to the vehicle, ready to rip the door open and expose everyone inside, but apparently, special agents locked the doors when spying on people. Instead, I yanked so hard I almost toppled over. There would be no more crying even if I had to remind myself on a second-to-second basis.

"I'm ready to tell everything. Tell your friends to open their stupid door."

"Skylar, calm down a minute. Let me talk to you."

"I'm not telling you anything. I'll talk to them."

"Fair enough."

Brent did a slight knock, and the door opened. Three men wearing big earphones sat around monitors. I recognized one of the men—a bit older than me with gray starting to speckle his brown hair. He had been at the office earlier, which also meant that the whole time I'd been texting Brent, he'd known exactly what had been going on and had played dumb.

"Hello, Ms. Skylar. I'm Special Agent Kemp. It's nice to meet you officially."

"Hello," was all I could say.

Kemp then turned back to his equipment. "Why don't you come on inside and we'll go for a ride? We'll go to the field office where we can sit and talk."

Without looking back at Brent, I crawled in and heard the door swing shut behind me.

Through the tinted glass, I saw Brent climb onto his motorcycle. My helmet dangled from the side, making me feel discarded. He drove off, and the silence in the van became deafening.

"So, where do we go from here?" I asked. "Do you read me my Miranda rights or something?"

"No need. You're not under arrest. After we talk at the office, you're free to go." Kemp paused. "Why don't you start by telling us what you know?"

I forced myself to face him. "Diversion," I replied in a tear-stricken state.

"What do you mean?"

Panic seized me. I was alone with people who owed me nothing—no understanding, no sympathy. There was a real chance they might not believe me. "I mean, I was all diversion."

"Do you have proof of that? The evidence paints you as a pretty willing participant."

Even though they hadn't read me any rights, the words ran through my mind, warning me to shut my mouth.

CHAPTER 18

THE VAN FELT like a hundred degrees inside with no circulation of air, although the men appeared at ease. I chalked up my too-hot sensation to being nervous. For a moment, we all scanned each other.

"This is Special Agent Hall," Kemp said. I nodded, trying not to show how petrified I felt. Hall appeared to be about thirty and had an air of cockiness that I guessed made up for his lack of experience. He had dark hair and a thin layer of scruff shadowed his square jawline. Liz would like him. "Special Agent Bailey." Kemp tipped his head in the other agent's direction. Bailey had a full head of red hair, and a beard covered his face that, in a different situation, I might have described as kind. He leaned forward, giving me his full attention. The gesture almost looked polite, but something told me he only cared about the entertainment factor of watching me crack under pressure. Being outnumbered didn't concern me. If I could survive hours with Henry, then I could survive this.

"So, are you going to begin?" Kemp stared at me with penetrating eyes.

I searched my mind for every scene from movies resembling my situation and stumbled across my saving phrase, "I want a lawyer."

My saving phrase brought laughter, of what kind was yet to be determined. Were they laughing because I had found my out, or were the men laughing at me because I thought I had found it?

"We can go that route, sure, but we have what we need. This case is a special agent's dream. It's so cut and dried with the amount of evidence we have." Kemp smirked. "We don't need you to share what you did. What we're giving you is an opportunity to share why. Save yourself, Skylar. That's what our friend Brent was hoping you would do, anyway. Here's your chance."

I made eye contact with each of the three men in the van as if I could decide my future with a probing stare.

"I can save myself, or better yet, I can make that job of yours that you are pretending is so wrapped up even easier. We both know it's not me you're after. You're bait fishing right now so that you have something to throw back into the water to catch the shark. Don't play mind games with me. I'll be your bait, but I'm not talking to you. Not yet. I need to see Brent."

After a few stolen glances with each other, the cocky young bastard spoke into his shoulder.

"Come on back."

Brent had been listening to us the whole time. I should have known, yet my jaw still clenched in anger. We sat in silence until I heard the motorcycle pull up next to the van parked in the same spot. We had not moved before they'd realized I would not be speaking to them.

I stood, staying slumped over to prevent knocking my head on the ceiling. "Let me out."

They opened the door. Brent waited like a nervous husband, holding my helmet with a look of fear on his face. I took the helmet from him, motioned for him to hop on the bike, and positioned myself behind him. Holding on only because I had to, we drove in silence until we came to an apartment building that I had barely noticed existed before then. We both got off the motorcycle, and I followed without a word into the place he called home.

When we entered, he motioned with his hand for me to head toward his sofa, which I did. After taking a seat, I scanned the room. I saw nothing personal, no sign of who he was. There were no pictures or collectibles; nothing but basic furnishings. His apartment was evidence he'd never intended to stay for long, and that fact stung even now.

"I'm sorry, Skylar. I never meant to be dishonest, but you have to understand, I couldn't tell you."

I had no idea where to start. What was safe to say? Even though I was now sure that he wasn't working for Henry, I still didn't know if he was on my side or against me. What I wanted to ask, beyond anything, was if his interest in me was all due to the case. Did even a small part of him care for me? I feared I would only look pathetic as he scrambled to let me down nicely.

"So, now what? Those men in the van did not seem to want to help me. I am guilty, but I'm innocent, too." I paused before it dawned on me. If Brent had heard us in the van, then the other agents were probably listening to me now. "Do you have a wire on right now?"

He stood, opened the patio door, placed his wallet on the table, and came back in, shutting the door behind him. "We're alone now."

"Your wallet! That's why you always put it on the table."

"It's actually the credit card, not the wallet."

Stunned, I stared at him. "I don't know whether to be impressed or pissed."

"I'd understand both feelings but would like you to stick with impressed."

I put my head in my hands and took a deep breath. "I don't know where to begin."

"How about at the beginning? But, Skylar, you will need to go to the field office later and give a formal statement. For now, you can talk to me as a friend."

I looked up at him. "Did you know Henry's people were on the beach the night we watched the crabs?"

"No, I didn't know."

They took pictures of us." I laughed out loud. "It seemed so big at the time. They were going to show Adam, so I signed off on a few FBARs that weren't accurate. That's how it started, and from there they tightened the noose. I didn't know how to stop it."

"We've been watching Henry for some time. We believe he's smuggling in drugs and hiding the money in offshore accounts. He makes some of it clean through a shell company—a construction firm—that works hand-in-hand with his hotels. He puts up bids for construction. The construction company may or may not do the work. The money is then put in banks anywhere from Wyoming to the Bahamas," Brent said. "We also believe he hides the money by buying Bitcoin and purchasing yachts in the Netherlands. He buys the yachts legally, brings them to the U.S., and before selling them, he sells off the drugs he stored in them. Unfortunately, we don't have the evidence we need to crack the case yet. My job was to listen and report back what I heard. It didn't help that Henry made you leave the office so much and not work in the same computer system as the rest of us."

"When did you start to suspect me?"

"It didn't take long with the trips to Miami, the Bahamas, and the secretiveness when it came to Henry's account. It was obvious, actually."

"Pretty funny they were sending someone with the FBI on those assignments. Won't they be shocked when they find out? But why me?"

Brent turned with obvious uncomfortableness. "Skylar, they targeted you. You fit the personality that they could control—a little bit of a loner, a rule follower." He cleared his throat. "I think Bruce sensed something about you when it came to me. The moment on the beach worked right into their plans. I'm sure it's why Bruce had the bottomless glasses of wine. He wanted us to let our inhibitions down and see where the night took us."

Heat rose to my cheeks. "Well, I don't know what Bruce thinks he was sensing."

"So, you know, with or without the case, I still think you're the most interesting woman in the office." Brent smiled. Warmth and sadness washed over me and mixed into something too painful to handle.

"Please don't. I understand. You needed information. You used attention and flattery. I don't blame you. Let's move on."

"Skylar."

"No, really, please don't. It's better that way. I want to see reality even if I don't like it. I need to work on finding my life again and making things right with Adam. Maybe this is a good thing. I don't have to hide all the things I did wrong from him anymore."

"Skylar, you know the truth."

"No, I don't. Please, help me clear my name so I can prove to Adam that I still deserve him."

"That's what you want?"

"Yes, that's what I want." My insides may have been screaming otherwise, forming an ache so real I felt nauseous. However, Adam was my lifeboat, and I was going to cling to him.

"Okay, then." Brent stood and reclaimed his wallet from the patio. "It's time to talk. Let's head to the field office, where they will record the conversation. Do you feel comfortable telling them everything?"

"Brent, as a friend—and I hope with all the time we've spent together that I am not wrong to call you a friend—should I talk?"

"I'll make sure you're protected."

"Can we practice here?"

"Yes, if it makes you feel better."

"I think you're right. Bruce and Henry set up the trip to Miami to see if we would slip up, and they could trap me with the pictures. I didn't do anything there." I paused, knowing that explaining the next event would prove tricky. "Something happened when I went to the Bahamas with Henry, though."

"What?"

"I'm not sure. Henry slipped drugs into my drink. I'm certain of it. And the fact that Bruce told me I was a diversion."

"That's all you remember?"

"Yes, besides some embarrassing side notes that have nothing to do with anything, and I have vague memories of signing papers."

"What about when you went to the Bahamas with me?"

"I opened accounts in a woman's name—Brenda Carter's. I've put a great deal of money in those accounts over time with money orders and transfers."

"Brenda Carter? What more can you tell me about her?"

"Not too much. I've never met Brenda, but she owns the

shell companies you discussed earlier. Oh, and I also opened an account for me. I know it was to make it look like Henry was paying me off and that I was a part of his scheme, except I wasn't."

"Then, why do it?"

"I failed my drug test. Bruce could fire me, and I know Henry had Adam fired. Bruce told Adam that I wasn't on a business trip, so he left me." I started to cry even though I hated myself for it. Brent came and took a seat next to me. I'm sure he sensed I wouldn't fight his embrace, so he wrapped his arms around me and let my tears dampen his shirt.

"You're doing great, Skylar. Anything else?"

"Yes. On our trip to the Netherlands, I had to buy Bitcoin. I knew that it was shady, but once again, I didn't know how to save myself. At least, I tried that time."

"What do you mean, you tried?"

"The banker, Lucas, gave me some papers to give to Henry. I opened them and wrote down what I saw. It was gibberish; twelve words that made no sense. I didn't know…."

"What did you say?"

"I copied down the words before giving them to Henry."

Brent took my face in his hands and like a happy parent, kissed my forehead.

"You're amazing, Skylar."

"Will it help?"

"Like I said, Skylar, you're amazing." Once again, he kissed my forehead; only this time, Brent's touch didn't feel like that of a parent. The warmth in his touch caused my feelings of longing to battle with my desire to make things right with Adam.

I lay in bed that night listening to the silence and wondering where the makers of my noise were at that moment. Were Adam and Ted curled up together watching television in some pet-friendly hotel room, or was he shacked up with a friend from work? I begged for that friend to be a man.

At some middle of the night hour, maybe two, another dream haunted my sleep.

Something shifted in my mouth. I sprinted to the bathroom mirror and studied my reflection. One of my front teeth was missing. Suddenly, many of my teeth slid out of place and then fell from the sockets into the sink. I knew if a tooth was returned to its rightful place, it might retake like an uprooted plant. One by one, I forced each tooth back into its hole. The mission was futile. For each tooth I replaced, another one fell into the sink. With each clink on the porcelain, panic filled me. The final clink jolted me from my sleep.

Going to my trusted internet site, I learned I was regretting saying something. My subconscious knew that even though I had begun the process of getting my life back, I had also ventured into unknown waters. Only time would only tell if they were friendlier ones.

Despite knowing it was pointless, I decided to text Adam yet another time.

Are you awake? I glanced at my clock, which read 2:35. Adam was never awake at this hour.

Praying for something, I stared with heavy eyelids at the screen, and then it happened. The little bubbles appeared.

Yes.

I sat frozen as my mind tried to find a way to continue. The only sensible way was by telling the truth.

I miss you.

Floating bubbles lit up my screen.

I miss you, too.

Where are you? I pleaded.

I don't want to share that right now. Soon.

How's Ted?

Good, but he misses his mother.

Tell him I miss him, too. Can we see each other?

Not yet. I need a bit more time. Good night, Skylar.

I thought about the dream and how it had meant I wished I hadn't said something. I typed anyway.

Adam, I think someone was in our house the day you left.

There was a definite pause.

Why do you think that?

I thought I heard something when I walked in, but I'm not sure anymore.

Is anything missing?

Not that I can tell.

Do you keep any work files at home, anything someone might be interested in?

No. I can't do that.

You can't, but have you ever? Is there anything someone could be looking for in our bedroom or the house? Think about it.

No, nothing. It was too late to begin the conversation about the Bitcoin, the gibberish words, and the FBI. I needed to do that in person. Besides, I had carried the paper with the words on it with me until earlier in the day when I'd handed it over to Brent.

Did you see any footprints outside the house or by the window?

No. Had I mentioned the opened window?

It must have been your imagination. I would let it go.

I was sure I hadn't mentioned the opened window. Although Adam could be attempting to think as a criminal would, my instincts told me otherwise.

Your mom was trying to reach you, I texted, knowing Adam's mother had passed away years before.

Tell her I'll call soon.

I stared at the phone as if it had grown a face and given me a demonic sneer, and then I forced myself to text.

Okay. Good night, Adam.

I let the phone drop from my hands. How long would it take whoever had been on the other end to realize his mistake and decide what to do about it?

CHAPTER 19

KNOWING MY SECRETS were as evident as a second head sprouting from my neck, I walked in the office that morning and headed straight to my cubicle. Before I could get my computer booted up, Brent slid a cup of hot coffee in front of me. The perfect softened color of a well-poured creamer relaxed me a bit. Next to the java sat a small piece of paper with the words, *Lunch, noon, Metro Diner*, written on it.

"Thanks," was all I could muster.

"You're welcome." Brent turned to leave.

The hours ticked by at a painful pace. The world of debits and credits was merely an interruption of my more pressing thoughts. Now and then, Bruce would come out of his office. Each time, the hair on my neck rose as I waited for him to approach me, but he never did. About a quarter to noon, Brent headed for the door while telling someone he passed that he would see them in a bit. I waited for an appropriate amount of time before I left as well, not speaking to anyone on my way out.

I found Brent in a booth with two cups of coffee and two water glasses already on the table. Things had changed between us, and I wasn't sure if all the truths had buried my feelings for him or if they were lying dormant, transforming into something new. I hoped I would be able to handle what emerged from the cocoon.

"So, were you able to use the information I gave you?"

"They're working on it." He set his wallet on the table.

"Are you serious?" I said in a whispered yell.

In return, Brent gave me one of his charming smiles. "Wallets are uncomfortable to sit on."

I eyed him with suspicion until he took out the infamous credit card and slid only that into his back pocket.

"It's just us. Promise."

"What were those words on the paper I gave you?"

"That, my dear, was the recovery backup phrase. With those words, we can get into the wallet you created, and from there, we can get the keys. There simply hasn't been any activity that we can tell of."

It was all a foreign language to me, so I returned to the matter that concerned me most. "Adam didn't leave me," I blurted out.

"Excuse me?"

I handed him the lines of text and waited for him to finish reading them. "So, what makes you so sure?"

"Adam's mother died years ago. If your people want any more help, they need to find Adam today." Adrenaline pumped through my body as if none of it were real until I had spoken the words, and then reality hit me with the force of a Mack truck. "He's missing. He's actually missing. Oh my God, Brent, do you think he's still safe?"

"Skylar, I know it's hard, but calm down." Brent glanced around the restaurant. "We don't need everyone's attention on us. I believe he's safe for now."

"For now?" I whisper-screamed. "What is that supposed to mean?"

"I mean they want you to be their puppet and the deeper they pull you in, the stronger the strings need to be. Adam's safe

211

and will stay that way until you make things difficult, or they decide they're done with you."

"Where does that leave me? If I help you, then they'll hurt Adam, and if I don't, they may still hurt Adam, and I'll be their puppet forever."

"Not forever. Henry and Bruce have a plan. We need to figure out what it is, that's all. Right now, play it cool. Don't let them know you suspect anything strange concerning Adam, and do what they tell you to. Then report back to me at the end of the day."

"Are you saying they won't hold me responsible for anything?"

"I wouldn't run off and murder someone, but you can shuffle money all you want. Make sure you record what you can."

"He takes my phone away whenever I'm there and keeps a camera on me."

"We figured, so we're setting you up with a microphone that will look like a button on your sweater. The sweater is a token of appreciation from us, but in reality, you get it so we don't have to buy a million buttons."

Brent leaned down to pull a gray sweater from a little bag he had carried in with him and handed it to me.

"Go ahead. Try on your first official spy gear."

Overwhelming gratitude and excitement rushed over me. The garment was a tool; one that would help get my life back. For whatever reason, the little piece of spy gear empowered me, and I finally started to see a way out.

My shaky hands brushed over each button. "Which one is it?"

Reaching over, Brent placed his fingers on the second one

from the top, somehow avoiding grazing my shirt, which was fine with me because with Adam missing, all other feelings had frozen inside of me.

"It looks exactly like the other ones." I stared at the innocent-looking thing. "I'm officially the coolest accountant in the office now," I said with a failed attempt at a smile.

"You can buy these things on Amazon for about thirty bucks."

"Way to wreck my excitement."

Brent's hand drifted back to his space. "This one's much better quality, I assure you."

"Can I mention Adam to see how Henry reacts?"

"Not yet. There's a better chance he'll read something into your comments than there's a chance you'll decipher what little he gives up. No offense. Let him talk when he's ready or when we tell you to pry."

"You're kidding, right? I'm supposed to just stay quiet and let Adam suffer somewhere?"

"Henry's not someone who commits murders for the pleasure of it. He wants money. That's what it's all about for him. He's not torturing Adam to find out information. I'm certain he thinks Adam doesn't know anything. He's holding him to keep you in line. We'll know when Adam's life begins to be in danger, but it's not now."

"Are you sure?"

"It wouldn't make sense. Henry is the type of criminal who kills for advancement or to hide information. He's not a serial killer type to kill only for enjoyment."

"I'm trusting you."

"I know, and my colleagues and I will do everything in our power not to let you down. I promise."

"So, what's the next step?"

"Do exactly as you were doing before and try to act the same way you have been. We'll tell you when there's a change."

Besides a few other details, lunch went by with little conversation. Brent paid the bill, and I watched as he tucked his credit card into his wallet and slid it back into the pocket of his right hip. When he looked back up, we locked eyes, and I held on as if somewhere within his gaze was my salvation.

"I'm scared, Brent."

He paused before cupping my hands in his. "Skylar, I'll do whatever it takes to keep you safe. You know that, don't you?" There was a line, and Brent was standing on it, waiting for permission to pass.

"And Adam?"

"Of course, Skylar." Brent's hands slid from mine. "We'd better get going before people start to wonder where we ran off to."

I let Brent leave first and rested my head on the steering wheel for a few minutes before taking off. With my eyes closed, I was more aware of all the sounds around me, each engine holding a personality of its own. The sounds of the passing motors stole me away from my reality. Trucks, motorcycles, and cars with jacked-up engines raced by the parking lot. Each one stole a piece of my anxiety and sped off with it as I meditated to the rhythmic noise of traffic. Then the soft purr of an engine settled into the spot next to mine. I should have cared about what I looked like slumped on my steering wheel, except I didn't. A sudden rap on my window jarred me, and my eyes flew open to see Bruce standing by the door.

"Get out of the car, Skylar."

"What? Why?"

"Get out of the car."

I thought about grabbing the sweater that lay next to me, but it would look suspicious on this warm spring day. Dragging myself out of the door, I stood before him.

"What's wrong?"

"Get in my car. *We need to talk.*"

"Okay." Bruce headed around to the driver's side. I glanced back at the sweater sitting in the front seat of my car, useless, before I slid into Bruce's passenger seat.

We settled in, and immediately I noticed how jittery Bruce was acting. His eyes scanned the surroundings, while he gripped the steering wheel with clenched fists.

"I'm sorry," Bruce said, sounding panicked.

"About more than the obvious?"

"Oh, there's so much more than the obvious, Skylar."

"What are you sorry for?" My insides twisted. I dreaded what could have him so agitated, petrified it had to do with Adam's safety.

"I called Adam. I told him you'd phoned in sick."

"I know." My heart pounded in my chest, and the twist in my stomach increased to a churn. "But why?"

"I was trying to make things right, Skylar. I wanted Adam to question things, so he could help you get out of this mess. I know you didn't want him to see the pictures. It was a desperate plan I should have known wouldn't work. I had to try something. I was responsible for telling Henry about your weakness."

"What weakness you are talking about?"

Bruce either decided to ignore my comment, or he was too frazzled to have heard it. "After that, Henry had you snared. I sent Brent with you on the other trips because I worried about your safety. I should never have involved you in this. Henry was okay with it because he thought he might get more incriminating stuff against you."

"Do you know where Adam is now? Please tell me he's safe."

"I tried to get you out, and instead, I brought Adam into the whole thing. Somehow Henry found out. Henry made me call Adam to have him meet me at a hotel for proof of what you were doing. Henry met him there. He showed Adam the pictures, and they took his phone without his knowledge so he couldn't contact you. That's the last I saw of him. Henry had me go back to your house to get Adam's suitcase and a few things to make it look like he'd left you. That's when you came home. I almost told you everything right then, but, Skylar, well, I don't know what Henry is capable of doing."

"Bruce, where is Adam? Are he and Ted safe? Tell me that much. Please." My voice shook, and I swallowed the cry that fought to escape from my throat.

"I have Ted."

"You have Ted?"

"It was that, or we had to dispose of him. Henry hadn't planned on a dog coming along. Ted's safe. Don't worry."

"I want him back."

"Not yet. Henry will know I talked to you."

"What about Adam, Bruce? Where is he?"

"I don't know, but I don't think he's in the country. But, Skylar, he's met Henry."

"Why are you telling me that?"

"Henry is holding him for leverage, but I want you to think this through before doing everything he tells you. If Adam has met Henry, Henry never intends for you to see your boyfriend again."

The truth set in, and I bawled into my hands.

"I have to go now. I trusted you with this information, Skylar. Tell no one."

"Tell no one? Do I let Adam die?"

"I don't have the answers, but it could be him or us, Skylar."

"Then let it be us. Adam's innocent."

"We can't win, Skylar. I needed you to know that. You can go now; get into your car."

I opened the door and stood on wobbly legs as I reached for my door handle. Bruce reversed out of the parking space at such a frantic pace he almost ran over my heels. Beaten, I settled in my car and stared at the gray sweater as if it were a deflated balloon. What good was it? No one could save me. There was no stopping what had already been set in motion.

When I got back to the office, I sensed a pervasive air of discomfort. My coworkers resembled students in a classroom that I had entered late. All eyes were on me as if warning me of the teacher's agitated mood. Some of my coworkers glanced my way with a look of caution while others busied themselves, hoping to go unnoticed. Retreating to my cubicle, I hoped to stay under the radar despite knowing the secrets behind the teacher's foul mood.

Bruce had beaten me by only minutes, which meant his mere entrance into the office had unnerved my colleagues. I feared he might be losing his mind. Bruce stepped out from behind his door, and everyone's fingers punched at their keyboards with intensity. He headed to the breakroom. The sound of his mug hitting the counter and his exasperated sigh made it evident someone had neglected to refill the coffee pot. The water ran, followed by the hostile sounds of slammed cupboard doors. We hunkered down, waiting for the storm to pass. After several moments, we heard Bruce's door bang shut.

I waited a few minutes, scribbled the words, *We need to talk*, on a small piece of paper, and went to get myself a freshly brewed cup of coffee. On my way, without uttering a word, I laid the note in front of Brent. Hours passed before we could speak.

That night, for the first time, Brent came to my home. I told him everything that Bruce had said and waited as he paced in my kitchen.

"Why take Adam?" I asked. "Why are they so desperate to think that they could get away with murder?"

"Their plan must be coming to an end. When's the next time you go to Henry's?"

"Tomorrow."

Brent paced a bit and then paused in front of a picture of Adam and me standing arm-in-arm. Genuine happiness lit our faces. It had been our tenth dating anniversary; before I had started wanting more. I'd been content, and so had Adam. Brent looked at me, and I hoped he could see everything I wanted to say spelled out on my face. I needed Adam back.

"Let me see your phone. I need to check if there are other incriminating texts to Adam that Henry could have read." Brent paused. "If you don't mind."

"I don't mind, but I do know that I said I was about to tell him everything."

Brent looked at me. "They would never let that happen. Once you'd told Adam everything, he would have made sure you went to the authorities."

"So, my text endangered him?"

"Don't think like that. Adam was in trouble the minute

Bruce contacted him. What else could be on your phone? You did say Henry takes your phone whenever you are at his house."

"Yes, he does."

Brent's brow furrowed, creating a serious expression that concerned me. "Skylar, where's your phone now?"

"In my room charging. Why?"

"Don't speak, just go get it."

As I walked down the hallway to my bedroom, I guessed what Brent had been thinking. Without a sound, carrying my phone like a hand grenade, I made my way back to the kitchen. Brent opened and closed drawers as I entered the room. When he saw me, Brent again signaled to be quiet, and the sinking feeling in my gut settled into complete nausea.

Skillfully, he pried at the crease in my phone until it popped open. To me, it was only a bunch of electronic components that meant nothing, but Brent pointed toward a small square gadget. He glanced at me with a raised eyebrow and then, with care, replaced the cover. Then Brent motioned for me to take my cell back into the bedroom. When I returned, he was pacing again.

"We should have thought of that."

"Why'd you leave it in there?" I asked.

"For now, Henry can't know we're aware of it. I need you to write down everything that you may have said when the phone was near you. Think hard. But Skylar, one thing is for sure, Henry knows about me."

"What are we going to do? They know about the sweater. They know I've spoken to the FBI. They're going to kill me, and then they'll kill Adam."

"They don't know that we are aware of the bug. Carry the sweater with you. They'll be expecting you to have it, so we'll change where the bug is. We'll figure this out, Skylar. I promise." Brent paced some more. "I'm going to get you a tracker. Something he won't find. If things go wrong, we'll be able to find you." He stopped, placed his hands on the counter, and took a deep breath; trying to recapture his FBI composure, I supposed.

"Are you okay, Brent?"

"Yes." He looked at me. "Some cases mean more to me than others, I guess."

"Thanks for your added concern for my safety." I forced myself to look away, to picture Adam scared and alone because of my actions.

"You don't have to thank me for something that wasn't my choice."

I gave a slight nod, understanding that as much as we tried to control everything, we were never in as much control as we hoped.

"I need to make some calls," Brent continued, "but Skylar, I think I should sleep on your couch and get some agents assigned for outside your house."

"Thank you." To be honest, I couldn't imagine being alone.

All night I tossed and turned thinking about Adam and the danger he was in, but I also thought of Brent, only a short distance away, and hated myself for the warm feeling his presence created.

When I tried to come up with a list of what Henry might know, I found the better question dangling in front of me was what did he not know? I cursed my generation's habit of always having our phones within arm's reach; we should rethink that habit. I fell asleep with the not-so-crazy feeling that Henry was in the room with me.

The next morning, I raced to get ready. Brent had gone

home to change, leaving other agents to man the site. As I scrambled to find my other shoe in the back of my closet, the doorbell rang. Racing to answer it, I knocked over the framed picture of Adam and me on the nightstand. As if it was fragile, I placed it back the way it should be, allowing myself a moment's glance at the man I knew so well and missed intensely.

Brent stood in the doorway, his motorcycle a silhouette behind him.

"So, do you have a plan?" I blurted out, knowing my phone was still in my bedroom.

"We need more information, Skylar, and you have to help us get it. We simply don't have enough on Henry, and we'll destroy our case and endanger Adam if we move too quickly."

"I'll do whatever."

Brent saw the gray sweater on the counter. "I brought you another mic and a tracker. You're going to have to snap one button onto either one of your bra straps, and a second one that looks identical will go onto your other bra strap. That's the tracker, just in case. You'll work the accounts exactly as he expects you to, except this time, we need you to get as many of Brenda Carter's account numbers as you can."

"How? I'm on camera the whole time. He'll be watching like a hawk. I'm sure he'll notice."

"One time, that's it. And then you never have to go back to that house. See if you can get the account numbers and see if he'll say anything. He probably won't, knowing we're recording him. This is buying us a little time. If you don't show up, he'll know something is up."

"He's too smart to say something to me."

"We know. We're getting a warrant to tap Henry's lines through the phone company, but to find Adam, we need to hear conversations that go on inside the house. That brings me to your next job. We're going to give you a small bug to put under Henry's desk."

"How am I supposed to do that with a camera on me?"

"The doorbell is going to ring right about noon. The delivery will require that the recipient, Henry, sign for it. When he goes to the door, you need to install the bug."

"Are you kidding me?" I cried. "I don't know how to install devices."

"There's nothing to it. You'll know everything you need to by the time I'm done with you this morning."

"Won't Henry know something is up when he receives a bogus delivery?"

"It won't be bogus. Henry's expecting a package. We're simply controlling the time and the fact it needs a signature. We're hoping he won't overthink that part."

"How do you…never mind. I guess it's a perk of being in the FBI."

"Exactly."

"What if he rewinds the recording?"

"Act cool, and he won't have any reason to suspect he needs to. Now, let's teach you a thing or two about planting devices."

Henry opened the door, and I stood in front of him, wearing my sweater that was no longer bugged. Henry would not suspect the bug to be on my bra. Once inside, I would hand over my phone that I now knew Henry had bugged. An insane laugh built deep inside me, and I swallowed it down. My mind raced. Did I generally say good morning first, or did he? Maybe neither of us said good morning.

"Is something wrong, Skylar?" Henry asked.

"Excuse me? Are you actually going to pretend that nothing is wrong when you are the cause of my life falling apart?" My feisty, angry side finally appeared like a protective friend on the playground. Except it had waited until I was about to get pummeled to make its appearance.

Henry refusing to answer, stared back at me long enough to make me sweat around my collar. I resisted the urge to pull at it to give my neck some air.

"Come on in." Without a verbal request he held out his hand, and I placed my cell phone in it. "May I take your sweater? I find that the office gets quite warm at times."

"No, thank you. I prefer to have it handy in case."

"Your call. You can show yourself to the room. Instructions are waiting for you when you get there. Use the intercom if you have any questions."

"Will do," I replied with the stiff tone of a teenager.

Once upstairs, I went to my desk. Each movement was deliberate and uneasy; watchful eyes followed me everywhere. I was happy to have a tracker but also aware that it wasn't foolproof. What if Henry found it? What if the FBI were wrong about the battery life being months?

I looked over my list of duties for the day. For the most part, they were routine. While on his computer, I would log into Brenda's account since the password was in the keychain, and I was never able to know it on my own. If I whispered the numbers when I wasn't facing the camera, Henry wouldn't see what I was doing, or so I hoped. I tilted the computer only enough that I would not create suspicion and plugged in the bank website. Instead of the regular login page with the username and password filled in with the mysterious dots, there was nothing. He had blocked me. A chill ran up my spine as more evidence of Henry's awareness sank in. Did I dare delete the history of my search, or would it only make my prying more apparent? I decided to leave it as is and went back to my list.

There were FBARs to file. Enough to take me the better part of the day. At least, they seemed legit. Could it be that Henry was finished with me? The thought relieved and terrified me at the same time. About eleven-thirty, I began watching the clock obsessively. My only distraction was when the door opened, and one of his servants brought in my lunch. My stomach was in knots as I scanned the room for the best place to hide the microphone. Henry's desk looked too neat for one that was often used, but it was the obvious place. As soon as I heard the doorbell, I would run over and attach the device to the underside of his drawer.

Twenty minutes left to wait. The idea of eating disgusted me, but due to the dryness in my throat, I guzzled down the iced tea served with the lunch. It was impossible to complete the FBARs in front of me, but I needed to minimize any suspicion. In an attempt, I plugged away, stealing glances at the clock hands that refused to move beyond a sloth's pace.

Over time, Henry had created a world where he almost looked legit. The FBARs would keep him from being legally charged, even though Henry might pay fines for being delinquent. His accounts in the United States seemed in line with those of a hotel owner. He had, through the past few months, opened many accounts with much money in Brenda Carter's name. I was sure she would be next in line for an FBI investigation, or else she legitimately was doing an absurd amount of construction on Henry's hotels. He had purchased some rather run-down ones that were in desperate need of repair.

Nevertheless, Henry wasn't stupid. He knew it was too late for his plan to be successful. The authorities had gotten too close before Henry could hide it all. All the FBI had to do was prove that he was profiting in some illegal way, but beyond suspicions, they still had nothing. And without Bruce confirming the story, the special agents couldn't prove Henry had anything to do with Adam's disappearance.

The clock struck noon, and moments later, the doorbell rang. I resisted the urge to run to the door and listen for footsteps and conversations. Henry, thinking his staff would take the package for him, could still be watching me. I waited until I heard the faint sound of the front door. I pictured the slow, steady steps of his servant walking to the intercom button, uttering the words to Henry that his signature was needed. Then I envisioned Henry's irritated footsteps as he left his office and only then, did I spring to my feet and slide under the desk.

After locating a spot an arm's length from the front, a place he wouldn't feel unless he was trying to find something, I attached the device. The task would have proven easy if only I could have stopped my hands from shaking and dropping the bug onto the hardwood three times. Begging the air that the FBI made quality gadgets, I finished my job and ran back to my seat moments before the door slid open.

"Are you almost done with the FBARs?" Henry asked.

"Yes. Another half an hour should do it," I answered without looking up.

"When you finish, your work here is officially complete. You can go back to the office permanently."

I staggered, not ready for him to kick me out of the world that still held Adam captive. "But you said you would help Adam get his job back."

"Oh, yes. Well, I also said it wouldn't be easy. I never made any promises to you."

"But…."

"That's all I need, Skylar. If I hear something about Adam's case, I'll let you know."

He shut the door and left me alone. When I headed down the hallway for the last time, I expected a wave of relief to wash over me. After all, the FBI was on my side now. Instead, as I turned my back to Henry's home, the hairs on my neck stood alert, waiting for a machete to strike a fatal blow to its wounded prey.

CHAPTER 20

S O THAT WAS it. Henry had kicked me aside before we could find Adam. All we had on our side were some Bitcoin keys and a useless bug stuck to the bottom of a desk Henry seldom if ever used. As I drove to the office, leaving Henry's house for the last time, I took with me a small comfort. I was no longer alone. Somewhere nearby, a van full of opportunistic partners was listening in when needed.

I stopped for lunch on my way back to McClurry & Associates. Neither Brent nor I suggested meeting up. The fact I was no longer someone on the inside was concerning to both of us. Yet, his concerns were work related and mine delt with issues of much greater value. He arrived at the office hours after I did. We barely spoke the rest of the day.

That next morning, I decided to leave for work extra early. I grabbed a coffee and a doughnut, a treat I seldom allowed myself, and took my time savoring every bite. Then I drove at a snail's pace, not ready to act like a typical accountant preparing mundane tax forms.

When I reached the office, the realization that the day would be anything but ordinary hit me like a tsunami. Crime tape sealed the doors off to the staff. Police cars, undercover and public, lined the road both in the front and in the back where I usually parked. To my relief, I saw Brent's motorcycle amid them. Numb and petrified, I climbed out of my car. What had they found? My feelings still wavered between fear of being caught and the excitement of being saved.

Off to the side of the parking lot, a group of my colleagues huddled together. Some of them were wiping their eyes; some were consoling each other. Brent had his arm around Liz, but the sick feeling within me was so overpowering that no other emotion could squeeze in, not even jealousy. I drifted more than walked until I stood next to them. Over Liz's shoulder, Brent met my gaze. Despite his attempt to explain, a look could not translate what would take pages to say. Brent whispered something consoling into Liz's ear and headed toward me.

"What's happening?" I asked, terrified of the answer.

"It's Bruce. He shot himself."

"Oh, my God, Brent," I cried. Despite all my mixed emotions about Bruce, I realized one feeling had always been prominent—pity. He'd been so much like me, only a bit more pathetic. Bruce had been chosen for his weaknesses, his seclusion from the world, yet he had never wanted the isolation. Henry had molded him, with little effort, from a lump of clay into a criminal. Bruce had suffered alone; more alone than I had ever been in my life. Hatred of myself and my lack of strength to turn our misery into a bond overwhelmed me. We could have fought together. Maybe I hadn't missed a chance because I couldn't remember any opportunities; in hindsight, though, there must have been at least one.

"Henry must have told Bruce about me. He didn't see a way out," Brent continued. The sob in my throat silenced me, but even without words, Brent seemed to hear everything I was thinking. "There's nothing you could have done, Skylar. Henry will slip up, and we'll catch him. He'll pay for what he's done to both of you." I continued to cry as I tried to believe all Brent had told me. "The police will ask questions. Tell them nothing. We need to take care of Henry on our end. We can't have police getting involved right now."

"Can I tell them about his ex-wife?"

"Yes. That's what most everyone else has mentioned. The investigators heard about Chrissy coming in angry a while back. That should distract them while we figure out what Henry is up to."

"Can I leave, or do I have to stay?"

"We should both leave. Where will you go?"

"I'm going to get my dog back. Know how to break into a house?"

Brent smiled. "I'm sure we can figure it out."

When we got to Bruce's, ready to break in, we found the door unlocked, and to our relief, the police had not ventured that way yet. I guess if Bruce knew he was going to commit suicide, he no longer cared if someone robbed him. Walking into Bruce's home while he lay dead at his desk miles away felt like walking through his soul. Pictures of his life with Chrissy covered the walls and shelves. Candles and flower arrangements collected dust as they stood as a reminder that, at one point, a woman's touch had made its mark within the home.

Being so immersed in Bruce's world, I almost forgot why I was there until I saw the dog dishes. Ted wasn't rushing to see me. That meant he was no longer there. The thought of Bruce throwing the dog toy to Ted saddened me. Now, the plastic ball sat motionless next to Ted's dish, and I hoped that somehow, my dog had brought Bruce joy in his last days.

"Ted's not here," I said. "Let's get out of here."

Brent and I drove separately to my house. He pulled

up next to me on his motorcycle, and we headed to the door together. I noticed that the planter hiding our extra key was out of place. Brent and I exchanged looks as we walked cautiously to the door. As we approached, the most beautiful sound in the world arose from the other side. Ted barked with unconfined excitement. I opened the door and fell to my knees, letting Ted cover me with kisses and dog paws. As if my eyes had become open faucets, tears flowed down my face. I cried for Adam, and Ted, and for the man who had thought enough about me to return a piece of my family before ending his life.

For the next week, we all had to work from home. Keeping us all under close supervision, the police had allowed us to go into the office and get what we needed. After hearing from my colleagues as well as myself, it wasn't long before the authorities ruled Bruce's death a suicide. It was a closed case, nothing more than a man depressed about a woman, and in many ways, they were right. My hatred for Henry had gone through the roof, and my fear for Adam was immeasurable. Henry didn't need my boyfriend anymore, and for that matter, he didn't need me anymore, either. Brent would still play bodyguard at my house until things had settled down. Now that I could explain everything to Adam, I was sure he would understand and, in time, be thankful that Brent had been there looking out for me. If only I could get that chance to explain it to Adam.

Having Brent in my home was comforting in a few ways. The first way was obvious; I felt safer. The second was much harder to explain, even to myself. I wanted him to know me more. Not only who I was alone, but the me I was with my boyfriend because Adam was so much a part of me. If Adam and Brent could be friends, I would like it, or so I told myself. I needed it to be appropriate and pure because what I felt for both men was so special. Because I knew that without a friendship between them, I couldn't be friends with Brent either, and I would have to let him drift out of my life. The thought made me ache inside. I would rather stand beside someone and feel confused than never stand next to them again. Brent needed to know Adam and to like him; to like him enough never to want to hurt him or us as a couple.

Sipping coffee and looking lost in another world, Brent sat across from me at the kitchen table. Often, he would step into the garage to take a call, telling me he didn't want to be rude while I tried to work. I would nod, yet I knew the real reason. I wasn't an actual partner in this case, and some secrets would never be shared with me. It was mid-afternoon when he came in from outside; his face beamed with excitement. "Good news. Awesome news, actually. Henry did not hear you tell me that you had the Bitcoin keys."

"How do you know?"

"Because he just spent some of his cybermoney."

"And."

"And he became an open book."

"What's that mean? What have you found out?"

"He used the money to buy a yacht in the Netherlands. It's a step toward having solid proof."

"Great."

"There's more. There have been some leads on Adam's location." Brent smiled, but it didn't reach his eyes. "There's evidence he's in the Netherlands."

"Bruce said he thought Adam had been taken out of the country. The Netherlands would make sense since Henry had recently bought a yacht there."

"Maybe, Skylar. Maybe." Brent's expression dimmed, and I saw his doubt. I didn't know if he doubted the Netherlands or that Adam was still alive. I looked back at my computer, no longer excited.

"Skylar, why don't you wrap up what you can, pass off the rest, and let's go find Adam."

"What do you mean?"

"Let's go to the Netherlands."

"Are you serious?" My breath caught as I waited for an answer.

"I got permission for us both to travel there." Brent's words were layered with emotion, a fake coating of happiness covered his sadness. "If he's there, and we find him, I have a feeling the first person he would want to see is you."

I jumped from my chair and ran into his arms.

The next day, Brent and I were on our way to Amsterdam's Schiphol Airport. Henry's house had been under constant surveillance, but since the day I'd left, no one had seen Henry.

On the plane ride over to the Netherlands, after I thanked Brent profusely for allowing me to join him, he came clean. On one of his trips to the garage, he had learned that my bug had been successful.

"That's so awesome. Did you get information that will help us find Adam?"

"Skylar, I'm going to let you hear the recorded conversation because we owe you that truth."

"Okay," I replied with hesitation.

He reached in his bag, pulled out a pair of earbuds, and found the recording.

"Are you ready to hear this?"

"As ready as I'll ever be."

He hit play.

"It's time. You know what to do with him," Henry said with a coldness that chilled me to my bones.

"Are you sure about this?" answered a male voice I didn't recognize.

"There's no way around it."

"I'll be back in Amsterdam in a couple of weeks. Levi rented a place because the present place won't work much longer. He's taking him there soon."

"Where's that?" Henry asked.

"Some red light district apartment; Noorderkerk Deluxe Apartment. Levi will need to keep him either bound or too loopy to go anywhere, but Levi stops there. He won't take care of this problem for us."

"You said you had it under control. Finish it."

"I didn't agree to murder anyone."

"Don't start having morals now. The problem can't wait until I get there."

"I wasn't planning on adding murder to the rap sheet. I sell drugs. I don't like to get my hands that kind of bloody."

"Just because you aren't pulling the trigger doesn't mean your hands aren't already bloody."

"I don't want this traced back to me."

"Impossible. I've told you that."

"And what makes you so sure?"

"They won't find him out in the middle of the ocean. Besides, even if they do, good luck connecting a body found in the Netherlands to a man missing in Florida. She'll regret talking, but it doesn't matter anymore. We're done with her. It's only a matter of time before she joins her boyfriend."

"Just tie things up there and get over here. This is your mess. I'm not doing your dirty work."

"You can expect this to come out of your percentage, and you'd better keep him hidden," Henry said. "I'll be there before you know it."

The phone went dead—as did a part of me.

"Brent, they're going to kill Adam, and then they're going to kill me."

"I know this must terrify you, but you're missing the more important detail here."

"What could be more important?" I whispered in panic.

"We have some time, we know where Adam will be, and they have no clue we know. We're going to save him, Skylar."

Somewhere on the plane were the men from the van. Whether Brent was right or not, he believed what he'd told me.

"I'm trusting you, Brent."

He squeezed my fingers gently and then moved his hand back to his lap. "You should, Skylar." A moment of silence passed. "Would you like to see pictures of the yacht Henry purchased with his Bitcoin?"

As if he was a boat salesman, Brent reached down and pulled out a pamphlet. With a humorous boyish excitement, he opened the brochure.

"How can you get excited about this when so much is at stake?"

"We're getting so close, Skylar. We know where Adam is, and we know what they bought with the Bitcoin. It's exciting to see what we're chasing. If we find this yacht, we get even closer to arresting Henry."

After giving myself a moment to let Brent's words register, I asked to see the pictures.

"First, they purchased it with sixty million dollars in Bitcoin, we're assuming. The price is more than the amount of Bitcoin we know they acquired. Still, we can assume there was more, and whoever is working with Henry had money as well."

Brent opened the pamphlet to pictures of a pool on a deck, a glamorous round tub, and a spa. Underneath all that was a garage that held another boat that they could drive off in if they desired.

"Where does Henry come up with sixty-million dollars? The hotel business is not that profitable."

"Not with the hotels he's buying up. That's all a cover, just as the yachts are a cover, albeit more fun. People use their illegal money, likely earned through drug sales, to buy up things to resell later. It's their way of making their money clean. Then they can spend it as they wish. Henry's problem was that he became too good at what he does, and he tripped over his own income. He couldn't hide it fast enough.

Henry's been very diversified; I'll give him that. The number of offshore accounts that he hadn't accounted for tipped off the IRS. In turn, they tipped off the FBI since they suspected international crimes. Henry buys hotels and works side by side with the woman who owns the construction companies. Together they move their funds enough that they go unnoticed until there is a little slip or a bit too much money to launder. Together they clean up the hotels enough to sell them off for a profit."

"Are your people going after Brenda Carter?"

"Working on it. There's a good deal of suspicious activity for a crap construction company. A few employees have said they go out to Henry's hotels and repair things or remodel. They gave us specific jobs that checked out. As for Brenda Carter, she's a bit of a mystery. However, when you're hot on the trail of the pack leader, the little guys sometimes fall to the side for a bit."

I took the pamphlet from Brent and browsed through it. It sickened me how the need to have money could control people. The brochure represented the greed within Henry that made him lose his conscience, that is, if he'd ever had one at all. Why some people, above all else, sought the glamour of what money could buy was beyond me. I stared at the pool, the deck, and the crystal blue waters. How many people, attempting to buy a heaven that was never intended to be purchased, fell into darkness? I handed back the pamphlet, and Brent tucked it away, as though sensing he shouldn't be quite so impressed, either.

After hours of talking, sleeping, and gazing out the plane window, we began our descent into Amsterdam. The natural beauty of the countryside greeted me like a gift-wrapped time bomb. Hidden beneath its beauty, evil people threatened to destroy the man I loved.

Once at the airport, I watched Special Agents Kemp, Hall, and Bailey drift into the crowd like strangers, while Brent stayed close by my side. Outside, we hailed a cab.

"Waarheen?" the driver asked.

Brent answered, "We moeten naar de Ramada Apollo gaan," Brent answered.

"What the hell?" I replied in plain English since it was all I knew.

"Second languages help in my line of work."

Why was I annoyed? I couldn't quite say. Maybe I merely needed to know things were going to be typical and expected. Surprises were beginning to tire me. I looked away at the futuristic-looking design and cleanliness of the airport terminal building. I was no more capable of appreciating its beauty than a deaf person was of enjoying the symphony.

"When we get to the hotel, rest and freshen up. Tonight,

we'll imitate a couple out enjoying the red light district. I thought you might like the warning."

"Thanks. Probably a good thing to warn me about."

As soon as I was alone in my hotel room, I slipped off my shoes, and fell into a deep sleep. The sleep brought a dream I often experienced when I felt unprepared for what lay ahead.

I walked along the paths of my college campus, going somewhere. I recognized the buildings, but suddenly, nothing made sense. What class was I going to? Had I even set foot in the classroom this year? Another realization hit me from nowhere; the final exam was today. I searched my bag for my schedule, hoping it would reveal where I should be heading. Frantically, I pulled out all my books, realizing I didn't recognize any of them. The paper was nowhere. My mind in my dream reality drifted as if I were on drugs. I couldn't capture my thoughts or recollections.

I walked, hoping something would rekindle a memory but nothing came to me. Finally, I saw a blond, curly-haired friend I hadn't thought about in years. I ran toward her, but she kept getting farther away until she disappeared into the crowd. I stopped in my tracks, waiting for clarity, until reality brought me back.

This was not the first time I had dreamed of being lost on a college campus, or not being able to recall the combination to my locker padlock. In fact, I was surprised the dream had not visited me earlier. I stared up at the hotel ceiling thinking of the events to come. There were so many possible outcomes, but even the one where Adam was rescued, did not guarantee a happy ending.

The address they had given Brent was within walking distance— in the heart of the red light district, where age-old crimes were cast differently in the glow of the lights. Shoulder to shoulder, I walked with Brent. Shocked and horrified, I took in the displays that surrounded me. Framed in each window, in the skimpiest of lingerie-type attire, stood a woman on sale to the next buyer. If my glance was quick enough, I could mistake them for mannequins rather than humans. They modeled themselves as nothing more than amusement park props. In my world, they served as the displays engineered to distract me as I closed in on the dangers that lying ahead.

Brent took my elbow to hurry me along, pausing only to scan the road signs before stopping a passerby. He was an older gentleman, obviously comfortable with the culture surrounding him.

"Excuse me; I'm looking for an apartment." Brent reached in his pocket and looked at the piece of paper. "Noorderkerk Deluxe Apartments."

"Ik spreek geen Engels," the man replied, which apparently was not the answer Brent sought.

"Waar is Noorderkerk Deluxe Apartment?" Brent asked again. I tried not to act as shocked the second time I heard him speaking Dutch.

The man pointed down the road. "Twee blokken verderop en aan je rechterkant." He never released his gaze from the twenty-something-nearly-naked woman beckoning to him from the window.

"Dank je." Brent took my hand. "Just a couple more blocks." He saw me staring at my hand in his. "I don't want to lose you in the crowd."

"Or are you trying to tell me we could get killed at any moment?"

"It's quite safe here, considering." He glanced back at the

windows. "It's even safer for these women conducting business without pimps. Instead, they pay their portion of their income to the government like everyone else."

"So, you think this is a good thing?" I said, appalled.

"I don't remember saying that. What I'm saying is it goes on one way or the other. This way has its benefits. If it makes you feel better, the area's future could be at stake. Many people in the world share your distaste for the culture."

We continued down the street in silence. The red lights reflected off the waterways, creating beauty and disguising the sinful interior of the city. Was this how Adam had gone unnoticed? How many people had seen him in distress and had been too dazzled by the glamour and mystique to notice?

Brent stopped in front of a brick building. "This is it," he stated.

"Now, what?"

"We wait. The other agents have been watching the building. They're close. They'll go in do what they need to do while we wait outside. If Adam's in there, they'll bring him out here to you."

We found a bench and watched an endless flow of people as they passed by the building. The chilly night air crept into the folds of my clothes. I hadn't predicted the coolness of the weather or the fact that Brent's body would be pressed against mine as we sought warmth.

My frozen hand remained curled within his, while I searched the door for a sign of Adam. The moment summed up every sensation my tortured soul was experiencing. I could sit and hold Brent's hand while he helped me get Adam back because we both knew it was what had to happen. There wasn't a demand in his hand for more; only tenderness. He understood that he served as my strength, and when Adam walked out of that apartment, Brent would let go, and I would let him. I had to let him.

Time passed. Finally, we saw four men dressed in jeans and jackets. They appeared casual enough that no one would notice them if they weren't watching for them. They walked through the front doors of the apartment building. Unless someone was paying attention, they would not become suspicious of the dark-colored bags slung over the men's shoulders. When the door closed behind them, I stopped breathing, or at least it felt as if I had. Brent's hand tightened on mine. I kept my focus on the door except for stealing a glance at my watch that flashed nine thirty-two. So many people, blocking my view like a speeding train, walked by the door. I studied the backdrop of the building, that appeared as flickers of a movie viewed through the passing traffic.

Breaking the silence, I uttered, "I'm scared, Brent." To my surprise, the same words from my dream slipped into my reality.

"Trust the plan, Skylar."

"But, what if…."

"Skylar, trust the plan. If it doesn't work, make a new one." I glanced at my watch again. The numbers nine thirty-six lit up my wrist. Brent squeezed my hand again, which made me look up at him. He smiled. "It's going to be okay."

Another group passed by the front of the apartment building right before the doors swung open. I made out the vague shapes of bodies. My mind counted them: one, two, three, and four. Searching the figures between the moving crowd, I counted again and again until I could make out one more figure. Not until they headed down the steps did I trust my vision. In the middle of the agents stood a frail-looking Adam. Without knowing the exact moment it happened, I released Brent's hand and flew across the road, only slightly aware that Brent followed. I plowed through the nameless heroes and wrapped my arms around Adam's neck. He blinked several times, likely while his eyes adjusted to the brightness of the red, glowing lights.

"Skylar? Oh, my God, why are you here? How did you find me?"

"I'm so sorry, Adam." He stood dumbfounded as I cried into his shirt, and he eventually settled his arms around me. "I told you I could explain everything. I just couldn't right away."

Brent talked with the other agents. "Skylar, we need to get you guys to a safe place. There wasn't anyone in the apartment with him. They could be back at any time."

A car pulled up, and Brent, Adam, and I got inside. I caught my breath, did a final sniffle, and looked at Adam with a smile plastered across my face. For a moment, I forgot that although he had to feel ecstatic about the rescue, he was not sitting in the backseat of that car in the same world as I was. His understanding of his ordeal was only beginning. His expression of pure confusion reminded me, and I knew that no matter what the distance to the hotel might be, Adam and I had a long road ahead.

Adam sat on the bed as I spoke. I sat in a chair next to him, which allowed me to hold his hands and look him in the eyes as the details poured out of me. I told him everything from the beginning. Even though my explanation showed, or least I thought it did, that I had not betrayed him, I could not know if he believed me. I left no detail out, except for my feelings. As I told of the pictures on the beach, I spoke in a hurry, hoping it downplayed the tender moment caught on film. When I finished spilling out the entire story, Adam sat up taller, took a deep breath, and looked away from me. For several moments, I was not sure if my words were like vinegar hitting baking soda and forming something new, or wax dripping down a candle that would, in time, harden into nothing more than an altered form of what it once had been.

Finally, Adam reached for my hands again and pulled me to him. Before I knew it, I was lying next to him, his hands tenderly touching my face and neck and stroking my cheekbones. Still silent, except his actions held promise. The tenderness shifted into a forceful passion. Letting go of the fear of this unknown us, I allowed the emotions to twist into an intensity of my own. My hand slid under his shirt, and I pried it up over his head before moving on to his belt buckle. His hands, sometimes colliding with my own, followed a similar path across my body.

Later, when Adam lay next to me, I noticed how thin he had become since he'd disappeared. When my eyelids became too heavy to hold open, I pictured Brent lying alone in a bed somewhere within the hotel. Sadness overwhelmed me, and for the first time, I felt unfaithful.

On the plane trip home, I sat next to Adam, and Brent was far behind us. My thoughts drifted so often that I feared my distracted mind would be obvious to Adam. His mind, however, was too busy trying to swim its way back to reality to notice. Adam rarely let go of my hand, even as he became lost while staring out the window. Occasionally, he would turn to me with a question that would randomly pop up out of nowhere. "So how did Henry get you to go to the Bahamas with him?" "Why did Bruce send Brent with you?"

Some questions I seemed to answer a million times, maybe

because I'd left out pieces, the ones that would hurt him most. I couldn't tell him Bruce had sensed I had feelings for Brent. Instead, I explained Bruce had been hoping to stir up trouble. My answers fell short. Even though I'd apologized for the moments caught on film, I knew doubts lingered in Adam's mind.

Beyond those concerns were much bigger ones. How were we to continue our lives when Henry was still out there wanting Adam and me dead? Instead of going home, Adam and I were being sent to a new location until things settled. According to the phone tap, Henry would be wrapping things up and joining the mysterious man in the Netherlands. The authorities had tipped off the airports, so it would be difficult for Henry to leave the country. Still, we all assumed that he was aware of Adam's rescue. The man who'd rented the apartment had paid in cash for the month. None of the neighbors admitted to knowing anything about him. At least one of them had to have known him well enough to tip him off because he had yet to return to the building. According to Brent, a search of the apartment had not helped much.

Holding Adam's hand couldn't keep the panic at bay. My life felt upside down. For the moment, both Adam and I were out of work. My boss had committed suicide. Adam was still struggling to prove his innocence at work, and Henry wanted us dead. Even with Adam beside me and the FBI taking over where I could never be successful, I saw no end in sight. Exhausted, I rested my head on Adam's shoulder and fell into a deep sleep. The hours of flight across the ocean disappeared, and the dreams took over.

A frozen river surrounded me. Up ahead, I saw a group of people and realized they were my childhood family. I raced toward them. The experience of running across the slippery floor thrilled me. The white backdrop sparkled, and the crystal waters splashed up the sides of the ice. My heart raced as I closed in on my parents. Right before I reached them, the ice cracked, and I dropped into the freezing waters. I swam with stiffened arms to the underside of the hole and climbed out. Panicked, I scrambled toward my family while calling out that the ice was melting.

Much of the ice around us disappeared before I could reach them, leaving only the shrinking island we stood upon. Below us, killer whales bumped into the underside of the island and, one by one, bounced each of us into the freezing water. Each time, whoever fell, scrambled back to safety. Images of the unlucky victim being tossed around like a ball at SeaWorld haunted me. We stood in the center of our island, our hands clasped together, until a whale's head jarred into us, and I was jolted awake.

I later learned dreams of ice often represent frozen feelings that are not allowed to flow.

CHAPTER 21

BACK IN JACKSONVILLE, Adam and I stayed in a hotel near the St. Johns Town Center. We weren't allowed to leave, even for groceries. Whenever we were at the pool or the gym, the special agents remained nearby, watching and acting as other patrons. For days, we busied ourselves with nothingness until finally, Brent knocked on our door.

"We found Henry."

"Thank God. Do you have him in custody?" I asked.

"Not quite yet," Brent replied with a lingering pause I took to mean something terrible.

"Why not? What the hell else does he need to do for you people to bring him in?" Adam was beyond frustrated, and after days held up in the hotel, his usual mild temper had transformed into a mood I seldom witnessed.

"It's not about what else he has to do. We're pretty sure he's done plenty. It's about proof. When we bring him in, we want the charges to stick, and we want to hold him accountable for all his crimes."

"So, what's the plan? Are we supposed to sit here for weeks while your people figure out how to get your evidence?"

Brent paused before answering. "No, it's not that easy. We need you to do more than just sit here. Well, actually, we need Skylar to do more than sit here."

"Not a chance. Skylar is not going to do anything that could put her in danger. Find another way," Adam demanded.

"Adam, I want to help," I said. "If I can make Henry pay for everything he has done to Bruce and us, then I want to do that."

"No, Skylar."

For a moment, I pretended Brent was not in the room with us, and I spoke only to Adam.

"I know you want to protect me, but you don't understand. As much as I can tell you about the past few months, I can never explain how everything has changed me. I can't just sit back and watch. I need to be a part of putting this man behind bars."

"But…"

"Adam, I was alone and terrified through this. Henry made me weak. He changed me into someone I never thought I could be, and I hated myself for allowing it. I can't be weak anymore. If I'm going to regain some self-respect, I must help. I need you to understand at least that."

Adam took what seemed like forever before releasing my gaze and turning to Brent.

"You'd better keep her safe." Adam's jaw tightened; the tension visible through his stubble.

Brent walked toward the door and looked back, his eyes only on me. "I'll be in touch, Skylar, and I will keep you safe."

Brent picked us up the following day, and we drove for hours to another hotel near Port Everglades in Fort Lauderdale. There, I said my goodbyes to Adam, and we left him pacing in the hotel room. Brent didn't speak a word to Adam, or to my knowledge, make eye contact, as he placed his hand on the small of my back and guided me out the door. In the van, the FBI special agents outfitted me with a vest and wires. Of course,

Henry would expect such a thing, but only if Henry didn't think he was in complete control; only if he didn't believe he had found me by chance.

The FBI had traced Henry to a hotel near a port in the Everglades. They suspected the mystery man would attempt to smuggle drugs in through the port. Henry would then use the speed boat as his getaway ride to a larger yacht awaiting him nearby. The FBI also had to assume that Henry knew Adam had been rescued, but not necessarily that he was back with me. This detail gave the FBI the ability to provide me with my bodyguard. If Adam had left me, then I was free to be with Brent. They did not reveal any details to me until after dropping Adam off at the hotel. The plan was for Brent and I to wander the shops where agents had watched Henry walking the previous days. Once Henry had noticed me, Brent would then leave me like bait for Henry, while I shopped alone. Simple enough.

Agents kept watch from different locations, while Brent and I strolled past the cafe where Henry was having breakfast. I hardly recognized him in his Tommy Bahama-style clothes and hat. Brent held my hand as, admiring the window displays, we walked past the shops. We were, after all, playing parts; Adam had left me. If Henry believed Adam had stayed away from me after the FBI had rescued him, then Henry might lose interest in him. This was the theory I went with, anyway. Brent, skilled in undercover work, pulled me close, allowing our lips to hover within inches of each other's. With a smile that flooded me with adrenaline, he whispered, "Have you ever done any acting?"

"Not an ounce." I whispered back with a matching smile.

He leaned in and kissed me, letting his lips melt into mine as if we'd always been meant to be one. "You're quite good at it," he whispered. "You make it feel almost real."

Brent politely ignored the obvious flush that heated my face. He led me past Henry and down another block. We were still in viewing distance when Brent got the word in his little device that the trap was set.

"It's a go." Brent rested his hand on the side of my face and again kissed me, letting his lips linger for much longer than our skit demanded. "Be safe, Skylar. I'll be close."

He walked backward, smiling that smile that would either save or destroy me, before disappearing into the crowd. As instructed, I window shopped, stopping here and there to fake interest in the occasional garment. I checked my phone, and then made my way to the car someone had parked in a convenient out-of-the-way spot. I never saw Henry following me. Despite this, I could feel him as if he held the power of lightning before it strikes its victim. I unlocked the car and got in, taking my time before turning on the ignition. For a moment, I thought he had jumped off the hook. Then the passenger side door opened, and immediately, I saw the gun pointed at my ribs.

"Drive, Skylar."

I didn't need acting lessons because I was genuinely petrified. We drove to a crappy dive of a hotel, and suddenly it made sense that he would be hiding out in one of his money-laundering covers.

"Stay put until I tell you." Henry walked around the car and, acting as if he was a gentleman, opened my door. Instead, I found the gun pressed to my side. "Walk."

Henry's potential evilness had always intimidated me but being face-to-face with the reality of it was a whole other story.

"Glamorous place. There's a hotel called the Elephant

Butte Inn, which is a little more interesting name than Affordable Rooms. I take it this is one of yours?" I asked, more to make sure that whoever was listening knew where I was in case the GPS was glitching.

"Shut up."

We got to the room, and even though I knew I was in trouble, I was still shocked by the forceful push that sent me sprawling to the floor.

"Oh, for God's sake, stand up. You're pathetic." Henry locked the door.

I pulled myself up from the filthy rug and rubbed off the grit covering the palms of my hands.

"It's over, Henry. You wrecked my relationship with Adam; you destroyed Bruce. Walk away from me now and deal with your own shady accounts. There's nothing more I can do for you, so leave me alone."

"You amuse me, Skylar, but I can't do that. When people turn traitor, there are consequences. I don't think you'll like them."

"I didn't turn traitor. I was caught the same way the authorities will eventually catch you. You went too far when you messed with Adam and me. I had nothing to lose."

"You don't seem too upset."

Remembering I was supposed to be on a getaway with Brent, I added, "It's not what I chose. You destroyed everything else."

"Believe what you want, but I saw you and Brent together, and it's obvious you are happy that Adam dumped you."

His words stung because mixed in with his poison, there was also the truth. I decided to get down to business.

"What are you covering up with all those offshore accounts,

crappy hotels, and Bitcoin? Let me guess. You got a deal on the drugs you slipped me since you know the business pretty well."

"Playing games doesn't suit you, nor will it get you anywhere. You won't be any better off than Bruce shortly."

"I'm sure you're proud of yourself that Bruce cut himself out of the deal. You know you're responsible for Bruce's death as much as if you had pulled the trigger?"

"Oh little, naive Skylar, I didn't have to do anything to Bruce. He was never cut out for this line of work and you know those Ecstasy blues. Let's say it's a powerful drop from the happiness high of the night before."

"If you know that much, you should never have given him his first pill."

"He's a grown man. Or was." Henry's laughter sickened me. Was Bruce's life so meaningless to him?

Brent and his gang were in their van, listening to everything I said. So far, I had given them nothing in return. My mind scrambled for words that could lead the conversation into incriminating waters.

"Is that why you chose Bruce? Because you knew he was in way over his head and he wouldn't know how to get out? Just like you chose me?"

"That's an interesting question. Who chose whom? Bruce was looking for a way to earn his wife's love. Silly man, like he could ever hold the love of a woman like that. Have you met her? Never mind. I don't think you would run in the same circles."

"I wouldn't choose to run in the same circles with someone like her."

"You're a bit hypocritical, aren't you? I remember some intimate moments between you and Brent." The words slammed like an invisible fist, making my heart race. Brent was listening, and even though my feelings felt out of my control, I still experienced shame.

"Do you think that my photographers just happened to be there for one little moment?" Henry added. "They were always there, watching your wannabe romance. To give you credit, you held out, or more likely, Brent has better taste in women." It was hard not to hear those words through Brent's ears, and I struggled to remain composed.

"Are you surprised how closely I had you watched? Motorcycle rides, lunches, walks on the pier. All so romantic, really. It's no wonder Adam left you; yet you think you're too good for the likes of Chrissy? She's too good to wipe her red-soled shoe on your, what are those by the way, Dickies?"

"Do you treat all your business partners this way?"

"Only the ones who nauseate me."

The words hit places where I didn't even know I was weak, and some little girl inside me curled into a ball. That is until I remembered my secret microphone that held all the power in the world to destroy him.

My eyes watered as though I was the pathetic girl he felt he was attacking. In reality, I coiled like a rattlesnake, a funny oxymoron moment where I had to fake weakness for my strength to grow. "You're telling me that from the moment we met for that first lunch, the moment you blackmailed me into signing the first wrong FBAR, I nauseated you?"

"Pretty much when you stepped out of the car."

"Is that why you had Adam fired?" Actual tears began to fall. I was good at this. "Is that why you destroyed our relationship with lies?"

"Lies? Maybe the pictures were more truth than you are willing to admit to yourself."

"Is that why you drugged me and had me sign papers? What were those papers? You might as well tell me since you plan on killing me."

"First, hating you was a perk. I rather liked Bruce. It was a shame about him. I enjoy turning people I dislike into my puppets. It's quite entertaining watching them dance around in a pathetic attempt not to hang themselves. Second, I don't just plan on killing you. I am going to kill you. There's no way around it. Third, you will never get the chance to know what papers you signed."

"So, how are you going to do it? I'm curious."

"When my ride gets here, we'll unload all the goods and rake in the profits. The transaction will make me a very wealthy man capable of hiding anywhere. Then I'll take you on a nice little boat ride. Somewhere between here and the Netherlands, I'll beat you badly enough that you're too weak to swim, and then I'll throw you into the ocean. For a short time, you will have glimmers of hope that Brent will ride up and save you, but sharks can swim incredibly fast when they smell blood. I might stick around and watch for a bit before riding off into the sunset with more money than you can dream of with your simple little mind."

The FBI had to have enough evidence at this point. A shipment, a planned murder; it was time for the arrest. "I think you would be amazed at what dreams my simple little mind is capable of." That was my moment, my one-liner. Now Brent would come in with his buddies and take the bastard down. Nothing. Honestly, Brent, wasn't that enough? Where was he? Everything should have been recorded and ready to be used as evidence to clear my name. I looked at the door that hadn't crashed open as I'd expected. The second hand continued to tick in time with my heart. Where was he? Henry walked to a drawer and pulled something out that he kept hidden from my view.

"You know what, Skylar, I think I've heard enough. It's time you took a little nap." The last thing I remembered was a cloth covering my mouth.

When I woke, I was on a boat. The rocking motion and the interior of the small cabin led me to assume so, anyway. My hands were tied, and my bulletproof vest hung from a pole, mocking me. I had no idea where the wire was, but it wasn't on me. I was alone. Above me, I heard footsteps, presumably Henry's. To my surprise, I wasn't scared. Only anger fueled me as I fought with the knot that bound my wrists. I had never felt more determined in all my life. My hands had to be purple due to the tightness of the ropes. Freeing myself would take some time.

I listened to each step, envisioning Henry's movements until finally, he stopped at the hatch leading below deck where I sat. He swung open the door, and a blinding light filled the room. He turned away from me as he climbed down the ladder. That's when the soreness of my body made sense. He must have thrown me down the hole. Due to the cloth tied around my mouth, I couldn't use my witty *I'm not bothered* line. Instead, refusing to show anything except annoyance in my eyes, I waited for him to speak.

"Well, good morning."

Good morning? How long had I been out?

"It's amazing how long a person can sleep with a little chloroform and a good knock on the head." He paused as if the silence in the air was my part of an ongoing conversation.

"I'm going to head out for a bit. I think it's safe to say no one followed us since we've been here overnight. You'll be happy to know all your tracking wires never left the room. I must say, I'm impressed. I fell headfirst into your trap. I didn't know until the sun set when I picked you up to throw you in my trunk. That's when I felt the vest and found all the other fun undercover stuff." He placed his hands on his hips and studied me. "But I am still mystified why no one came to your rescue in the hotel room."

If he was waiting for information, he wouldn't get it. For one, I kind of wondered why no one had come; and two, I still couldn't speak.

"I have a couple of errands to run before our ride shows, so I'll leave you to your thoughts."

He turned and went back up the ladder he had come down. I heard him reach the end of the boat, and then the sound of footsteps stopped, and an engine started. The cloth had sucked my mouth dry, and I hadn't had a sip of anything in hours. I was beyond parched. Then again, it had also been hours since I had used a restroom, so it was best to be thirsty.

I wriggled my hands until the skin became raw. Refusing to give in to the burning sensation, I pushed my joints to new limits until I needed to rest. Tears stung my eyes, but I held them back. Even if I didn't survive this, Henry wouldn't win; he wouldn't break me. The vivid image of sharks devouring my body made my stomach turn. It couldn't end that way; I couldn't end that way. I twisted my wrist in the rope until my skin was raw, and the pain became too much. The knot wasn't budging.

Without the warning sound of an engine, I was positive I heard a footstep landing on the boat's edge, and then another and another. The cabin door swung open, and the silhouette of

Brent stood above me. Relief washed over me as I watched him climb down the ladder to me.

I expected him to come running to my rescue. Instead, he only untied my gag.

"You're doing great. Let me get you a drink before Henry returns."

"What?" I said as soon as the gag gave way. "What the hell are you talking about? I'm not doing great. You knew I was here?"

"Of course. I told you I wouldn't let anything happen to you."

"He chloroformed me, gagged me, tied me up, and threw me into a boat headfirst, and you're telling me nothing happened to me." I was too angry to cry, and my hands were still tied so I couldn't hit him.

"Skylar, I'm so sorry, but you wanted to help. The plan is working better than we thought. He brought you right to the drug deal site. We're going to be able to bust him for dealing and get the guy he's working with." Brent looked at me for a moment. "If we move you now, he'll call off the deal, and we won't have the evidence against him. But you only have to say the word, Skylar, and I'll take you off this boat right now. We'll do what we can without you."

I thought about everything Henry had done to us all. I thought about him getting away and me living in fear of him coming after me again, and I said the only thing I could. "I need to pee."

With a smile, Brent untied me, led me to the tiny boat bathroom, handed me a bottle of water and protein bar, and after I scarfed down a bit of both, tied me back up.

He replaced the gag. Staring into my eyes, he promised, "I'll always be closer than you think, Skylar."

I believed him.

To my best estimate, an hour had passed when I heard tires roll over what sounded like a gravel drive. Footsteps followed shortly afterward, and then the door swung open again. A boyish grin spread across Henry's face as if he experienced some sinister Christmas morning, and gift time was approaching. A part of me was thankful for the gag. Otherwise, I would have wiped his stupid look off his face by yelling out, *Brent was here, and you're about to watch your years of planning go up in flames.*

Instead, I watched as he pulled a rope and a few bricks out of a bag.

"I had some purchases to make, as I was saying, and I want your opinion. Do you think it will take three or four of these bricks to make you sink?"

My silent pause was again allowed its moment.

"I agree; four would be best."

In the distance, I heard a boat motor. Henry's body went on alert. Scrambling, he stuffed the bricks back into the bag. "It's time, Skylar. Isn't this exciting?"

The sound became closer until it slowed to a stop very close to us. Henry hurried up the ladder.

"Man, it's good to see you."

"Have you heard from them?"

"They'll be here any minute."

As if on cue, I heard a vehicle pulling up on the gravel, and the voices went quiet. Even from the bottom of the boat, I sensed the tension. I closed my eyes to let my ears become more in tune with the sounds from above. The clamor of footfalls alluded to the fact that many people were now outside.

"Is it all here?"

"It's on the boat," Henry replied. "Do you have the money?"

I expected to hear the click of a suitcase as it opened. Instead, the gruff voice replied, "Do we have the money? Of course, we have the money."

"Then let's see it," Henry replied again.

Guns clicked.

"Let us see the drugs, my friend, and then you will see the money."

"Go get it," Henry said, probably to the man with him.

After a few quick moments, the man returned. "There are five more cases like this one."

"Bring them out here and set them on the dock."

For the first time since I had met Henry, he was not the one in charge.

"Go get them," Henry said.

I pictured Henry, awkwardly trying to keep his power, standing guard at the crates. There wasn't any conversation as they brought the containers out, but I counted the trips by his footfalls. After the fourth trip, the man from the vehicle spoke again.

"Get the money."

Again, a pause as they followed the order. All seemed to be going as planned until suddenly loud car engine sounds muffled their voices. Car doors opened, and an authoritative voice shouted, "Drop your weapons and put your hands on your heads."

In case they had not heard the conviction in his voice, the noise of the chopper engines came out of nowhere. And for the longest time, it was as if I was watching a movie with my eyes closed. Not until the vehicles had pulled away with Henry and crew in tow did Brent come down the boat stairs and untie me. He held me until voices from above called to us, making us return to reality where painful choices awaited me.

For the next couple of nights, Adam and I remained hidden away in our hotel room. The agents needed to finish investigating some of the details before confidently releasing us. For the most part, I was no longer needed. I had told them everything I knew. My only job now was to lie low while they decided whether it was safe for us to resume our daily lives.

On the third day, Brent knocked on the hotel room door. No longer fearing Brent had plans of stealing me away, Adam let him in. Brent went to the desk chair, pulled it out, and had a seat, letting the silence build intolerable suspense. Finally, he began.

"The two of you are safe to go back home and start living your lives again."

"Thank God," Adam replied.

"How can we be sure we're safe?" I asked. "Are you positive you have everyone?"

"We're still working on Brenda Carter. We're watching all her accounts for activity. So far, nothing. At the moment, she's in hiding, but we don't feel she has any reason to harm you. Right now, she has an incredible amount of the money in her name. If she's smart, which we can assume she is, she will stay quiet. When the time is right, she'll turn up in some foreign country and try to live a life of luxury with the money Henry helped her make. If she were to come after you, she would risk losing all that. She has no reason to do that."

"What about the other man you arrested?" I asked.

"We're still seeing how deep the connections go, but as I

said, there isn't a reason for any of them to want you dead. Even when we tapped the phone, only Henry had it in for you. The other guy didn't want to take part in a murder. He was after the money, nothing more."

"Is the guy you arrested the man you heard on the phone?" I asked.

"We're not sure yet. The speed boat he came in on is linked to a yacht, like the one I showed you, where you park the boat underneath in a garage. We traced the yacht to the newest owner, but the man bought it in an untraceable transaction without the speedboat. Whoever drove the yacht knew to dump it when the deal went bad. They're in hiding too, Skylar. They want to stay that way. Coming after you would only bring them to the surface. They don't want that."

"But?"

Brent reached in his shirt pocket and pulled out a business card. Hoping I would have Brent's contact information, my heart skipped a beat, but when I read the card, there was only a number and some FBI business crap.

"If anything makes you suspicious or if you think of something else we should know, call this number. You'll never be as alone as you might think, Skylar."

Brent studied me. Was he trying to see if I understood his hidden message? How could I accurately detect what he was trying to say when hope blinded me? I couldn't trust my senses.

"So now we go home? That's all?" I asked.

"Now you go home," Brent replied.

"What about....?" I searched for something to prolong the inevitable, something to give me one more moment. "What about the diversion? What did they mean?"

"I suspect Bruce was trying to clear his name. He might

have wanted out, and when he realized it wasn't that simple to peg you as the corrupt accountant, he gave up."

It was possible, but I suspected there was more, and I would most likely never know the whole story.

Not until I heard Adam plop the suitcase onto the bed, did I realize I had been so unaware of his presence.

"Did I hear we get to go home now?"

"Yes, you did," I said while trying to tell Brent otherwise with my eyes. "Soon, we will be able to put this whole terrible fiasco behind us like it never happened."

Brent stood, and, as he raised to full height, wiped his hands on his khakis. "Just like it never happened," he repeated, and reached for the door handle.

"Will we see you again?" I stammered.

"I'll be around for a few more days. After that, you probably won't." He didn't look at me when he said it. "I'll make sure I say goodbye."

"Okay," I responded in an almost whisper.

"Come on, Skylar. Let's get packing. In a few hours, we can be picking Ted up from the kennel and curling up on our own couch. I'll run by the grocery store while you unpack…"

His words trailed off, and I began preparing myself for the journey back home.

The door shut behind Brent.

CHAPTER 22

WITHIN A WEEK, life almost looked normal in my house. We'd brought Ted home from the kennel where I had left him at the last minute. Adam had gotten his job back since the women who filed the suits had dropped the charges. The investigators had allowed us back in the office, and corporate had regained control over the chaotic tax season. The mundane walk through other people's debits and credits resumed.

The temps, including Brent, had moved on. I clung to the promise he'd made me that he would let me know before he left town. When Friday rolled around, Adam took me to Caps On The Water for dinner. As we picked away at our appetizers, a sunset more radiant than any I could remember dazzled us. My second glass of wine helped me block out every thought not conducive to Adam and me reconnecting. Yet even with my best effort, one thought crept in uninvited. I envisioned me gazing out over the Intracoastal, Brent by my side. The memory warmed me to the point of pain.

Adam cleared his throat, bringing my thoughts back to him. "Skylar, these past months have made me reevaluate our relationship." Adam must have sensed my confusion because he held up a hand. "Let me restart. The past fourteen years we've been together have been, well, in my opinion anyway, perfect. I believe we were both happy, but I admit, complacency set into our relationship. I didn't mind, but you've changed. I'm not sure who you are anymore."

My heart pounded, fueled with both fear and excitement. Adam saw it, too; we had changed. Life had changed. He grasped my hands and looked down at them for several moments.

"I've thought about this long and hard, about what went on that I know of and all the things I don't know about as well." He paused again. "We've been together for fourteen years. That's a long time, Skylar. I know you. I know the you that will still exist when all this chaos fades away, and this messy time in our life is over. And it will end. Life will return to normal again."

Adam released my hands, and waiting for him to continue, I looked back over the water. From the corner of my eye, I noticed him slip his hand into his pocket and pull out a velvety red case. I faced him. The case sat open, revealing a ring beyond what I deserved. Adam's expression pleaded with me for a sign he should continue. He must have read the tears in my eyes as a yes because he began to speak. "I want us, the us before life interfered with everything. I always said we didn't need a ring to prove we loved each other, but something tells me it's time to rethink that. I want people to know we're a unit," he added with a smile. "Will you marry me, Skylar? Can we try to get *back to who we were* before all this, but this time, do it as husband and wife?"

He placed the ring on my finger, and his words echoed through my mind. Back to who we were. In my heart, I knew we could not, but I also believed the new me could find a way to exist in the old world. I could breathe a new life into us. It was possible that when Brent altered my world, the universe never meant for everything to change, only some things. I would forget Brent; in time, the ache would subside. I laid my hand in Adam's and gazed at the silver ring with its one-carat diamond on my finger. The ring, almost perfect in size, slid sideways slightly, making the diamond point toward the sunset. A small adjustment would make it sit straight; I was sure of it.

That weekend we attended a memorial service for Bruce, the first of the goodbyes I needed to say before I could put the past behind me. Adam came with me, for which I was grateful, but I was also aware that it might be my last time to see Brent. Not precisely the goodbye I had wanted, at a funeral with my new fiancé. Brent sat in the set of rows across the aisle with Liz by his side. How could I blame him? It wasn't like he could ask me to join him, and no one liked to go alone to funerals. What did surprise me was Chrissy sitting in the front row, wiping her eyes with a tissue. What right did she have? Didn't she know his death had been in many ways her fault?

After the service, Chrissy headed to the restroom, and I could not resist following her. I ended up at the sink next to her while we washed our hands.

Feeling bold, I asked, "Aren't you Bruce's ex-wife?"

"Yes," she said with a sniffle I presumed to be fake. "I guess you saw me the day I embarrassed myself in the office."

"I would say you embarrassed more than just yourself. I wasn't there that day. Still, I've seen your picture in Bruce's office. He was quite upset about your visit."

"Are you trying to make me feel worse? You have no idea. You don't know what I went through, so don't judge me."

"All I know is that he would have done just about anything for you. I'm not trying to make you feel worse by saying that"—or was I? "I just thought you should know."

Chrissy wept more openly and reached for a tissue from the box on the sink.

"You may not believe me, but I loved Bruce more than any person I have ever loved. But there's more than one kind of love. Some love is too big and doesn't fit in the boxes that life offers it. Then there's love that works. It simply works. Never mind. How can I explain a feeling to a stranger when no one in my life ever accepted it? I walked away because the part of me that loved him wasn't brave enough to resist the things that made up my life before him—clubs, tennis, my dad's money, my family's approval. I wasn't brave enough to throw away what I knew I had so I could grab onto what I wanted to become. It will always be my one true regret. I should have, at least, let him know that he was enough. I just wasn't."

The door opened, and the atmosphere changed. Suddenly, we were two strangers aware of an unplanned intimacy. Chrissy chose to turn and flee. I stared at the person in the mirror who looked a great deal like a woman who I had despised moments before.

When I had regained my composure, I walked from the bathroom and found Brent and Adam talking in the hallway.

"There you are," Adam said. "I thought I was going to have to go in after you."

"Sorry, I ended up talking to someone."

"Adam told me the news," Brent said.

"Oh, yes." It occurred to me that Brent had had no way of knowing about the engagement before that moment. Adam lifted my hand that had become very heavy, and Brent held it in his, allowing him to study my ring.

"It's beautiful." His eyes met mine. "Adam's a lucky man." My stomach clenched into a knot of sadness. I squeezed back tears I would never be able to explain to Adam.

"Yes, I am. I've taken too long to put a ring on that pretty hand."

Brent's fingers slid from mine before he spoke again. "Well, I'd better get going."

"When are you leaving?" I asked, trying not to sound too anxious.

"We're wrapping up a few things. After we're done, I'll find out where my next assignment takes me."

"I guess you'll have to be checking in now and then," I said as casually as I could.

"I guess so."

Liz appeared from nowhere. "You ready?"

"Yes. Until then." With a small wave of his hand, Brent headed toward the door.

We rode home in a silence broken only by the sound of Adam flipping around radio stations. Comfortable silence was one of the perks of couples who had been together for a long time. When conversations paused for a minute, no one concluded that something was wrong. I stared out the window and thought about the past year. The universe had sent me spiraling out of control and down a strange path. Part of me was nothing but grateful for the mysterious pulls, the prophetic dreams, and the misguided emotions. I remembered myself in the car during the very first dream when a zombie had bitten me. Yes, I was aware of how completely bizarre my dream sounded, but the meaning was clear. A desire for something more had bitten me—something I'd doubted I was capable of handling as a mere accountant, yet the past few months had proven otherwise.

My journal was only half full. The ending had yet to be determined, and no matter how many times I'd read through it, I couldn't decipher the universe's code. There was more to be written and more to discover. And I was good with that. I had already learned so much about life and myself. No longer would I view the future as daunting and exhausting. What awaited me contained mystery, and that's a good thing.

The past, I promised myself, would not become a screenshot of the most terrifying and tragic moments. I would remove my hands from my eyes and see that life continued. I would look at what I'd already overcome, and I would see my strengths. The hardships, once perceived as punishments, could reshape themselves into badges of honor. Most importantly, I'd learned that if I let go of the fear, the universe would guide me exactly where she wanted me to go, and I should feel pretty good about that.

Adam took my hand, and when I looked over at him, he smiled, so I smiled back. The only problem with the universe is that she doesn't always write clear-cut messages in the clouds, pointing us in one direction. Maybe it's because there isn't one path but two; perhaps sometimes it's nothing more than a flat-out choice. We pick the road, and the universe continues to throw in the lessons. I was ninety-nine percent sure I'd chosen the right one for me. How could I forgive myself if I didn't find out who this new Adam and I were? I would always wonder. But then wondering was inevitable when we are only allowed to choose one path. The woods between the two would grow thicker, hiding any glimmer of what lay on the other side.

I remembered the time Henry had told me that someday I would thank him for the education he'd given me. Would I thank him? Well, not to his face, and not for the knowledge of Bitcoin. My gratitude was for a deeper, more essential understanding that somewhere inside my slacks-wearing accountant self, regardless of the path I chosen, stood the person I wanted to be. On wobbly legs, still learning how to stand with confidence, I took my first steps down the road toward Adam.

EPILOGUE

TAX SEASON WAS over. Bruce was gone and, in his office, sat a new man we were all yet to know. My relationship with Adam was rebuilding, despite its foundation being a shaky rock in the middle of waters that had only recently stilled. My body didn't feel my own. Some part of me was too big to contain within the walls of the McClurry accounting firm. The flimsy chair that Bruce had bought so long ago felt as if it would not hold my weight, and the cubicle walls had shrunk to a suffocating size.

Not knowing how to find myself, I tried to begin with the old routines. Even though the office coffee could never be strong enough, I walked toward the breakroom anyway. Without thinking about it, I froze in front of Brent's empty cubicle.

At first, I only peered inside as if I could catch a glimpse of the man who had once filled the space, but that wasn't enough. With no one looking, I took a step in and turned the chair so that it faced me, allowing the emptiness to sting. And then for a moment, I sat in the chair that had once held him. I closed my eyes, letting my hands grab the arms as if I could make the memories tangible. When something hurt so intensely on the inside, shouldn't there be something on the outside to grasp? But there wasn't. I returned to my cubicle without any coffee.

My phone lit up. One would think that I would have grabbed it in eager hopes that Brent's voice would answer my greeting. Instead, I waited for the second alert, for in that small in-between moment all possibilities still existed. Once I looked, I knew, those possibilities would narrow into one truth, and the fear that it would never be him again was too much. Slowly, I reached for the phone. I didn't want my heart to leap. I didn't want my eyes to fill with unwanted happy tears, but they did.

"Can you meet me at the pier?"

"When?" I asked.

"Now would be an awesome time."

Without taking precious moments to respond, I fled to the back door, mumbled to some coworker about going to lunch, and drove the miles to the spot that would always be ours. Brent stood at the end of the pier. I would say I ran to him, but it was more like a force pulled me to him. When I finally reached him, I curled up in his arms and rested my ear against his chest. I listened to his heart beating hard and fast, matching, I'm sure, the sound of my own. His hand ran through my hair, and his chin rested upon my head. I feared I might never again feel as safe as I did at that moment. We stood without words until our hearts slowed, and we both knew it was time to let go. For a moment, we gazed out over the water in silence, not knowing how to begin.

"These past few months have been amazing, Skylar."

I chuckled through my tears. "Work's going to be pretty boring now, that's for sure."

"I doubt it. You have the bug now. You'll be seeking out excitement. Maybe pick up a skydiving hobby."

"That might be pushing it." A tear slid down my cheek.

"It's incredible how strong we can be when we dig deep. The things we can do when we believe in ourselves."

"And the things we're strong enough not to do." I stared

off into the distance toward the horizon. It was a place far more than where the water met the sky. It was a place you could never reach because, with each step you took, it slid another step away—a realm that existed yet didn't, the only place where Brent and I could exist.

When I dared to look his way, he was staring into the distance as well, at the unattainable possibilities. When his focus drifted back to me, I studied his face, his skin, his whiskers starting to show. I guess the word was familiar, but what a dull word to use to try to describe how one person's skin had become a part of another's. How could that word express that the sound of someone's voice, of his name on your lips, had become synched? How would the world remember that Brent's name should never be spoken without the thought of Skylar trailing in the air behind it?

"I promised I would say goodbye." Brent's warm smile stung like vinegar in a wound.

"I don't know what to say." Words stuck in my throat. "There's so much I want to...." I stopped because I stood at the base of mountain I had already decided not to climb.

Brent held me at arm's length and looked me in the eyes. "Come on now, you're practically FBI," he said with a playful grin. "You know to trust your instincts. If you have a feeling about something, then there is probably some truth behind it. And if there is a lead, you need to follow it until you know it goes nowhere. You wouldn't ever feel completion until you're sure you left no rock unturned."

"And then what?"

"Well, that's when you can officially let it go and move on to the next case."

"Sounds so easy."

"Oh, Skylar, you know better than that. This work is never easy."

As he stood next to me, I tried to take in every inch of the man who had changed everything for what I feared would be the last time. Many feelings battled inside of me, but mostly I felt thankful for his existence. Even if his future would not involve me, knowing he was out there somewhere eased the pain.

"Then I'll just say I'll miss you," I whispered because it's all I could do.

"And I'll just say I'll miss you back."

We walked hand in hand down the pier and stood by his motorcycle in the parking lot.

His smile tried to light his face, but apparently, knowing it could not, he turned to grab his helmet. Before I could yell the loud panicked, "Stop," that I wanted to, he was on his bike, and the engine roared. Brent smiled at me one more time. I smiled back and gave a weak wave. Then Brent drove away.

I watched him disappear into the pattern of traffic. That's when the fist reached in and pulled out a piece of me. Actual physical pain emanated from my chest. Perhaps I'd never had to choose to say goodbye or maybe had never cared that much when I had. Could it be that was exactly how a person was supposed to feel when they lost a friend?

That night I dreamed.

I stood in a field, and out of the grass arose an impossibly large group of balloons. The blue sky hid behind the array of colors clumped together and held by a hand slowly emerging from the ground below it. Even though my very brain was creating the image, I had no clue what was coming next. Who would have expected to see an enormous Superman balloon being lifted by all the other little ones? For a dream, it was quite an impressive, colorful sight, and I stood mesmerized by the image of the floating Superman until he'd drifted far enough into the distance that my brain became bored and brought me back to consciousness.

Even the reasonable interpretations of why a balloon would rise to heights no longer attainable—blighted hopes, the need to release feelings, to let people go—could not stop me from wondering: Why, at least in my dream, why hadn't I run after them? Why hadn't I tried to hold on to even one little harmless balloon? But then, when the universe speaks, when it decides to close a door, who am I to question it?

THE END

ACKNOWLEDGMENTS

Without the help of others, I would be lost. First, I must thank Edward Mickolus. Not only did he help me understand the FBI, but he also supported me with the many aspects of taking a story from a thought to a published book. Other professionals that were resources in the areas of government organizations, banking, and accounting include; Andy Macey, Tim Proper, Jordan Jenks, and Lisa Cascanette. I also need to thank Catherine Kean for her editing services. I take full blame for any errors or stretches of the imagination.

I am indebted to my family and friends that read and sometimes reread versions of this story to help me with revisions and editing. Thank you to Gail Sheehan, Judy Deon, Karrigan Deon, Lisa Cascanette, Kim Stone, Dorri Hall, and Steve Tripp. I also must thank my book club, Reading Between the Wines. These ladies have been a source of continual support: Cathy Klein, Kathy Bravo, Donna Nuckols, Charmaine Brooks, Renee Schreck, Cecile Spiegel, Anne Warren, Tatiana MacDougall, Maritza Ochoa, Leah Maltz, Christine Schmitt, Meg Balke, and Stacey Horan.

The following sites were used for dream meanings and interpretations:

http://www.dreambible.com,
https://dreamingandsleeping.com,
http://www.dreammoods.com.

AUTHOR NOTES

Tracy Tripp is the author of the novels *Parting Gifts* and *Still Life*. She also has two children's books titled *The Wealthy Frog* and *Sammy the Snowman*. Learn about her blogs and future publications at tracytripp.com.